This is the Country

William Wall

This is the Country

SCEPTRE

First published in Great Britain in 2005 by Hodder and Stoughton
A division of Hodder Headline

The right of William Wall to be identified as the Author of the Work has been
asserted by him in accordance with the Copyright, Designs and Patents Act 1988.

A Sceptre Book

2

A CIP catalogue record for this title is available from the British Library

Hardback ISBN 0 340 82215 5
Trade paperback ISBN 0 340 89679 5

Typeset in Sabon by Hewer Text Ltd, Edinburgh
Printed and bound by Clays Ltd, St Ives plc

Hodder Headline's policy is to use papers that are natural, renewable and
recyclable products and made from wood grown in sustainable forests. The
logging and manufacturing processes are expected to conform to the
environmental regulations of the country of origin.

Hodder and Stoughton Ltd
A division of Hodder Headline
338 Euston Road
London NW1 3BH

For Illan and Oisín

O quanto è corto il dire

– Dante, *Paradiso*, 33.121

This is the Country

The shades are waiting
where it all began.
It wouldn't hurt to lie,
walk away from everything,

the cross, the pills,
the death of children
the surprise breakfast.
There's no such thing as dead even.

Things to believe in –
My child's sleeping face,
a hatful of mushrooms,
a bird's nest in the wall.
We play happy families

in the glass eye.
Old friends,
old times –
the ark of gopher-wood

swimming in the oily waste.
White socks, tennis shoes,
a rabbit teddy bear
dreaming of evening.

I'm a careful man.
Normal is perfect.
Kids go fast:
and I hear the wake-up call,

the lonesome whistle.
The blackbird watches from the shadows,
arriving and departing
while we sleep,

a happy family,
repentance, love,
a long way down the track,
a pool of tea, islands of broken cup

and no going back.
Way up over everything,
a place of safety,
I see a good day coming.

I shake hands with my soul
in the multitude of the slain,
the place I came from,
planning a comeback,

practising funny faces
in the shrink-wrap,
waiting for the day
the old men have their say.
This is the country.

The Shades are Waiting

The shades are waiting on the steps. It's a damp morning. I look up and I see that since I was away they gave old Justice a steam cleaning. She has a shiny new dagger and scales, and she's as white as ash. The scaffolding is still there. One or two people I know are walking around in their good suits, talking to solicitors, getting good advice. They have that anxious look like maybe guilty is better. I see someone I think is Micko coming out of the antique jewellery shop. I notice that his taste in clothes has gone downhill, then I remember that he's dead. A Baker Kab pulls up but it's only a woman getting out. She pays the fare. I think maybe I know her too. I'm moving towards the entrance hall when I see two men on the top step. The thin one is smiling at me.

Well, well, he says.

How you doing? I say. What's the story?

We were wondering if you'd show up.

I wouldn't miss this for a million.

How's the care?

Mint. I'm seeing her every weekend now. I'll probably get her back. I'm sorted now, know what I mean?

A man of property.

This is Ireland, I say, property counts.

They look at each other. The fat one is the bruiser. He

opens his big pig fists and turns them up helpless. He tells me they're all depending on me. Like the whole force. I can see the boys in blue down the station waiting for the word. Then it comes down the line. He's all right. He won't let us down. Spontaneous applause. He tells me to give good clear evidence and not to let counsel for the accused get up my nose. He says I should just tell the truth and put my anger to one side. He asks me if I ever say a prayer. He tells me this big cop secret that he often says a little prayer before he goes up to give evidence. It steadies his nerves. Then he tells me again that they're depending on me but they have the DNA so it looks good. DNA is a killer, he says, you know that as well as I do.

This guy, the one I don't know, is smoking. He sucks deep now, who'd have thought he had space for so much smoke, and breathes out in a sudden spurt. He watches and says nothing. His fingernails are stained brown like flitters of scorched paper.

Then Pat Baker arrives. He's wearing a three-piece suit. He looks over at me and I can see he's thinking about having a quiet chat until he sees my company, the three of us watching him, conspiring against him in our heads. This is one thing we have in common.

So instead of coming over, he waves. I don't move but I feel like I'm rushing across the steps and falling on him like the angel of death. I trust in my anger. I feel his hard, twisting fear like some unknown muscle. The fat one puts his hand on my arm.

Take it easy, sonny.

I see Pat Baker's solicitor shake his hand and together they go in through the big timber doors. The mist seems to be lifting, a weak sun suddenly switched on over my right shoulder, and the morning feels a little warmer. As if someone turned the volume up the traffic gets louder. I hear a radio playing in a car waiting for the lights to change. A man in white overalls is standing on a ladder across the street brushing a big poster in place, a Smirnoff ad maybe. I see what looks like a million rats queuing for a funfair. I don't get it.

We could use your help in that department, the fat one says. You know he gave the nod. He mightn't have been there on the night but he gave the nod all right. You know that as well as I do.

The thin guy names Pat Baker, casually, taking the fag out first and breathing smoke at the same time. All air and blue. Pat Baker, he says. Your man.

I told you already, I say.

Come down to the station. Make a statement.

They say I could be valuable. They're sure I have things I could say. It all helps. It all fits into the big picture. They talk like they've seen it, like maybe they're all together down the station painting the big picture themselves, like they know where everything goes. A police masterpiece with Patrick Harold The Baker Baker at the centre like Jesus Christ with the light shining on him and the guy that's going to kiss him and turn him over sitting down to dinner with all the gang, looking very like a photofit of me.

The thin guy stubs out the cigarette with the toe of his big black pig's shoe. He says: We're going to be interviewing you anyway. One of these days. I don't feel like having to look for you.

You know where to find me.

Do a runner on us and we'll fucking throw the book. Understood?

You won't, will you, sonny?

My name is not fucking sonny, I say.

Look, come down during the adjournment. I'll be waiting.

Is that him? I say. But I already know. I saw him before.

I'm looking at two prison officers taking a boy out of a van. He's wearing a suit. His head is shaved. He looks like a small bouncer on a hunger strike. Max's brother used to call him the langer. He has a neat thin moustache, a big bony dog's face, but his eyes are dodgy. They never rest on anything for more than a second. He walks up the courthouse steps and suddenly, from nowhere, the cameras arrive. He looks at them, cool, giving them nothing. They ask questions and he just looks. His minders pull his arms. Come on, one says. For maybe three seconds he doesn't move at all, then he mock-head-butts a woman who is talking into a microphone, a small movement but it's plain enough. Even though she's ten feet away she pulls back like she felt the heat of his head. The hard hot skin of his bald head. Then he nods to someone at the back of the crowd, a cool nod, a howya, and then he goes up between his minders and in the same door as everyone else.

He's going for not guilty? I ask.

They nod.

And?

Open and shut, sonny boy, open and shut. DNA, remember? We have him by the balls.

And what's the story with The Baker?

They look at each other. The quiet one catches my shoulder and turns me round. He points at a building down a side-street. A block of apartments. See that? he says. Know who owns that place? Our Pat is moving up in the world. He's a respectable businessman with no visible means of support.

I'm thinking: I slept in that building once, a long time ago when someone gained access through a broken window that led onto a stairs, upwards into a high room. Maybe five or six of us, like totally goofed off. We lit a fire with bits of furniture. I think we had some sweet shit that brought comfort and purpose for several hours. Who the others were I can't remember.

You could do us a favour, sonny.

I shake my head. I'm still loosening that memory that has half a hold on me, of people I once probably loved like brothers, lighting a fire with the legs of a chair and bunches of wallpaper. I can smell the burning paper. Someone is standing sideways at the window and saying: Boys, you can see Justice from here. Someone is divvying up the deal. Someone getting the spike.

There's witness protection . . .

No way. That bastard did enough damage to my family already.

Still . . .

I see they're smiling at me. I recognise the big generous smile of people who want to buy and sell me, who think they can do it too. Just to get the bid right. They want to wreck my head. The fat one has a kind face. I think his children must love him, the people he plays cards with, he's probably well known around his estate and people feel safer with him. He serves communion on a Sunday with a sad smile on his face, he knows the moves. But he has one false tooth, whiter than the others, where someone hit him hard. It's in his smile. He touches my shoulder softly like he loves me. His voice goes down almost to a whisper.

You're sticking it to this bastard, you could stick it to Mr Big too. You know he's the main man.

Revenge, sonny, the thin one says. Think about that. Look, never mind the bastard that's just gone in. He's finished. Think about The Baker. You know as well as I do he was behind it. What do you say?

I say nothing. I put my hands in my pockets. I'm not happy for people to see me in broad daylight talking to someone like this. The shades taking an unhealthy interest in me. And I'm thinking Pat Baker was a child prodigy, even when we were kids he could turn his hand to anything. He was gifted.

We'll take care of it all. Go in now and give the man your name and let them know you turned up. They might have been worried about you. Come down the station during the lunch break. We'll talk it over, know what I mean? We'll sort it. Come down, will you?

So I go in and find I'm down for that day, but it's still two more days before I get to give my evidence. Counsel for the prosecution talks to me. The world is half full of waiting rooms. All the time I wasted expecting my name to come up, maybe days, maybe weeks, courts and hospitals and clinics and places where good money was going on maybe bad product. When I was a kid and I should have been somewhere else.

*   *   *

6

I give my evidence.

I was away, I say. I should have been there.

I have issues around that but I don't tell them. They nag at stuff I don't give a shit about but they don't touch the truth, the crystal-clear truth, which is that I was somewhere else on the night in question. The defence asks me if I consider myself a responsible person and I say: One hundred per cent. He has a shiny blue suit and the same ratty wig as everyone else. He asks me if I ever saw the defendant before. Once, I say. I told you already. He probably thinks I should know the accused because the two of us are Norries, like all Norries are related or something, or we socialise in the same dole queues. He looks at a piece of paper. He was driving up and down outside your door, he says, counting houses. He says it like nobody is going to believe it. Like the defendant can't drive or he can't count. Like any minute now he's going to pull out a piece of evidence that will totally kill me. The sworn testimony of an expert. But he just moves on. I think he's bored.

Afterwards.

I sit at the back and for the first time in a few years I miss Max. Cool it, boy, he'd say. I can hear him. One look and he'd suss everything. He had an eye for situations. They're coming in from lunch.

Pat Baker's big head is two benches down, following the proceedings. Pat has things riding on the verdict.

I see someone has added a new line in graffiti: PIGS R PIEDERFILES is scratched on the rail in front of me. Beside it: SCRUFFY 4 EVER.

It won't be everything, no matter what they say. They

7

say The Whole Truth like the whole truth was available to any of us. All the people who could tell this out, but nobody makes a full statement. Maybe close to true or just off being wrong, things other people might believe, things you think you believe yourself, gossip and stories and hearsay evidence. How much is dream and how much is just a consequence of some weird shit with ingredients not mentioned on the label? Everybody gets more than one version. You say: I only know what I saw. Like this is some defence. Or what I heard, or whatever. But you don't. Better to say: I can't talk about that. I've spent years trying to get my head together and there's things I can't talk about. Things that can't be said.

I look around the court and see pale faces I used to know well, people I grew up with, always on the edge of happening, or waiting for something to happen, waiting for the news. Famous anonymous people, witnesses, people known to the police, people who deny the charges, victims, passengers, residents, inmates, eyewitnesses, accomplices, neighbours. On the street they're invisible but in here they come into their own. The sun streams in through a high window and the oak benches glow like glass. Old people in gowns are drifting about on the floor, talking, smiling, making the magic. It looks like nothing is happening but there's not a man or woman in the crowd that doesn't know where everything goes. All this chaos is moving. In the end the people on the floor will put a little something by for their old age and everyone else will wonder where the time went, deciding, maybe, this is the way it is, they better get used to it, it's nothing special.

Then counsel for the state stands up.

May it please the court, he says.

He catches at the edge of his gown and hangs one fist on it. Someone hands him a sheet of paper.

Where it all Began

Max fell in the river, and later he got tetanus and died. We were on the run from something, the kind of thing we did in those days. We borrowed a boat down the river and rowed out into this perfect day. Our first time in a boat, we couldn't see how it worked. The river drifted us along and we got the oars into their places but we couldn't turn it into action. Stuff was happening but we weren't doing it, bottles and sticks were passing us, headed for eternity, and we couldn't catch up. Fuck, Max was saying, we're all going to die. If I die first, eat me. Promise me you won't let the rats get me. He was kneeling down with his hands joined. Please please please, he said, all them tiny sharp teeth. Then I got one oar working and we started to turn and Max stood up and said thanks be to Jesus we were saved. He started to sing 'You're My Wonderwall'. There were clouds in the water and swans up-ended and further down there was a guy fishing. He looked like nothing ever happened, one quiet satisfied customer with his baseball cap and his little green jacket with fifty pockets and his long boots. He held the butt of the rod against his heart and the rod went up into the air and the ghost of a line connected him to the fish. Or maybe just to the shit at the bottom of the river. But just then he looked like the best friend anyone could have, the kind that'd tell you to get a grip if you had an unwise plan.

At that time I was mad at a girl who seemed to me to be offering more than she was going to give. That morning we went out to her house and did a bit of shouting, hoping she'd come out and maybe change her mind and lighten up a bit. Instead her mother came to the door – which took us by surprise – to tell us to fuck off. Go away, she shouted. Go away or I'll send for the guards. Tell her I was asking for her, I said. Tell her I send my best. Her mother wore an apron that had flour on it in two dustings, one at each side. Max said we should go. Tell her I said I know what she is. What is that supposed to mean? her mother said. Later Max asked me the same question. Like, is she a whore, is that what you're getting at? For Christ's sake. He was on the mother's side. Max thinks every mother is beautiful except the alcoholic ones. Max has his own problems that we don't talk about, but I know the story somehow, the way when you're close with someone you just absorb things from the air, the way you know the story even though nobody ever said anything about mothers. It's not like that, I said. She'll know when she hears it. She knows what I'm talking about. Max says that someone like her would never have anything to do with someone like me. Her father is a doctor or a lawyer. Actually, now I remember: he's a surgeon. He works at the Regional Hospital. He drives a beautiful car and he looks like he has everything sorted but he has an ex-junkie for a daughter and there's nothing he can cut out of her that will make her normal.

Max was a porter in the hospital for a while. He wore the uniform but he never looked like a normal porter. His face is too small and a little pushed in here and there, and his arms are too long, so he looked like one of those postcard monkeys in a uniform. He knew the names of all the surgeons, each in his own speciality, and the names of important nurses and ancillary staff. He once said: Anybody who is anybody comes in here. But the fact is the money goes somewhere else, to the private hospitals where there's a fixed number of beds in every ward and a private room is private. They only came under Max's care when something serious went wrong. Max talked about the machines they had, the best in the world, he said, for seeing inside. The body is mostly water, he said. They have a way of looking in and seeing the tide turn, or if there's shit floating in the water. They can count the number of thoughts you have, but they still didn't figure out what the thoughts mean. That'll be the next generation. Inside the head, he said, is all this silent fizzing and sparking and things communicating. Dots and lines and tangents and loops. There is no rest. They slide the body down a tunnel and they can see everything that happens without knowing what it means. It drives them crazy; it's the only secret left.

This girl was a plastic surgeon's daughter, but Max said they don't use plastic, they make you grow your own skin. He saw people with their faces glued to their arms. The highlight of his whole time there was bringing trolleys of dead people down to the morgue. That's the thing he talked about most. One in particular was when this kid came in. He had to have a wheelchair and Max rolled him in and he said that, apart from having to have the chair, the kid was fine. About fourteen years of age. Chatty and not pale or anything. Not smelly or anything. Max says sick people have a special smell and the smell is different for every disease. Then Max is on duty the next evening and he's called to bring someone dead down to the morgue. Max said the dead make noises. You hear them at night, resting in the dark, waiting to be brought home one last time, farting softly and sighing. It was the only place Max ever felt safe. It's my family, he said, and I love them all. He brought the trolley down and like always he took a peek at the face. They had a green sheet covering him from head to toe and it was the same kid. He just came in and died.

This was some kind of road to Damascus thing for Max. We never know, he kept saying. It could be any day. He was right. So he stopped doing stuff. We both did. Up to that time we were not wide about where we got our drugs. Max would turn up with something in a childproof plastic bottle, or a silvery blister-pack or maybe a twist of paper with a few tabs inside. Or we would acquire some serious money and buy hash or whatever was going, like there was no better way to see the seven wonders of the world. E was still on the dear side at that time and we needed to save up to go for that. But after Max saw the kid just die we thought we saw the writing on the wall. We decided to get a grip. This priest took us under his wing. He said we were bright kids and we were wasting our lives, which was strictly true; although we were up for anything and enjoying things, it was doing our heads in at the same time. And possibly affecting our internal organs as well. Max's liver was not too good. If he pressed on that side he could feel it sort of tender. Max said you should not be able to feel your own liver. His face looked sort of shrink-wrapped. Like we knew we were fucked. The priest got us going to the meetings and counselling. Going to school again, although I can't say we were welcomed back with open arms, but with a certain kind of hostility and suspicion, like we were in danger of polluting all the other people, not to mention the staff. We got cautions all the time. People were saying: I know your kind, like we were yellow-pack criminals and all you had to do was read the label once and it was good for everybody. The priest told them all we were bright kids and we were making a fresh start. Then he was moved away. He said his tearful goodbyes and fucked off to another parish where the takings were better. A Southside parish with good addresses. So Max and I went back on the shit with renewed interest.

But this happened while we were still attending the meetings and owning up like mad. Thanking God. Taking advice. Hearing confessions. The surgeon's daughter stood up at the meeting and said the same thing everybody else says. It's all about guilt first. That's the way it works. Like you have to believe in sin – which I don't. You have to keep going until you get to the positive things. After a while you start to see a piece of sky and everything starts to move slowly. I saw her standing there and I thought to myself, maybe these meetings might be worth it. If I could click with someone like her, not taking drugs might have an upside. She had small hands, too small for her arms, and when she was talking she closed her little fists and held them about level with her heart. She was telling the truth and it was her truth and it hurt, only it was the same truth everyone else had and it was cheap and flashy because of that. But she stood up another night and said she was lonely. She said this was not an excuse, but it was still true. Everybody looked at her like she broke the rules. Like lonely had fuck-all to do with drugs. Like everyone is lonely. So I waited for her, and when she came out I told her how deeply touched I was. I told her two people can't be lonely together. I told her the director's cut version of my life story. We made up our minds to stick together, and maybe we both thought about screwing each other, even though I was the only one that really needed it bad. I think I was in love. And for a while it worked out that way. But I was also a virgin as a consequence of concentrating on chemicals and different kinds of pleasure. I was a real virgin – on a scale of one to ten, I was ten. Even Max wasn't as bad as me. It was like something terrible that I was going to have to do, like a dangerous operation that I had to decide about or anything huge that you put off too long. Maybe I was the only virgin, I don't know.

With the surgeon's daughter I never got back as far as the real past. Her father operated on people's faces and gave them a new identity. Someone comes in with a birthmark they've had all their life and they feel like a piece of shit. They have very low self-esteem. He operates on their faces and when they wake up they're perfect. They're someone new. Their skin is so shiny they have to stay out of the sun. Or someone was burned in a fire and he saved them. Or some bitch wanted her double chin taken out of circulation. He was never home. He was in love with the knife. So she started on the drinks cabinet and then there were other things. She had access. After we fell in love we stopped going to the meetings and went other places. We'd lie down together someplace nice, usually in a park, and talk for a bit. I'd lift her shirt, loosen her belt. She was soft. She sounded different too, lying down, her voice getting lost in the sky. Who knows how far the sound went up there without any obstacles. It was like a different way of being herself. We sampled various drugs and tried to organise ourselves. We tried to keep the shapes and names and colours in our heads. It was a kind of religious moment just before we took something, like this was God. Sometimes she'd put her tongue out and close her eyes and I'd just rest the pill on it. We never knew, would we get high or die. Once she said to me: What if it's just fucking rat poison? And I said at least we die together. We'll be found lying down side by side staring at the universe. The headline would be Suicide Pact Lovers. If it was good we'd try to make out. Sometimes we were too lazy or sleepy. We slept more than was good for us. Sometimes we couldn't stop our hands. We learned several kinds of touching, but she never went too far.

Now I wonder if she was able to let go, if maybe she was never as stoned as me. Or maybe there was something wrong with her, some kind of obsessive-compulsive thing, or she might have been a tad schizo. She said: That's as far as I want to go tonight. Then she zipped herself in. Jesus, I wanted to drink her. I wanted to die in her. I wanted to absorb her. I wanted to be her soul. But I waited. I remembered the word. I respected her.

So after her mother came out to tell us what to do with ourselves, Max and I went down to the river. I might have been a little depressed. I thought the surgeon's daughter was being unreasonable and her mother was a cunt. Max told me stories to cheer me up. He had all the gossip about who was in the money and which people we should be nice to, and which one of our neighbours was going into the market or showing entrepreneurial skills, and what was affecting the balance of trade. It was a beautiful day. The river was the same glass as the sky. Max was messing on the edge of the boat we borrowed. He was standing up. He had a small cut on his hand, a splinter from the boat, a little straw of fibreglass. He held his hand up to me and I pulled it out and a thread of blood came too. That was how the tetanus got in. He hated doctors and by then he was sleeping rough because the hospital fired him when they found out what he was doing in the morgue. I remember a swan came down the river, ignoring us, this beautiful unlikely white shape with the long neck. The river was a greeny-brown colour but the swan was pure white and not in any way involved with the shit, like some people slide through life and never get touched by what fucks up the rest of us. Like a baby – pure and simple even when the parents are lying through their teeth. This swan didn't even look at Max when he fell in. The splash never reached him. I don't know if swans can hear, but if he did, he didn't let on. I hauled Max out of the water and he was laughing. Someone on the shore was shouting. It might have been someone who was worried because he fell in, or it might have been the owner of the boat. We just drifted down-stream in the sun.

It Wouldn't Hurt to Lie

It must have been about the same time that we first heard of an acquaintance dying due to circumstances beyond his control. A man we had a commercial relationship with, as it happens. We were watching it on the news. This man we both had issues with. Among other things we owed him money. Max said: Jesus Christ, he was shot while laying patio slabs. How fucking weird is that? He moved out there so his wife and kids would be safe. Doing the quiet business from a desirable residence in the suburbs. No planning permission, no change of use. People said he looked like an insurance man. Later Max and I drove down with Pat Baker in Pat's DIY Merc. Max was older than me by a couple of years, and Pat was older than him and he had a provisional licence but no insurance. We wanted to see the holy place where someone was shot dead on a half-laid patio. We couldn't get near the house and Pat lost it when he saw the estate swarming with shades. He reversed back the full length of a terrace and into someone's carport. Then he stepped on the pedal and took us out of that small world. We went through three estates and the houses got bigger in each one. By the time we stopped, it was like we changed languages. Every garden had this weeping tree with kids in Benetton playing on the grass. The cars were all clean. Women walked big dogs. They wore sunglasses and smelled like fields. We had no name for this place we found ourselves in, but we wanted it bad. It's a funny old world, Pat said. You'd think you'd be safe doing something like that. Max said people were shot in all sorts of weird places but Pat said nobody ever got shot laying a patio. Pat said maybe it was Max's brother whacked him. He heard Max's brother was working for someone now. Doing pro stuff.

We don't keep up, Max said. He went his way and I went mine.

Pat said it was handy to know someone.

Just because you know me doesn't mean you know my brother, Max said. We don't get on.

Since before he was inside or since he got out?

Before.

A brother thing, hah?

He hammered me once too often.

Maybe he thought you were going astray. Bringing the family name down.

This was Pat Baker's sense of humour. But we didn't know he was saving it all up. Nothing was wasted on him. He was a memory man when he needed it. He was also big on family name.

We knew where the dealer was shot because I was still having trouble with that girl and we decided to drive down to the hospital in the Merc and see about her old man. We thought we might teach the surgeon something about plastic. So first we scored something to smoke. We all clubbed in. This was before Pat became a business tycoon with a fleet of Mercedes cars and an import and distribution branch and female employees. Nobody noticed that while he was fuck-acting about with us he was shooting to the top of his profession. It was magic. He never drove like a waaboy, always a steady and a careful man.

We stopped outside the dealer's old place in Michael Collins Avenue and asked after his health. His daughter gave us the bad news that he moved out. Some bastards superglued his hand to the boot of a car containing a quantity of Class A substances and called the shades. It was a warning. Probably the IRA, she says. At that time he was on bail for possession. So then we enquired among the neighbours about who was up and who was down and someone gave us the new location. It turned out he was still doing business in a small way in this good address with roses round the front lawn and a bird table in the middle, not rich but comfortable. There was a scruff of crumbs around the edges of the bird table and some streaky white shits at the bottom of the hole where the birds went in. This was the summer so the birds had to be sleeping out. There was nothing inside the little house. I looked in and all I could see was the hole at the other side, the back door, I suppose, unless I was looking through the back door. It reminded me of home. Yermano with the hashish came out and did the deal and we had just enough as it happens on this occasion, though he reminded us that we owed him some from a previous incarnation when he was living in the council house in Collins. Keep away from my fucking bird table, he told me. You want the birds to smell you on it? They'll never come back.

So a couple of nights afterwards Max and I did a job on the bird table about three o'clock in the morning just for fun. We poured a little petrol over it and we shoved a deodorant can in the little hole and when the wood and the paint started to burn the can exploded and blew the roof off. That was Max's plan. It was cool to see the way it all came apart, like blowing up a real house. And the lights went on all over the place except in his window. We knew he was looking out though because the curtain moved. He was standing in there, in the dark, watching his bird table burn to the ground, and he was afraid to come out in case one of us had a weapon. The neighbours came out to see what was going on like New Year's Eve.

Somehow he found out it was us. So we have this langer drug dealer barking at our ass and we're making sure we sleep in different places every night. That was when Max decided to sleep in the morgue. He got his hands on a spare key. I think it affected him a little. He told me once he talked to them at night, maybe other things, I never found that out.

We're telling our friends to say we emigrated. We're wearing our hoods up and then thinking we should get rid of the hoodies and try to look normal. We're spending a lot of time in crowded places. We feel like we're walking a tightrope and nobody's offering us a safety net. And then we see the house on telly in a shop window and there's the burned-out bird table leaning against a wall. We go in and pretend we're looking for an expensive stereo system, but we're actually listening to the news.

He was shot dead laying a patio, they say. Neighbours say he was a quiet unassuming man but vandals burned his beloved bird table and he was so upset he decided to patio the front lawn. The crime correspondent says he was known to the police and maybe a target of rival gangs. So who shot him and why? The shades are keeping an open mind. Another gangland shooting, the crime correspondent says.

What we did to the surgeon's car was we scratched something on the paint. This was an expensive car. The thing is Pat looked around for the camera and he looked straight at it. They have good cameras in that hospital. Oh Jesus, there it is, he said. I looked straight at it. Think they'll be able to recognise me? Max and I didn't look. We ran. That's how we ended up only scratching YOUR DAUGHTER IS A BI, which wasn't true. I heard afterwards they made her go to counselling to burn the lesbian out of her.

Why did you write that about me? she said sometime later when we met by chance.

I didn't write it.

I know it was you.

It's just I never finished it off.

Like what were you going to write?

You're a bitch, I said. I didn't mean it. I just wanted to hurt you.

Thanks a million, she said.

She had these low-level jeans and a high-level top and all I wanted to do was touch her belly, just touch the soft round of her belly. I wanted to cry. I could remember the feel of my hand down her pants, flat against her, the scruff of hair like soft springs giving to me. *Tonight*, I wanted to shout. *Tonight* is the *night*. In those days I was close to igniting with sex. She was so near but I was never going to be able to even talk to her again. She was still in counselling. The sun was shining down the street like oncoming headlights and people passing were wearing only the smallest clothes. There was an old dog tied to a parking sign, waiting for the boss to come out of the bookie's with a fistful of money from the horse that finally came home. That dog was watching me closely like he saw a million of me in his time. Did you kill that drug dealer? she said. Everyone knows you burned his bird table. I thought it wouldn't hurt to lie.

Walk Away from Everything

This part of the story is not clear to me. A period of maybe years that works out to be mislaid somehow. There's uneasy dreams and things that might or might not be dreams or fantasies. Uncertain allegations that Max makes up or that someone tells me are true and subsequently prove to be unfounded. But I remember the blackbird because I met him again. I know what that old bird means. What did Max tell me about the house? I remember he tracked this gay down to a good old address, a big brown house with a lawn. He told me we had to do something about him. Max said he was dangerous, like he knew somehow. So we spent a lot of time making small adjustments to his comfort, the way he never knew what to expect, whether his house would be there when he got home, whether his cat suffered an unexpected anaphylactic shock or something had been written on his wall. Max had this secret plan that he didn't confide, but he told me it was there because, he said, morale is important. The people in that distant place don't look at us, though we're only ten streets from home. They're going to where we came from, what they call a good night out, hoping for a little something to make the night be fast, hoping to score, hoping for something pure and hot. We walk down streets with trees and lights and warm houses. We were here before, we're as good as neighbours. We do not disturb the peace. We slip through the gate and stand under his chestnut tree. Chestnut trees have candles but there's no light. A bird is singing, a blackbird probably. Over the other side there's a pond with a life-size statue of some kind of skinny bird looking into the dead water in case a fish shows up. A light is on in the old fag's room. Max is annoyed. The patio door is open and you can hear the usual crap. We know without looking that the old guy would be sitting in his armchair looking out, waving his hands around. The voice of the woman, that's the bit that gets him going. Max saw him standing and holding his hand over his chest and singing his head off to the voice of the woman. I'm standing so still this bird comes down and starts walking around me. Once an uncle or some-thing showed me how to make a bird-trap. It was too easy. You make a cage out of twigs tied together or using insulation tape and there's a hinged trapdoor which you prop up with another twig. You lay a trail of crumbs in the winter and the birds just follow the trail. When they follow it into the cage you pull a piece of string and the prop comes away and the trapdoor drops down. Some-times the bird dies of shock. I think they're weaker in the winter. But when you have a bird in a trap what do you do next? I never saw the point. I stopped doing birds early. Max is like a bird sometimes. He's so thin and he moves kind of fast and darty and sometimes he's slow. There's something wrong with him inside, I know that. He knows it too. He worked in a hospital, for Christ's sake. He's seen everything. He knows the names of incredible diseases. He has a dictionary and he looks up the words and sometimes the explanation in the dictionary is harder to understand than the disease so he makes up the meaning. Systemic lupus he saw. Lupus is a wolf, he says. It's when a person is changing into something awful, any frightening kind of animal, not necessarily wolfs, only they're still human inside. No cure. And ankylosing spondylitis. It's this thing that grows around your ankle inside the skin. A spond. And scoliosis and uncommon kinds of cancer and tuberculosis of the bone and a virus that eats human flesh. Once he told me he saw someone who just expanded and expanded like a balloon with too much air in it. Somehow this started after an operation and they had to open this person up at both sides to let the pressure out. I might have this wrong. I don't remember everything Max told me.

It was Max who diagnosed Pat. Asperger's Syndrome, he said. Who was this Asperger? Maybe he was the first person to get this disease or maybe he was the one who discovered it. It means Pat gets things in his head. Like he knocks off cars. He only does Mercs and sometimes, somehow, incredibly he seems to actually own one. Maybe he started small the way millionaires do, and slowly worked his way up until he could actually own a car. The other side is Pat has no social skills. And he can be very unreasonable and he's incredibly strong and can take pain. Later when he took my mother I should have remembered that half of him was dead. That he didn't relate well to people.

I'm standing on the lawn, listening and waiting for something to happen. I remember that the uncle who showed me how to trap birds was fucking my mother and for the first time ever I start to ask myself why she always made us call them uncles. As if it was OK if the man that was fucking your mother was a relation. The bird-trap one was nice. He showed me other things too, like how to hold a teacup. I could sit down with the richest person in the land and drink tea and they'd never find out anything about me. And he taught me never to say: Max and me. He made me do my homework and learn spelling. When I think about it now he stayed the longest and he was the best and my Ma was happy. We used to go on picnics. He showed up at my grandfather's funeral and my mother hit it off with him even though he was an older man. That was in the days when my mother still expected long-term commitment. He could do card tricks.

The thing is the music is nice. I don't say it to Max because Max is into metal, but whatever the man is playing is nice. I wouldn't mind if we just stayed where we were and listened. The bird is trying to pull a worm out of the ground. The trees are dripping and it's getting evening. Max is able to tell people what's wrong with them before the doctor. Once a doctor said this woman was OK. Max was called to take her up to her ward after a consultation and he says to her: How are things? I'm fine, she says. There's nothing at all wrong with me, only lower back pain. It'll go away if I take regular walks. But Max could smell what it was. You better go back, missus, and get him to check it all over again. Get him to do an X-ray. She didn't and next time he saw her she had cancer of the spine. Then one time he comes on night duty and she's laid out in the morgue under a green sheet. He takes a look and he recognises her straight off. Max loves her because she's kind of his patient. Why didn't you listen to me, he says. He told me he wept. He held her head in his hands and wept like it was his own mother that died. Maybe they heard something. Maybe some doctor passing or a nurse or some busybody patient heard something in the morgue.

Let's go, he says. Let's stop this fucker before he queers up someone we know.

The bird gets the worm and he's kind of whacking it around. He eats it. I wait until he's finished.

Come on, boy. What're you waiting for?

Fuck you, I say.

Years later, after a certain tragic loss, I'm out walking. I happened to come across a pair of hill-walking boots that were a perfect fit and straightaway I decided to take up a sport. Now I'm walking along this small road. I'm hungry and desperate. I'm walking away from everything and I'm lost. There's these dark bushes on each side with tiny red flowers like spots of blood. The whole place looks like there's been a violent altercation. And I see the same bird. I swear to Jesus it has to be the same one. I wish I knew his name. I call him blackbird but he's not actually black. I stop and I look at him and he does the same thing exactly. He gets this worm and he whacks him around and then he eats him. And then he looks up at me out of one side of his head. This one eye. What's the other eye doing? Is it looking at something else, something I can't see? I'm standing there in my stolen boots and he's digesting his worm and watching me out of one side of his head.

The Cross, the Pills

The dead dealer came back at Max's funeral because I had ingested something to help me through. I might have been remembering or I might have been hallucinating a little. I see the scene of his death like I was looking down from a tree, the way a bird sees it. Or like a camera-shot from a helicopter. The flapping crime-scene tape, the shades with their flat hats, the tops of the neighbours' heads. I can see down chimneys. I can see a rat running along the ridge-tiles and down a chute. I can see broken blue eggshells in a valley of lead around a chimney. And I can see the dealer's cross is made of patio slabs, like he was laying out his own grave on his front lawn. This was the way things happened to me in those days. Something I never saw, or only partly saw, became the real thing for a while. Things came back after a long absence and went for the big impression. There were times I felt I was living in the past, going through occasions that maybe happened to other people I was related to, now deceased. I didn't know any better, I trusted everything.

I had the pills Max gave me because he sort of knew he was going. They won't do me any good, he said.

Maybe it wasn't tetanus. Maybe that was one diagnosis he got wrong. I should've kept my tetanus up, he said. I got one when I was four after I stood on a rusty nail. It seems this nail was in a plank that was just lying around somewhere and Max walked on it in bare feet, the way kids that age have bare feet. I don't think it came up through his foot or anything but it went in deep anyway. The doctor said that deep wounds with small entries are the worst for tetanus. So he gave him the shot. When Max was dying he was seventeen years of age, near enough, probably he needed a booster, his original shot wore out. He told me his birthday fell while he was in hospital but I wasn't there that day so I can't be sure. When I found out why he wasn't around I went out to the hospital. He was lying in the bed with the drip going into him and I saw the drip was electric. The wire was glowing so intense, so intense. Cool drip, I said. He laughed softly. You're enjoying that, he said. What am I going to do without you, Max? Shag Pat Baker's sister for me, he said. I'm giving you my blessing. She's some hole. He looked at the ceiling and his eyes were like wet stones. He knew I was sniffing her. He knew I wanted her. But he had the gift of prophecy that time, like people do when they're on the way out. Pat'll fucking slaughter you, he said, but you have to do it. If you don't someone else will and she's a nice kid. This hatchet-faced nurse came around and put something up to his ear and took it away when it beeped. She looked at it and licked her lips. Cool, I said. I saw the numbers: 38.4. She looked at me. He has a fever, she said. He's very sick. I hope you're not involved in anything. Me? Definitely not. Because you have your whole life before you. I know. I see it. How old are you? I'm eighteen, I say. She knows I'm lying, but I feel I want her to believe in me, that maybe I'm the legal age. But I know what she sees is a couple of fucked-up Norries, one dying. She's holding his hand now, with her thumb and two fingers. She has the two fingers on the inside of his wrist and I see the bones of his wrist and the veins. She has her finger on one of the purple veins and it's lit up from the inside. I can see muscles too but they're obscure. I love those fingers. I see the colour of the nail is purple. Each nail a perfect curve, a purple moon. Now she wraps a tube around his arm and pumps it up and watches the numbers again. She has a stethoscope in her head and the long end on his arm, up near the tracks. Can I listen? I say. She shakes her head. She's looking at me like what she's listening to is some kind of voodoo or something from outer space. She's dreamy and beautiful. I wonder if people's bodies have some kind of music inside. Then she folds everything up and leaves.

There's a kind of secret trembling in my hands. I feel it inside in the veins or the nerves, down in the heart too, fluttering and uncertain. I just remembered, I say. The slabs made a cross. He looks at me. What slabs? The fucking slabs in the patio, boy. The place we got the hash. The fucking bird table. It was a cross. Slow down, he says. I can see he's getting tired. Look, the slabs he was putting down. They were in the shape of a cross. It's like some kind of a fucking omen. You're out of it, he says. No. I went back for a look. It was a cross. He closes his eyes and folds his hands across his chest. The wire from the drip is in the skin of the back of his hand. There's a little plastic head with a plaster over it. I want to take it out the way I took out the straw of fibreglass the day in the boat. I want to save him. Except maybe that killed him. I'm thirsty. The stuff in the drip looks good. Think I could have a sup of that? I say. They won't give me pethidine, he says. They know I was getting it. Now how did they find that out? Then at the funeral I see the cross in the slabs. I'm looking down. And the bastard dealer is lying on them. He's nailed out to the slabs like Jesus Christ. The priest is saying things like ashes to ashes and I know that my redeemer. I'm crying. Max, Max, I say, what am I going to do without you. I hear someone snickering. Maybe Max's brother. He's looking at me over his shoulder. He has the blackbird's steady eye. Someone comes up to me and sort of moves me back. There, there, son, he says. But I'm not his fucking son. He goes back to the front line and I stumble and suddenly I'm leaning against a cross. This is too much, I say. No way is this happening. I need to get my head straight. But Max was still dead when I got clean.

The Death of Children

I'm hanging around outside the Tandoori Queen, not wanting to go home, a little depressed because of Max and certain responsibilities I took on by mistake, like The Baker's sister not getting two periods in a row, when I see the Merc go by. I'm waiting for something, I don't know what, maybe a deal, maybe someone I arranged to meet. It's hard after all this time to say how long it was since the funeral. Maybe, six months or a year. The length of time it took me to score with The Baker's sister plus plus. The state I'm in, everything shimmers a little. I have a dry mouth and I'm not taking Aqua Drops for it. Occasionally there's something electric, especially wire and sweet wrappers. I saw a Kinder Bueno that glowed like a cartoon. The Merc has this unreal thing, like a heat mirage, or something that might be seen behind glass. It goes down the street slow and then I see it turn around and come back. I don't see if Pat is in it or not. But I know he's looking for me because of my accomplishments with his sister. I have Max's blessing to protect me, but you can't depend on the paranormal. I go in the Tandoori Queen and duck under the counter and back through the kitchen and out the back door. Unbelievably there's actually an Indian working in there with a white cook's hat and an apron. He doesn't shout at me in English. It's raining in the yard and it stinks of rotting chicken and burned oil. I stand on a crate and get up on the wall. Behind the wall there's a garden. I jump down into some flowers and walk up the lawn. There's no way out except through the house. I open the back door really quiet and walk in. I'm in a hall. As I pass the first room I see an old guy in an armchair. He's watching some detective programme. I go into the front room and I look out the window. There's a green surrounded by houses exactly the same as the one I'm in. The Merc is parked right in the middle of the grass. I can see the tyre marks. He's watching the houses. He must have driven round when he saw me duck in the kitchen. Fuck you, Pat boy, I think. I go upstairs and look into the rooms. The first room smells like old people. There's old furniture and clothes and pictures. The second room is completely empty – no bed, no furniture. The third room is nice. I go in there and sit on the bed. There's no blankets or sheets, just this striped mattress. There's a row of glass animals on the windowsill, a dog, a cat, a rabbit, a pig, a snake, a giraffe. I open the wardrobe and there's girls' things in there. I open a drawer and there's panties and shirts. I go outside and look around. I find the place where they keep the sheets and blankets, a warming cupboard. The sheets and blankets are warm and dry. I think about when I was small. I go back in and close the door again and make the bed. I take all my clothes off and crawl into the warm dry and try to arrange myself so I don't feel too bad. The old guy locked the house up tight. I heard him opening and closing all the doors and putting chains and locks on. Then all the lights went out. I heard him come up the stairs. He stopped outside the door of my room and I thought: the door was closed or not? Then, in this kind of baby voice he says: Goodnight, Helen. I don't say anything. I hear him go to bed. During the night I don't sleep much and he doesn't either. He shifts around and goes to the jakes about five times. In the morning I'm feeling good. My head feels as if everything is coming back to normal size. My eyes don't burn any more. It's a sunny day out. The old guy goes out about ten o'clock and I take a shower. I feel clean for the first time in weeks. I open the drawer and I take out some nice silky panties and try them on. Then I try on one of her sweaters. Then I sleep a bit again. When I wake up the sun is shining through the glass animals. There's a rainbow on the wall beside me. How old are you? I ask myself. What is your date of birth? Sixth of January, my mother said it was meant to be her day off.

I'm thinking of my girlfriend but I'm also thinking of who this Helen might be. She's about my size. I'm thin and small. I have a small ass. I don't work out and I don't get much to eat. Generally I'm too fucked up. I need performance-enhancing drugs to get up in the morning.

I'm wondering if the girlfriend is going to keep the baby or get rid of it. Pat has the money to send her to England. I'm hungry so I go downstairs and grab a bite. I grab a bowl of cornflakes and some milk and a chicken leg from the fridge and I take it up to my room. On the way I see myself in the mirror and I'm wearing this girl's sweater and this shiny pair of panties and I look like a fag. But it feels good if I don't look.

Back before I knocked her up, I tried to square it all with Pat.

Patrick Harold Baker never fails to surprise me. He gave me a lesson in humility for my trouble. And at that time I didn't realise how far gone he was, how big his thing was that he was into. I was hammered drunk and I saw him parked someplace. Dutch courage made me tap on the window. He looked at me for a bit up through the glass like he was trying to work out if I was there or not. Then he pressed the button and the glass rolled down.

Fuck off, I'm busy.

I want to explain, I said.

We don't have a relationship, he said. You don't even buy from me.

This was something new. This commercial personality. A fucking chameleon.

Look, Pat, I told him, she's a sweet kid. But you know.

He knew all right. He was keeping a close eye on her for months. Keeping her in his sights. He was driving her to discos and picking her up like she was his daughter. Once I saw her freaked out in a club and I mentioned it, just casual. He found out who gave it to her and he broke his fingers. With a claw hammer. Now there was four or five guys working for him. Like bouncers. Shaved heads. Guys that worked out in a gym. Tight-assed fags in round-neck shirts.

Get in the back and stay quiet, he says to me, I'm going to give you a lesson in humility.

We drove around for about an hour. I got the feeling he was waiting for something. Next he gets a call on his mobile. Right, he says. Right. Right. Talk to you.

That was it. He dropped down to the speed limit. He turned to me confidentially. No point in getting clocked on the way to a job, he said.

Dead right.

I'm in no hurry.

Me neither.

He turned the radio on. I could see he wasn't relaxed though. His shoulders were all tensed up. He was going to have a tense nervous headache soon enough. I saw the ad.

Look, Pat, I said, I'm interested in your sister, right. I'm trying to be up front. I respect her.

I might have been getting sober a bit by then.

You're a fucked-up shithead, he said. Don't even look at her. She's not going to get knocked up by a fucking waster. Only we're mates, I'd fucking slaughter you.

Who's knocking her up, I said.

Don't even fucking say it, he said.

This happened around Christmas when the whole world was lit up by kindness and people were buying surprises. There was a snow scene in every shop window and Santa Clauses at street corners handing out advertising. All the music was about this very special holiday, like there was no other time worth living in. I spent hours going in and out of certain jewellers' shops and pretending I needed a digital watch. I was hoping to knock off a ring. But I could see that robbing a jeweller's shop was out of my league. I had this incredible longing to give her something surprising. Because she had this way of walking that drove me wild and she knew it. She walked with her knees straight no matter how high her heels were, like a model, kind of walking from her hips like someone in the flicks. I was crazy about her. She had small tits and a small waist and it felt like there was a kid fucking me she was so small. Jesus, she *was* a kid.

He couldn't always watch her. She had to go to school,

for example. I was more than a little cracked and she didn't care. That's the recipe.

Once I looked down at her and her teeth were bright white, like perfect things from a museum, her eyes were looking at me but her head was away somewhere. Away with the fairies, my mother used to say. Another time I ingested a substance given to me by a dealer who had access to unusual things. I was doing a little cash-machine job, introduced to me by an expert in the field, and I happened to have the money. This stuff made me feel like I could screw anything. That was the time. We were at it for hours, maybe days. Maybe years. I felt like I was stretched out on a beach, my head and legs going off over the horizon, and what was between was like some incredible deep place that I could never fill. I felt this mad endless affection for her and for every part of her including her soul. I felt like she was in my care and that I might need to die for her. She was so small. You're a little Shetland pony, I said. First she looked at me like she was going to get insulted, then she laughed. Then she said to me this incredible thing: I'm going to save you, she said. Later she missed her period. And I had to go into hiding.

I'm on the run from the posse and the claw hammer and I'm lying low in the old fart's house and every night he calls me Helen. I start to think he knows I'm in here and I'm wearing her clothes and he thinks it's her. His daughter maybe. One day when he's out I go through things and I find out he *has* a daughter. She's married. He has her wedding pictures in a drawer. Judging by the clothes she must be about forty now. Maybe fifty even. The letters are beautiful. I cry a lot. I know I cry at night because sometimes I wake myself up. More than once I woke up looking for Max, but he died. Max, Max, where are you. My head hurts. She's writing about her new life, about the house they bought somewhere down the country and the flowers she has in the garden, and the sea. Then there's a baby and the baby is called Theresa and she has no hair and blue eyes. *Cornflower blue.* What's a cornflower? They made us learn poetry at school but there was never any poetry like in those letters. I can see this house with small windows with too many panes of glass to be cleaned every week. I can see the chestnut tree. I can see water in the distance. Cornflowers or something in the garden and the baby with the same colour eyes. She's holding the baby up so the cornflowers are beside her face to compare the colours. She's wearing a blue dress and her tits are big with the milk. There's birds even. She had this robin that hopped at her feet. Like a pet robin. Like everything good came into this garden. And then the letters just stop. It drives me crazy. I sneak down about four o'clock and I go through every drawer and there's no more letters. There's no pictures of the woman or the child. Then I hear a noise. I turn around and the old guy is standing there with a poker. You won't find anything worth taking there, miss, he says. His eyes aren't too good. When he's watching telly he has to lean forward.

I'm sorry, I say. I didn't mean to wake you up.

He sort of looks at me, surprised. Then he tells me to get out before he calls the guards. He steps back.

Just tell me one thing, I say. What happened to your daughter? Helen? And the baby?

He shakes a bit. Then he says, Get out of here, you bitch, before I brain you.

So I go.

I see myself in the hall mirror and I'm wearing a dress and tennis shoes.

Sometime later, after I was in hospital, after I made good my escape into the country, I'm servicing this diesel engine. I have the oil filter in a chain-grip and the fucker won't come off. I say to the farmer: Jesus Christ, when did you service this bastard? Before Hally died, he says. Hally was his son. You shouldn't live longer than your children, he says. And I read someplace, or maybe Max told me, that time holds all things, and knows how to change name and shape and nature and fortune. That was the kind of thing Max came out with. Cool stuff that sounded like songs.

The Surprise Breakfast

I came out of that house running but I never ran in a dress before. It was tight and slowed me down. There was a car parked down about four houses but I didn't think it was a Merc. The old guy came out and stood at his door. I looked back and I thought he was wheezing, or maybe laughing. He didn't think I was his daughter. All the houses were closed up and I could see the blue underwater light of the TV in the curtains. There was no one in the car. I thought, fuck, I left my male clothes in her room. How many days did I hide out? There was only one place I could go.

Well, Jesus Christ Almighty, my mother said. I never thought you'd come to this.

It's a disguise, I said. Pat Baker is trying to kill me.

You got his sister up the pole. What d'you expect?

Let me in.

Fuck off, you little git.

Ma? Please.

She could never resist begging. Times we'd pass some knacker on the bridge and she'd pay out, it's not as if she believed the story. Down-and-outs, winos, addicts, refugees, she paid them all. Where she got the money is anybody's guess. She let me in.

She stood outside my door listening to me changing into a man. Can I have them when you're finished with them, she said.

The fact is the panties gave me itch. I was glad to get out. I dropped them inside my door and when I went back upstairs ten minutes later to get a few things together to go on the run, they were gone.

You're welcome to them, I said.

She thanked me. She hugged me when I was going. She was a slag but she did her best, I let her down, I could have been something.

I grew up on The Lawn, a famous place of ill repute. We had a bad name. There were times when the buses wouldn't bring people in. Times when fame reached out and touched us, neighbours' houses starring on TV, stories about entrepreneurs and cool people with undeclared income. We were coming up in the world when I was a kid, attracting attention. The rich and famous mentioned us at parties and we were a constant worry.

But before any of this there were days between uncles when we might have been a family. She'd cook something nice and send me down to the shop for a packet of John Players and I could keep the change. There was no one looking out of doorways to say: Tell your mother she's bringing down the park, or I seen the new daddy you have, boy, your mother is a right pony, put in a word for me. I might watch the game of football on the lawn or play on the swings. I could whistle a dozen songs or more and I could do the dance from the videos while I whistled. Big fellas used to get me to do it for the laugh. We went to a caravan at some beach. She wasn't drinking then. I played in the sand and she wore a bikini. We walked with our toes in the water. But the beach faced east. The sun set behind the land and not out to sea. By evening the sand was cold and the sea was dark as glass. We played the slot machines. She put me on the Ferris wheel and I revolved slowly out of sight into the sky and I saw the whole ocean without an end. At night I used to lie in the tiny cabin and hear her doing things. She made small shuffling sounds and sliding sounds. Now I know what she was doing but then I thought she was praying. All sons hear their mothers praying for them and they are comforted. Then, when I was maybe eleven, someone showed me how to smoke hash and I lay out on the lawn all one summer night totally fucked. Nothing changed in the sky. No clouds. The stars looked nailed to me. I never saw a moon if there was one that night. It was the beginning of all my trouble. There was this dog with three and a half legs that came and sniffed me all over. He didn't piss on me. That dog just went to sleep against my arm. I think I smelled like I needed a lame dog to be complete.

Other things that happened in the old man's house. I used to hear him snoring. I used to pretend this was my grandfather. Then other times, when I was dressed, I used to pretend I was his daughter. I'd wear her dress and stuff and when he was gone to bed I used to say: Goodnight, Dad, very quiet. Whisper. Then I'd take her clothes off one by one and put on her nightdress and get into her sheets. I'd listen to him shifting around and later, maybe, snoring his head off. Sometimes I'd look out her window at the sodium lights and the cars crawling by and pulling into driveways and I'd think about the normal people who lived in those houses. All these places called Baker Mews, Mornington Grove, Limeworth Downs. Other people naming the world.

They're inventing normal. To be inside the window looking the other way, two kids playing Lego in front of an artificial fire. The husband going for a few scoops down the local. The wife going to some kind of a club. They all wear soft clothes and smell nice. The smell of cooking and washing machines in the house. I felt like my head was inside a freezer and everything was setting solid and tight. My scalding blood. One night I heard him crying. Not everything has an end. There is a store of something that nobody can touch and all harm is made good out of it, and I believe that old man had something good coming to him. I was sorry for him. I wished I was his daughter, come home for a few days' break. I wished I could get up before he woke and go downstairs and make him a surprise breakfast with a fry and tea and bring it up to him on a tray. I was grateful that he loved us so much.

There's No Such Thing as Dead Even

This is later and I'm living in the country and trying to revive a dead-on-arrival diesel engine. The chain-grip is frozen with rust and whoever fitted the filter made sure it wasn't going to come off easy. I wrap the links around it again and clamp the levers. This time there is a rubbery movement and the cylinder gives a little. I lean against it and suddenly it's gone and there's blood on my knuckles. I twist the filter off and pick the withered ring from the head. The oil in the paper gills is an old wood colour. How long since he used the tractor? I fit the new filter and check the fuel lines. Clear fuel is coming through. There's birdshit on the cowling and the steering wheel. There's even straw on the block, however that got in, mouse shits on the seat. It's just a dead old tractor that used to hurt me to see it dying in the shed, but it starts first turn. The incredible guts of these old Masseys. The smell of fuel and carbon. I toss the tools into the timber box where everything is kept and climb back into the cab. I jam the gear into first and slowly release the clutch. We rumble out of the shed, and now in the open air I can see that corrosion is eating the outsides, the bonnet, and the mudguards. The tyres are freaked with cracks, per-ished away. The instruments are fogged with moisture. Everything is coming apart. It frightens me, like I'm the reciprocating end, getting solid, calcifying, no give any more. Like I'm somehow linked to the machinery, the two of us driving some giant system, that's breaking us down or setting like a frozen thread. I see Pierce Heskin at the door, laughing. He waves. The plough behind me is whipping from side to side, almost lifting the front off the ground. It reminds me of a whale I saw in a documentary.

After I got out of hospital I decided two things. Number one I would get a trade. Number two I would get that tool Baker for breaking my legs. I got rid of the crutches, the three longest months of my life, and went down to the Toyota and asked them to take me on. The foreman used to fuck my mother. I suppose he was ashamed of himself because he said he would. The thing is, straightaway I was good at it. He started me on diesel because that was easy. Anyway the cars were just getting into computers and you needed a laptop to fix anything, the timing even. That's the end of the mechanic, he said to me. Look at that son of a bitch. He was pointing at a guy in a white boiler suit. He had a laptop plugged into something under the bonnet. He's diagnosing it, he said. A shagging car-doctor. I thought about Max. He would've got a kick out of this.

First I started taking things apart and then I was put to getting things back together. My favourite part was the torque wrench. Every part in an engine has a torque rating. That means you tighten the bolt so far. Go a bit further and it'll explode under pressure. A bit less and it'll work loose or the engine won't get up to speed. There's this lever that bends. You watch a little indicator on the head until the correct torque rating comes up. Then you stop. It's called a torque wrench. You get the needle perfect and everything is under the correct tension.

I like things to be exactly right.

I get my overalls and my boots and bit by bit I start to work out how it all fits together. The day comes when he wants to move me on to petrol and I don't give a shit. I'll quit, I say. I don't want to touch that stuff. I'm a diesel man. I'm sticking with diesel.

So he has to let me go. He's sorry to let me go because he's maybe thinking I might put in a good word with my mother again. Except I don't talk to her.

What you going to do, boy?

Fix diesels.

He laughs. You don't know shag-all about engines, he tells me. You're half a cripple. I never seen anyone make a song and a dance about getting down on one knee like you. What happened to your shagging legs anyway?

I fell on a claw hammer.

You fell on a fucking pusher, I'd say. You're hardly here six months.

Seven.

Six or seven.

The last day I ask him if I can take two things. One tool, I say. Just an ordinary tool. And a pair of overalls.

What? I don't want you taking something expensive.

A chain-grip.

He laughs.

A chain-grip is a way of getting a grip on some very large cylindrical object, like an oil filter, or a head. You wrap the chain around the object and fit a link into the grip. Then you close the handles and the grip locks on

solid. You can increase the pressure a little with a
screw.

What are you going to do with the chain-grip? he says.

I have to kill someone.

He laughs again. You're a gas man. Tell your mother I
was asking for her.

Pierce Heskin swings up and perches behind me, one arm
wrapped around the roll-bar.

I thought she'd never start again. He has to shout
above the noise of the engine. Out there this past two
years at least. Since I let the place. How long is that? Two
or three? Since Hally went.

I shout: There's nothing wrong with her a drop of oil
won't cure.

But there's pinholes in the silencer. When I open the
throttle it's an anti-aircraft battery. And there's too much
smoke – a compression ring gone? an oil scraper? an
injector nozzle blocked? That depends on the colour of
the smoke – grey or blue – but I can't decide. Who names
the colours?

We swing down the road without meeting another
vehicle, into the empty field. White seabirds in the centre
like weird toys.

He lowers the lever and the hydraulics drop the
plough. He makes the necessary adjustments.

Give her fong! he shouts.

The tractor jumps and then settles into the groove.
We're going too fast – if we hit a rock at this speed we
could break the plough – but we don't care. I swivel to
watch the furrow opening behind and there he is staring
at me. I wonder where my girlfriend is, who she's with

now. How long till I can go back. I don't know what Pierce is thinking, except maybe that he hasn't been out to his son's grave in a couple of months. That, maybe, and the thought that he's never coming back.

He shakes his head and breaks the stare. He knows.

We have to be doing something, he says.

When I had the chain around his neck I told Pat Baker about his Asperger's Syndrome. I told him Max diagnosed it. I told him he's practically autistic. I told him he gets one stupid thing into his head and he never thinks of anything else. I told him his timing is off and it's going to need a fucking computer to fix it and no honest mechanic would touch it. I told him my legs still hurt, that every time I get a pain I think about him. I told him thanks for the memories. It's a year now and I'm still feeling defective. I told him his sister was the best looker I ever saw and I wanted her back and I wanted the baby because she's mine too. I told him things she liked to do. I told him I love her and I'm going to marry her as soon as he's out of the picture. He has a fleet of Mercs now, all bent taxis and hackneys, and I was in the back of one of them and there was a Nike gym-bag on the seat beside me and I knew it contained scores of coke and a couple of dozen Es. That Nike swoosh looked like some kind of rush, like something full and wet going into the veins. Like it was Pat's own logo. I'm feeling the chain-grip tightening and I'm thinking it doesn't feel like a cylinder head or a filter. All I have to do is turn the screw a little. Each turn is a mil less for his neck to fit into. I feel good. I have an erection.

Earlier he was parked in the car park back of Tesco's, waiting for customers to notice he was open for business.

I just walked up to him and tapped on the glass. I'm not fucking picking you up, he says, I thought you were a fare.

We're all square now, Pat, I say. You did me over and I paid the price. We're even, dead even.

There's no such thing as dead even.

I'm sorry I touched your sister. We were mates once.

All right get in, he said. For old times' sake. Don't touch the fucking bag.

I'm clean, Pat, I say. Since you hammered me I haven't scored.

You're working?

Was.

A mechanic?

Diesel only. They let me go today.

Celebrating?

Did you ever see a chain-grip?

Where d'you want to go, I have things to do.

Out the country somewhere. Somewhere there's a railway station.

He decided I was emigrating and he liked the idea. I wouldn't be anywhere near his sister or my child. I'd be someplace remote, out of touch. So we drove out the country. He explained to me why he respected the Mercedes. He said he needed quality and reliability in his line of work and you can't beat the Germans for quality and reliability.

The flowers are nice, Pat. Look at all the fucking flowers.

He sees nothing. It's his Asperger's Syndrome. All he sees is the road. I hope you can pay for this, he says. This place is all boggers.

I just got paid. I'm thinking maybe he should look at the scenery. The bushes are sprayed with bloody flowers and every now and then there's a plant that looks like if you shook it, it would ring with a clear metal sound through all the bells.

In the car park I put the chain around him like a necklace, but around the headrest too, and he doesn't know what I'm doing until it's too late.

This is how it works, Pat. The chain-grip.

When he broke my legs I felt the separation. Nobody deserves to be broken, not for love. I lay there in the dark, noticing not my legs but the world was cracked. It was a long time before I felt any pain. I was on waste ground somewhere – I couldn't say for sure – and I was going to die of pain but a couple of knackers in a Hiace van picked me up and took me to A&E. They were very gentle, they lifted me onto a blanket and slipped me in the back of the van. There was a disused fridge in there and what looked like the insides of a washing machine, a stainless-steel drum and a couple of chunks of concrete. The blanket smelled like an old dog. One guy sat in the back, up against the fridge. He held my hand.

The Mercedes is a silent car. It's a place wrapped in old cotton and used plastic, and what Pat was going through was not the shouting kind of pain. He was interested in getting the chain off but he couldn't get a grip. He didn't understand the principles of the tool. He wasn't working on his breathing. I could see this little station with red brick around the windows and one of those indicators with coloured glass. People were waiting on the platform. Country-people. I knew where I was going. It was like Jesus Christ or the Pied Piper was coming down the tracks.

I'm going to fix tractors, Pat, I said. I'm going to fix useful things.

If he knew how the chain-grip worked he could have freed himself maybe. I knew he didn't. He should have learned a decent trade instead of breaking fingers and legs. I left him there kicking the shit out of his second-hand Merc.

I bought a ticket. Where to, sonny? the guy said. The end of the line, I said. He stared at me. I could see him memorising my features in case the Murder Squad arrived with a warrant. Evil-looking feen, walks like his legs are mended glass, guilty-looking. Sixteen miles, he said. You're nearly there already. Three more stops. Shit, I said, I told everybody I was emigrating. He gave me the ticket anyway. Five minutes, he said, the next train. The poster in the waiting room says if getting to the end of the week is an uphill struggle maybe it's lack of fibre. Lack of fibre can make you feel snowed under. From the window of the train I could see the Merc at the back of the car park. I couldn't see inside because of the tinted windows, but I fancied I saw a little vibration, a little flexing of the suspension. That's Pat, I thought, trying to break the chain. Three stations on I got out.

Things to Believe in

Death sorts it all out. At the exact moment there's a balance. Here's this person who could change, and on the other side there's the whole thing like stone. That's what Max figured out in the morgue. He worked it out that he was safe because nobody in there was becoming anything. He had a box of DF118 one time and we had the best sleep ever, just flaked out someplace, on grass, I think. He says to me: There's more to life. I knew what he meant. First there's nothing. Then there's life for a time. Then there's a whole lot of death. Max had this big thing about a good death.

I was living in the back room in Pierce's and he was renting me one of his sheds to fix tractors. In six months I was making near enough a hundred and fifty a week, no questions asked, but I was going to have to get some serious equipment. I needed welding stuff and a hoist and maybe something to crane the engines out, and a proper bench. What I needed was to buy a garage or a machine shop. Crazy dreams. Pierce took me in to see his bank manager but the fat fucker took one look at me and just laughed. I think there's something, like a colour maybe, a secret mark, something that's invisible if you're wearing it. Besides, the bank manager did not believe in people getting out of holes, he believed in serious gravity. I thought it over for a few weeks and in the end I superglued the locks on his car. It was just a small thing but it gave me a sense of satisfaction. Guess what the car was? I could imagine the big mystery back at the works. None of ze locks vork? Vot iss dis? Dis never happen before. It was an '86 240D with a broken tail-light but it made him feel like a full-size man.

Pierce offered to make a loan but I wouldn't take it. Never do business with friends, Max used to say, share and share alike. Another time when he was putting something together for me, he was kneeling on the floor with the gear in front of him, he turns to me and says, out of the blue: Caring is sharing. A priest, like.

I won't take your money, I said to Pierce, and he asked me what was wrong with it, and I said, I just can't take it, what if something went wrong.

Well, I'm not saving it up for my descendants, he said. He had nobody.

So, one night I was having a quiet pint and this guy comes over to me. He shakes my hand. Timmy Stuart, he says. Pierce tells me you want to make a few quid.

Very mysterious. He sits down. He has a pint and a shot of vodka. He slowly reveals things. We have two more pints, two shots. He's very careful. The farmers come in and play cards. The women watch the telly. The football team arrives at ten with their hair wet and get into a corner for some serious tactical discussions about the bastards from the next parish.

What Timmy Stuart does is he videos weddings. When he talks about it his face goes quiet. Like he's about to reveal the identity of someone important. I've seen that look before. Maybe it was Max or maybe it was Pat Baker's dead-fish face. This guy is a serious case. I buy him drink and he's skulling pints and shots and talking and I hear what he's talking about.

He advertises.

He has the gear.

Everybody wants a moving picture of the day. They want it with beautiful music because otherwise they don't know what to feel. They want close-ups. Some people watch the day over and over as if they don't really believe it, as if they might spot something. As if the weather is different in the picture, the wind blowing or not blowing or rain and then they know it never happened. As if this will explain everything that happens afterwards.

But he keeps his own record.

Nobody is as beautiful as a bride, he says. And the bridesmaids. The way they move. The way they look at each other. White is for purity and innocence. Even the skin is not as pure. And everything is designed for the eye. The body wound in its veils of satin. Inside there's a little moisture, a little soft hair, things just held in place, but outside is a princess. When they get drink, he said, they're a different animal. All sweet in the church, like they didn't know what was inside the white, but later they dance the dance all right. I take the pictures, he said. It's all there.

He's telling me that he makes pornographic videos.

It's illegal, I say.

He shakes his head and laughs. They never take their clothes off, he says. You think they'd let me shoot that?

He downs a short.

They get their memories. I keep a little something for myself.

We drink to that.

He takes me home and turns off the lights and he has this huge wide-screen on one wall. He shows me wedding videos.

I see the beautiful girls.

He has cut all the shit. I see the faces. The moves. The light of the stained-glass windows, the beautiful fabric. One bride kneeling looking at her hands but she's not thinking about God, she's thinking about later. Two bridesmaids look at each other. One girl dancing with her hand just lazy moving up and down his spine. Is he her husband or someone who stepped in for the dance? Four girls dance together, the way they move. One moves her hands up and down her thighs, a jerky reachy movement. One looks and holds her arms out and sinks down. There is no music. This small girl with cropped black hair, so black, like night. Her face is small too and she dances for nobody but herself. Earlier in the church part I saw her and then later yawning at the dinner, an empty glass in front of her, a small hand moving to cover that perfect mouth, those stony perfect teeth. Timmy Stuart puts all the pieces together. A girl who talks in sign language, every finger meaning something. What do deaf people do for gestures? This man is a poet pornographer, a lonely boy at his sister's confirmation. I sit in the dark and I shake. I think of all the things I've done, the shit I've swallowed. I think of the girl who was lonely and the girl who had my baby. Max dying in the hospital, giving me his drugs, giving me his thoughts. There's more to life, he said. A girl looks a long distracted look straight at the camera. It must have pierced him to see that, how did he hold the camera steady? The human eye would blink, the soul should blink and step aside. She looks out from inside something and she's looking out of life into the empty future, a pale, green-eyed ghost on her wedding day. What does she see?

It's only Saturday work, he said. Nobody gets married during the week. He gave me the second camera. He gave me an hourly rate. He gave me the boring stuff, like the people in the church and he did the bride and the bridesmaids. There was this one wedding and I couldn't take my eyes off the women. Jesus, Timmy, I said, how do these guys pull these beautiful women? They're all auctioneers, boy, he said. They're all manky rich.

This blonde in a creamy dress that almost matches the colour of her skin like she's not wearing anything at all. There's sex just coming out her eyes. I watch her dancing later and she dances all to herself. Then she sees me filming and she starts to dance for me but pretending she isn't, pretending she doesn't know. She dances over by the disco lights so I can see the light between her legs. I can see all the way up the shadows of her legs and the divide at the top. I want to lie down and film her from the ground but I think the auctioneers would take me outside and beat me to shit.

When Timmy comes back from the bar he gives me hell. This is my job, he says. Don't ever touch my camera. Stick to the scenes I gave you.

Jesus, Timmy, she's beautiful, I say. Look.

He's holding a pint in one hand, a drop of Paddy in the other. He chuckles. You have it bad, he says. There's no cure for you.

How I met Pierce Heskin was I was sleeping in what I thought was a derelict barn. I scouted around and looked in the windows and everything was dead looking. It looked to me like the owner was recently deceased. There was a fugitive cat and a few beasts in the fields and everything looked ratty and run down. I didn't know then that farms can die of grief. Three nights I dossed down in the straw. On the fourth morning I found a toolbox and I started to mess with the engine on the Massey Ferguson. I got the cowling off and started to take off the fuel pump. I remember I was hungry and kind of drilled. I was running out of cash and it was a long walk to the village which I made the day before. The loaf of bread I bought was stale, maybe a little nibbled at one side. I couldn't face it. I opened the door to let the light in to warm my back. I got a sheet of canvas and spread it on the floor and I started to lay all the bits out as they came apart. The smell of old diesel and grease. I was happy. Maybe I started to whistle or maybe I started to talk to myself.

Suddenly I noticed that there's someone looking at me. It's an old guy with watery eyes and a double-barrel shotgun.

Well? he said.

I'm fixing the fuel pump, I said.

Did it not start?

I didn't try.

Are you going to steal it?

I thought you were dead.

He laughed. You're not the first.

Sorry 'bout that.

No offence. What in the name of Jesus are you doing with my tractor?

I'm fixing the fuel pump. The engine is fucked.

After a bit he went into the house and came back without the shotgun. He had a chair with him instead. He dropped the chair beside the canvas.

Beautiful morning, he said.

Mint.

Is there a problem?

The diaphragm is fucked. The gasket is withered.

Can you fix it?

Need the parts though.

How much?

Depends.

I bled diesel out of the tank into a bucket and I washed the metal parts in it. Every few minutes I gave him a look. The sun was warm and he seemed to be asleep. Then he said: Where are you living?

In your barn.

He laughed. Fair enough, he said, but you better move into the house if you're going to fix my tractor. There's a spare room. I can't afford to pay you but I'll give you room and board. In the meantime there's a few neighbours have tractors too. And diesel cars. All the transport around here, he said, runs on agricultural diesel.

What's in it for you?

You're going to fix my tractor.

When I'd stand on the floor first thing I couldn't feel anything. Then the pins and needles would start. Sometimes I sat on the bed and cried, waiting for the sparking to stop. I'd come down the stairs one step at a time and boil a kettle and fill out a shovel of tea. I'd hear Pierce shifting about. Then *he'd* come down the stairs one step at a time. He'd come into the kitchen with one hand pressed into the small of his back and one knee working overtime. He liked his tea strong. For the fuel pump, he always said. Private joke. It was the same in the pub. He'd order two pints of Murphy's and then he'd wink at me and he'd say: We're fixing the fuel pump. He told me once that stout lubricates the joints.

In the beginning I was able to get at the Rheumox and Ponstan but Pierce started to suspect. He started hiding them. My prescription is running out, he'd say, I could've sworn on the bible I had it for another two weeks.

Anyway Rheumox is hard on the stomach.

When they put the pin down my legs I ran into serious trouble. First thing is they start to swell. The pain is incredible. You got compartment syndrome, the doctor says. It's more common with redheads. We have to open up the compartments and let the pressure out. If we don't do it we'll end up having to amputate. There was all this meat inside and the skin that was holding it in couldn't stretch enough to cope. So they opened up the legs like a zip down each side. They gave me beautiful morphine. Then bit by bit they sewed me up again. Five operations. I had Technicolor in my dreams for the first time ever, and full-surround sound. Even the bad ones were more true than being awake. I remember floating above the bed and looking down and I looked dead enough. I could see out the window and there was a pattern in the traffic. I can't remember now but at the time I had the feeling I made a discovery that could make me famous.

In the end Pierce said to me: Why don't you go down to the dispensary and get something done about them legs.

What do you know about my legs, I said.

I hear you, he said. You're slower than me in the morning.

So I fixed his tractor and by the time that was working I had a waiting list. I bought a shitheap Volkswagen Golf diesel van and started doing house visits with my little bag of tricks. Not only their tractors ran on agricultural diesel but anything with more than two wheels. The van was holding together with rust and dirt but I got the engine running sweet.

I don't think about the legs. If I do, I start to think about what I should have done with Pat Baker's spinal column. I get angry and the psychologist said anger wasn't helpful in my case. After they nailed me back together they took a hand in my general medical condition. They sent me this limbo-dancer who wriggled under everything I said. I'd tell him something that was sure to put him off the track and a few minutes later there he'd be again, popping up just ahead of me with a stupid grin. Unresolved anger, he said. He wanted to know if I had suffered some traumatic event, some kind of abuse. I said nobody ever laid a finger on me. I told him about Max but not everything. I told him about girls. Tell me about your mother. Tell me about your father. Tell me about your grandfather. I told him I had too many ancestors with *not known at this address*. I had the feeling I was divulging too much. Like I was throwing things away I might need sometime. Go down to the centre when you get out, he said at the last outpatient clinic. Go to an NA meeting. To get him off my back I agreed I would. I said what the ad says: DON'T GIVE UP GIVING UP. He gave me a note. First of all the centre was off in the estates, big houses with lawns, places we only went about three in the morning for certain purposes, mainly to unlock some of the value in their homes. There's a chair for everybody, including me. It seems they were expecting me or someone like me. They say everybody has one good story. These people all had their story down mint. They all talked. They were accepting responsibility all over the place. Everything that ever happened to them was their own fault. Like they didn't grow up in a shithouse estate with junkies shooting up and friends and relations going down for things *they* never accepted responsibility for. I was waiting for anyone to declare his innocence. It did not happen. It seems they all had choices. At one point in their life they could have turned into something else, a contributing adult, a businessman or some useful member of the community with no habit and a happy family. They all could have had a good address if they made the right choice. But they all chose to be junkies. Like who ever chose to be a fucking junkie? I wasn't buying that. When it came to me I said: Not guilty, I blame everyone else. They all shook their heads and just quietly looked at me. I was sitting there listening to these no-hope heroin addicts and alkies and for the sake of the story I'm trying to think of one time, just one time, when I *decided* I would take a pill that might not be good for my digestion. I never came up with one.

My Child's Sleeping Face

But I forgot to tell what happened when I told the surgeon's daughter that it was me shot the patio man. She grassed me up. I'm at home, for once, asleep in my own bed. I hear knocking and I hear my mother answer and she's giving out yards. I hear her mention a warrant and I do a mental check to make sure I had nothing on me. My trousers is on the ground and I pick it up and I'm going through it when the door opens and two men in suits come in. Get the fuck up, one of them says. Don't try anything. I think: Like what am I going to try. I'm bollocks naked. Do I get dressed? I say. I'm shy. We'll turn our backs. But first they went through my clothes and did the room over, not that there was too much to do. They found a list of phone numbers I was keeping. We know one or two of these, don't we? I said I thought they would. Mostly they were drug dealers. This where you got the contract, one of them says. A cheap shit like you, it must of been easy money. You're moving up in the world, sonny boy. But first you're moving to Mountjoy Gaol. How much did you get?

The trouble was I didn't connect. I couldn't remember doing anything that would have two pigs in suits doing over my room. I don't get in fights. This was before we started in on the music fag and Max revealed to me that he had a secret. It was before I blew it with Pat Baker by fucking his kid sister and more or less lost it for her. It was before I started going to the club and getting thrown out. This was a time of innocence. All I did was blow up a bird table and smoke a little scag. Maybe Max was supplying me from time to time with things from the hospital, and maybe that was later too. I can't remember. They put me in the car and took me down to the station. They cautioned me. Then this big bastard I half recognised came in. He took one look at me. This is Theresa's kid, he says. How's your mother, sonny boy? All the fucking shades call me sonny boy like they're related to me.

What do they have you in for?

They didn't tell me yet.

I'll check. He went out and came back. You did the hit on Pakey Tynan alias The Masher.

I never heard of him.

Every fucking drug dealer in the country has this cartoon name. Like they're all refugees from comics. Like they're funny.

Someone came forward.

They're lying.

This party said you admitted it.

Oh no, I said. My ex.

Girlfriend?

I was putting it on. She grassed me up for it. She fucking believed me. I don't believe it. She never believed anything before.

You got lucky.

I told him about the hash, about the bird table. He nodded and looked at me with fish eyes. He was about six foot six and fat all over. He had fists the size of melons. I remembered him coming to our house when I was about four. He always brought me sweets. I remembered he was married too. My mother was always shouting at him. What my mother wanted was commitment and a long-term relationship, but what she got was married men and punters. The promise of a past. I mentioned my memories and he let me out. I believe the kid, he was telling everyone. He was very sure. He had to be a superintendent or something. Tell the missus my ma was asking for her, I said. He went very quiet.

I was doing about a bar of hash a week later on, when I could get it, more than an ounce a day. Also certain prescription drugs which were harder to come by. I did a little marketing here and there, among acquaintances. Sometimes I was more together and I raised money or visited friends and relations and held parties. Mostly I was someplace else. I borrowed a car and fell asleep at the wheel. I drove across the road, missing oncoming traffic, and through a concrete fence. Only that I was stoned I would have been killed. Drunks hardly ever get hurt when they fall, it's just they fall on other people. When all around them are losing their heads the drunk is the one in the middle, calm and controlled. Nothing is going in. There were many products available to those of us who understood the retail trade: I name speed, acid, cocaine, ecstasy, mushrooms, besides hash and a variety of opiates. Also things to make you sleep, to wake you up, to make you feel like you had power and owned something, like you had relations in the suburbs, a woman, friends, even happiness according to a certain definition. I got out of the wrecked car safe and sound and took off across the fields. I was cut in several places and later I needed stitches to my face, but at the time I just felt wet and surprised. This happened to Max's brother too, in similar circumstances.

The first time I saw my girlfriend she had hair the colour of old aluminium. Over the years it has become brown and blonde, like the natural tendency for someone as beautiful as her is to turn into silver in parts, like that's what evolution means. She has full lips and a small nose and eyes that are black at night and wood-brown in the daytime. When she looks at me from the bed, she rests her cheek on one shoulder and there's a line of muscle that goes down from her ear to between her breasts that I like to touch. If she's wearing a bra I slip my hand inside and touch the nipple and her eyes get big. When she's lying down her belly pulls the navel into a straight line and a ring glints in it. Just seeing her. When our daughter comes to sleep with us, like when she's troubled by dreams, she whispers and moves in long slow parts not to wake her. She leaves the curtains drawn late and slips out to get our breakfast. I lie there with my silent child and wish for the night again. Nights I looked out and there were moths and monster insects against the glass. The moths' wooden faces looking in from the dark, the metal bodies, bits of fur and strange designs. My daughter's face sleeping against my arm when she was a baby. Her breath was a feather.

And Jacintha Baker. I called her Jazz.

A *Hatful of Mushrooms*

I used to watch Pierce coping with the idea that he had
nobody left. He kept a few dry cattle and he used to drive
down this lane and out into the field. Sometimes he got
out and talked to them. Sometimes he sat in that wreck of
a Ford Escort with the windows closed up and the radio
on. Once or twice I had to bring the tractor and tow him
out. I can still see him out in the middle of some field with
the wheels spinning and the car digging him slowly down
into the earth like it wanted to die. Behind the wheel he
was just staring. He didn't care. In the autumn he'd bring
home a hatful of mushrooms from some field and fry
them with rashers. He'd ask me over and over, were they
the best mushrooms I ever tasted. This one time he had
me out picking blackberries. Jesus Christ, Pierce, I said,
the ditches are full of fruit. What's this?

Try it, he says.

I try it and spit.

That's a sloe, he says. He's laughing.

Who owns these fucking blackberries, I say?

God, he says.

Is there money to be made on them?

I never yet heard of a man who figured out how to
make money out of blackberries or haws or sloes. Or else
there's many a poor man I know would be a millionaire
for all the briers and thorns he has.

I never saw anything like this, I say. I'm picking the berries off the briers, the black juiciest one at the tip and red ones and black ones down along. Sometimes they just squash in my fingers and my fingers are blue black. We'll make jam out of it, Pierce says. He's excited too. By Jesus we'll ate well this winter.

But we just mashed them onto bread and butter when we got home, whatever we didn't eat on the way.

One time I found out he was a Protestant. You're the first Prod I ever met, I said.

May it be the first of many, he said, like people said when someone had a baby.

What kind of a Protestant are you?

The same kind of Catholic you are, not much of a one.

He'd sell a few beasts and buy a few, and he'd read the paper and *The Farmer's Journal*. He was trying to say that there was no such thing as nothing. He was whispering it, though. You had to listen to hear. I lived with him nearly two years while I was waiting patiently to get my girlfriend and my daughter back, laying my plans, making enquiries. I called up Micko, an old neighbour from The Lawn, and as it happened he had something against Pat Baker now. He gave me the news Jazz was out on her own in a flat.

I told Pierce the story. I told him about Pat Baker and his commercial interests, about how he warned me off his sister, how she wanted me, how love found a way. I told him Pat broke my legs over it and I finished up in hospital and didn't see her since. I previously indicated that my pains were caused by a car accident where I was the unlucky passenger. I told him how I was biding my time, making plans. I left out the thing about the chain-grip and everything about Max. I did not mention that a prolonged spell in hospital, for someone unenterprising like me, was as good a therapy as any for quitting a life of crime.

Christ Almighty, boy, he said.

He was excited about it.

She's the mother of your child.

I know it, I said.

Bring them out here. There's no bastard going to come out here to get them. They won't mess with Pierce Heskin.

I told him Pat Baker was a serious man.

Fuck him, Pierce said. He was seventy-one and thin and grey, but I felt the loss of his own son rise up in him, and maybe the early death of his wife from cancer of the oesophagus. He was a superman. He could crush some asshole drug dealer with his fist. Let him try me out, he said, and see whether he likes it.

So we called in to her one evening, not knowing what to expect.

And the funny thing is, later, after I fled the premises and they did come out to get me, Pierce saw them coming. He saw the silver Merc coming up the lane to his gate. He waited until they got the gate open and drove into the yard and then he opened fire. He destroyed the paint-work. He was using number twos. They took off fast and he called the guards to warn them and a car chase resulted with damage to a phone box and several illegally parked cars, though the passengers in the fleeing Mercedes got away, according to the news. They never came back for him. They probably cut their losses. I heard afterwards that they got a very bad opinion of farmers after their trip down the country.

The place she had was on Devonshire Street Lower. Wherever Devonshire is, they don't want this place named after them. The door was painted green and the top half was glass. There was wire through the glass like a net. Upstairs next door the windows were nailed. Two doors up was an adult store with the windows all pinked out. The first person she saw was Pierce. I think he looked like he needed something normal, tea or boiling water. Like someone working on the gas main, so she didn't slam the door. By the time she saw me she was talking to him.

Jesus, my brother is going to massacre you if he sees you, she said, after what you done to him. He still can't talk right.

He's lucky. One link more and he was dead.

If he finds out you're here.

Who's going to tell him?

She leaned out and looked up the street. Better get in, she said.

There wasn't a Merc in sight at that moment. I went first and Pierce came after me. Where's the baby, I said.

At me sister's.

Shit.

You took off. What're you worried about. She's not a baby any more, she's a little girl.

What did you call her?

None of your business.

I pointed out I was the father and she said she already knew. Pierce asked for tea. He was looking grey in the face. His angina was probably acting up. I kept starting everything with Look. She kept interrupting. After a bit Pierce said: He came back for you, girl. Your brother might kill him, but he came back for you. The way I see it he's risking his life for you and the child. He's mad about you. He never stops talking about you. Now, leave me drink me tea in peace. Sit down, the two of you, and stay quiet for three minutes.

I sat down and Jazz made the tea. Nobody said anything. Afterwards she told me that was the first time she felt safe since before the baby was born. Meantime I'm sitting there going: This is weird, like.

This all happened to me before, I was thinking. The way everything else seemed to be coming off alongside. At the time there was something bad going around, making people feel how precious everything is, life and health, how good it is to have the real buzz. There was an epidemic of anaphylactic shock among people I did drugs with and their friends and acquaintances. That time the first thing I noticed was that my face was icy cold. Then everything was too much. I had to think hard to move my hands and they wouldn't touch things. I got pins and needles in my legs. I looked down and I saw red spots on my wrists and up my arms. My eyes started to narrow down like I couldn't see things out at the edges any more, only through this round tunnel. The wall in front of me was so white it moved. I passed out and when I woke up I was happy. My whole head was icy cold and I didn't want to even lift a finger. I just stayed where I was, washing around in this happy pool. How long was I out? I could hear a radio playing somewhere and maybe the programme changed but they played the same shit day in, day out, you couldn't tell anything. Sometime during the night I turned over on my side and when I woke up all I could remember was the white. I was fine. Now it's there again without the drugs. Pierce is tapping his fingers on the table but no sound is coming out. My girlfriend is getting mugs out and putting tea-bags in the pot. I feel like I'm not there, like I'm watching it happen to other people. I think there should be a mute button I could press and release everything. Then her sister Stacey comes in just as the tea is ready. She takes one look at me.

Jesus, Jacintha, what are you going to do?

Is that my baby? I say.

I'm not in on this, her sister says, I seen nothing. I don't want to know.

I'm going with him, my girlfriend says. Her sister sits down. She looks at me, she looks at my girlfriend, she looks at Pierce. She's still hanging on to the child, pulled up close between her legs, half sitting in her lap. The child has on pink dungarees and a pink cardigan with square holes in it, light and soft and full of comfortable air. She has her mother's hair before she dyed it.

I look at the baby and back again. I look at my girlfriend's sister. I look at my girlfriend. When did she decide? It's like five minutes since we knocked on the door. Women are incredible.

Who the fuck are you? her sister says to Pierce.

Pierce gives her the wink. I'm just an interested third party.

She says: You sound like a fucking solicitor to me only I know he can't afford one. Is he in trouble? Are you Free Legal Aid?

I'm a farmer, Pierce says.

That explains it, her sister says. A fucking country wanker sticking his nose into what's none of his business.

Charming, Pierce says.

Up yours too, with knobs on, her sister says.

The child starts to cry.

We leave in the dark and there's nobody to see. My girlfriend kisses her sister more than once. Just tell him I ran away, she says. Tell him I took the boat. He'll murder me, her sister says. Pierce drives and I sit in the front saying nothing. He turns on the radio and it's some kind of request programme. I listen to this crazy religious tool talking about the little flower and people writing letters to him about *céilí* music and saying God bless every ten seconds and playing this diddly-dum bogger stuff that all sounds the same. I can't think of anything to say. My little girl is asleep. After about half an hour my girlfriend says: Does anybody live this far?

This is the country, I say. It's all farms and stuff.

Cool, she says.

A Bird's Nest in the Wall

I'm getting some pain from where they screwed the pins in the time Pat Baker broke me up. My legs sometimes felt heavier than bone should be and the dead places on the soles of my feet were electrified. I'm making good money on the video and good money on the tractors and I'm coming home at night full of desire, hoping Pierce is out, Kaylie is in bed, Jazz is alone. The same hope every night. Like this is how it should be. This one evening I remember. I park the van in the yard. I look up at the sky which is pitch black. The air is sharp the way you feel it breathing in. When I come in she's kneeling in front of the grate holding a sheet of newspaper up to get the draught going. She looks up and winks. You're not thinking about me, she says, otherwise the fire would light. That's what they say.

Oh I'm thinking about you all right, I say. And just then the fire lights and a black hole appears in the middle of the classifieds. She drops it and it's burning and I have to stamp it out.

See what I mean? I say.

The house is starting to look like it doesn't belong to a dead person. There's a fire every day and food cooked, sending its smell into every room. My daughter makes Pierce laugh out loud. He drives her around the yard on the tractor and sometimes he takes her out for a walk. In the springtime they find a bird's nest in a wall of one of the sheds and she spends hours watching for the birds to come out and look at her. The cat watches too with maybe something else in mind.

I'm twenty-one years of age. I don't remember getting this far.

Pierce says: Happy birthday. Who are you going to vote for?

The one in the suit, I say.

Everything is fine until I hear that someone is asking for me. Then I read in the paper about this fellow I used to know. He's driving a taxi. He gets shot at a traffic light, two bullets in the stomach, one in the upper thigh. He knows he'll bleed to death so he steps on the pedal. He goes through the red light, headed for the Regional Hospital, across a bridge which is one-way in the other direction, down a narrow street, hopping off stuff parked on the side, along under the cathedral where he forces three cars and a cyclist off the road. The cyclist is badly injured. Then he's roaring along the carriageway at eighty, there's a pool of blood on the seat between his legs; he's a very careful man and he never takes the plastic cover off the driver's seat, he keeps his taxi mint. He's through the red light and swinging right, the A&E is ahead, all he has to do is slow down and pull into the ambulance bay, maybe lean on his horn until they come for him, but he's drifting in and out and his foot is heavy. He goes straight through the ambulance bay and smashes into a Jaguar and a Lexus, neither of which moves. The car he's driving is a Merc. It's like this glorious battle of the car brands.

One place everybody knows is the A&E. We were all in there one time or another. We wait a lot.

I tell her they're going to get me. I show her the newspaper. I try to convince her that everything has got bigger, that monsters are growing in the back gardens. It's a big trade now, I say, no small stuff. This is gone international. Where the fuck do you think they buy this shit? That pistol had to come from somewhere. They used a nine-millimetre automatic, the paper said.

Jesus, she says, he was at my sister's wedding.

Who do you think owns that Merc?

'Member someone was asking for you? she says. Pierce told me. He bought Pierce a drink.

What did Pierce say?

He said they had the wrong guy. He said you were an old guy and I was your daughter.

We laugh about that. Pierce wouldn't like some city chancer asking around about his friends.

She says: If Pat finds me he'll kill me too.

He won't find us where we're going.

Where are we going to go?

I tell her I don't know yet. Then she starts to giggle. Maybe we could dress you up, she says. I told her about that time I escaped and about the old man and his daughter. She tells me I'm a poet myself. She says I have beautiful dreams. She already got me to try on her panties so I could fuck her with them on. It wasn't a good idea. Now I'm worried she might be serious.

We won't leave any clues, I say, and the lads won't talk, Pierce or Timmy. They won't let us down.

Someplace my brother won't think, she says.

I say: Anything that goes in the back of the van we

bring. I'm going to lay hands on some plates and once we get maybe twenty miles I'll change them round. Just in case someone gives them the reg. of the van.

I feel this responsibility that I have to organise everything. It's the man's job. Better not to know too much, I tell Jazz. She sees it that way too, I think. I piece it all together, thinking things over while I'm lying on the slide under an engine, looking up into the works and putting things into their exact place, every thread tightened exact, the torque exact. No mistakes. I make enquiries among friends and clients. I discover the location where we'll hide out from the posse. Where no one'll look for us. I have it sorted.

I call round to see Timmy to say goodbye. I bring a nodge of hash and we smoke some and watch his dirty movies.

The day job is shaky, he says. They're downsizing worldwide. Cutting the cost base. I'm only hoping they'll go for voluntary. I'm fifty-one, no way will I get another job. All I can say is I'm glad the mother isn't alive. She'd drop dead if she saw me on the dole. The bastards, the fucking bastards. We're the best production figures of all. I knew it. I knew. They're downgrading the plant the past two years. There was no turnaround. The place is only held together with Band-Aid. God rest her soul, my mother used to say they only came for the grants. As soon as the grants are gone they're off. They're only tourists, she used to say. She was right. She was nobody's fool.

The videos run and this commentary about downsizing is the only sound, the beautiful women in their ceremonies, the skin and the satin and the diamond rings, the child flower girls and the grandfathers.

Part-way through one of the best, I notice he's crying. He's sitting there pushed back in his seat, one hand gripping the remote like a weapon, the other brushing at his face. I can see the tears flashing on and off in the changing light.

I never told anyone else, he says. I never showed the videos to anyone. Not once.

I know.

It's good to share.

And there was me thinking we could do a deal with the hotel and get a camera into the honeymoon suite.

He laughs but he's not too sure. We have a different sense of humour. And then, maybe I was opening up a possibility for him. He stopped crying.

Pierce is turning something, a machine, and things come out in twists and shaves.

Feed, he says. Mangels. Fattening.

Jesus, I say, there's things I never even knew.

He comes back with me, slowly, like he dreads entering the house again. Like it's already back to normal. He makes a cup of tea. A cold breeze is blowing through the net curtains. He puts a nip of Paddy in each cup and winks at me.

To keep body and soul together, he says. Am I right or am I wrong – you're on the run again?

I just nod. I'm miserable.

When are you off?

They're making their enquiries, I tell him. I'll bring hassle on everyone if I stay around.

Stand your ground, boy. Don't be always running away.

I tell him I'll be in touch.

It was drugs, wasn't it, he says. Will I tell you one thing, boy? The way up is the same as the way down.

Fair dues, I say.

There's a kick in the tea. The kitchen is cold again like Jazz already left, that kind of cold damp that old people that live alone have. There's plates and cups stacked in the sink. Two empty Guinness Draughts gleaming in the winter sun. Jazz used to say: Tidy up, can't you, before you go to bed. But he'd come home after closing time with a couple of cans and they'd still be there on the sink in the morning. There's a black rasher in the cat's plate but the cat is nowhere to be seen. She spends her time dreaming about rats in what's left of the straw. Or sleeping on the seat of the tractor. Cats stop eating when they have enough. Humans and dogs never know. There's a triangle missing out of the small pane of the window where it blew shut in a gale. Six weeks ago he taped a piece of cardboard over it and the middle of the cardboard is soft with wet and the tape is lifting. I'm taking it all in because I know it all. I lived here. This is The House of Loneliness. Old people should die before their children, he said once. I believe it.

Did I ever tell you, he says. Then he stops. He looks at me.

The two of them had the same thing, he says. The big C. Cancer?

In the same place. What do you think of that?

There's something in his eyes that tells me not to say anything.

Ten years nearly to the day, Hally came home. At that time he was working for Avonmore, on the road. I mightn't see him for two weeks at a time. I'm after being in for tests, Dad, he says. I have the same thing as Mammy.

Jesus.

The genes are a killer, he says. Everyone on my side lived too long.

How long did he last?

Six months. It was rampant seemingly. The two of them are in the one place now anyhow.

That lady of yours, she's worth it. Stick by her. You have something now, don't throw it away.

Do I look like I'm throwing something away?

You do.

Next day we load the van and take off. I have a good idea where we're going. It's two hours from town, too far for anyone to come out, drug dealers get agoraphobia.

The guy that was asking for me had a husky voice. Who the fuck is that, she says, if it's not my bastard brother. You crushed his voice-box.

Congratulations, I say. You're turning over a new leaf.

Cool, she says. It's what I always wanted.

We're headed for the coast and we come over the saddle of some mountain and there's the water ahead of us.

We Play Happy Families

Now we're living in a seaside town. My girlfriend works nights in Mac's Fries and I work days because we're trying to get something going. I'm sitting watching telly with the sound turned down when I see one of my old neighbours talking to camera. I'm playing cards with my daughter. I see my neighbour and I wonder what the old bitch is on about now, and then I remember that I'm watching the news so I turn the sound up.

Too late. All I hear is that the shades are treating the matter as an abduction.

Max worked it all out one time, about how you could kidnap someone and pull it off. I'm not sure if Pat was in on it. The thing was, first of all, obviously, the kidnappee could not see your face or any distinguishing features, even clothes. The ideal victim would be blind. Next you need to get them about a day before anyone notices. You do not harm them. You post the note just before you do the job, at a time when the victim's whereabouts can be established. This is to lay a false trail. There was more that I can't remember, complicated stuff. Kidnapping did not interest me as much as getting good drugs and getting my hole. I could think of better crimes, but Max always complicated everything. Max got some whizz. Want to try it? he says to me. I was generally interested in extending my experience. We walked around a lot.

We went in and out of places. An old neighbour of ours from The Lawn was involved with this club and we went in and danced a bit. Everything was fast. This old neighbour asked us to leave sometime later. No offence lads, he said, but the boss is on to me. Those guys are messing, he says. Your friends. Go get them out. Sorry about this. No probs now. Nice and easy. We went nice and easy. We were afraid of bouncers. Max was doing a little marketing earlier, cold calling and working the crowd, trying to raise a little finance for some project, but he was out of stock by now. He just smiled his mad smile and did what he was told. No offence lads, he said. Fair dues. Take it handy. If I can get you anything ever. Et cetera et cetera. Max was into networking. He unfolded his kidnap plan to me outside the Yangtze River chip shop where he was eating chips at speed. There wasn't time for one chip to go down before the next was coming in. His face was filling up with used potato and he was trying to drink Pepsi at the same time. I saw the watery black falling down his face and over his shirt. Then he vomited into a litter bin and the polystyrene cartons blossomed red and white. That was a strange night. He held on to the pole and put his face over the bin. I think I heard the sound of the polystyrene shuffling to get out of the way. If it's a girl, he said, you could fuck her a bit, nicely, so she likes it. I read somewhere that Patty Hearst got to love it.

Do we know her?

He laughed and I laughed too, but I didn't know what I was laughing at. He had these twisted fantasies. Some of his dreams which I was in at times were like what you'd buy under the counter from select locations nationwide.

Some were things he read in the paper, rape and sexual assault charges against people who had drink taken and according to several character witnesses were decent people otherwise, that kind of thing.

Next news bulletin I find out it's my mother was kidnapped. I get my daughter to bed as quietly as I can. Go to sleep now. Mammy will be in soon and she's always tired after work.

She says she will. Ten minutes later she's down for a glass of water. She won't fall asleep until she hears the key in the door.

When my girlfriend gets back I tell her.

Jesus Christ, she says. What are you going to do?

We're safe here, I say. Nobody came looking for us. You're not writing home or anything?

How thick do you think I am?

Only you did last time. That's how they tracked us to Pierce's. The postmark.

That was only once.

She sent her sister a birthday card.

You're phoning her?

Only on the mobile. You can't trace a mobile.

This old neighbour that was involved with the club was Micko. He started as a bouncer. Actually, he started before that as a general asshole and liar. He might have been grassing people up for small things. A number of mutual friends got picked up and one or two got charged. He was no good as a bouncer but he got in early on the E trade. People going in the club knew they could pick a little something up on the way. This was a cool club and the clientele had money – private-school boys and blondes with careers ahead of them. It was all fock this and fock that. All solicitors and shit. I saw some of the places they lived. This friend, he buried the money, small stuff to begin with, but he had the motto of *waste not, want not* like my mother was always telling me. Before we knew it he was shares in the club. Now, I believe, he's sitting in the office. I never even knew he could add. Micko The Thicko we used to call him. I'm fucked if I know how I got him so wrong.

We weren't buying that night. We told him we already had everything we needed. We didn't say we were into a rival venture as a result of surplus stock coming our way. We believed in the benefits of competition in the market-place and below-cost selling. He gave us the wink. Be good now, he said. Don't do anything I wouldn't do. He was older than the two us, a few years ahead of Max, but it might have been twenty. He knew where he was going and we didn't. If Max had of known he was going to catch something and die young, everything would have been different. He would have done something big. But he fell in love with death and death came and took him. I knew it when he told me he was sleeping in the morgue. I knew he was sick.

Max is mint, he used to say.

How are you, Max?

Max is mint.

It was one of his jokes. He certainly wasn't mint. He was yellow-looking and his eyes were always dry. He got an eye-dropper from the hospital and started putting water in them but it made no difference. Don't cry for old Maximilian, he sang, the truth is I never left you. He panicked. He went a little crazy. He started taking antibiotics and other stuff. He got a key to one of those locked trolleys the nurses wheel around from bed to bed. Whatever the patients had, he had that too. He took the same drug regime as them. Even then Pat Baker had a deal going with someone at the Admin. He was collecting discharged patients in his Merc and bringing them home. Once or twice he drove Max for free. I could never work out exactly what Max had on him but they certainly had a commercial relationship of some kind. When I think of how far ahead of us that bastard was, even when we were kids. And now he was after kidnapping my mother to get me to come out of the sticks. Well, he could have her. I could see his small pig's eyes and his flat face, I could see the surprise. He doesn't want his mother back? What are we going to do with her, for Christ sake?

I arrange to meet Pierce and Timmy one night in Cassidy's Halfway Inn and Restaurant because Cassidy's is half-way, none of us would drink there by choice, people dressed up casual, sitting around drinking Cinzano and waiting for a greasy man in a monkey suit to take their orders. I don't tell Jazz in case she's worried. I tell her I have a nixer and I'll be late home.

We have a few scoops and I ask them if anyone was looking for me. I tell them things are getting rough back at the shop, people getting knocked off and kidnapped. They say they read the papers too.

They called on Pierce, Timmy says, didn't they, Pierce? Someone did anyway and if it wasn't you know who, I don't know who it could be.

I turned them away at the gate, Pierce says. No harm in that.

He tells us about the episode with the silver Merc and the number two cartridges. Timmy does a mock salute. Remind me never to call on you unexpectedly, he says.

I peppered the bastards. They'll need a good panel-beater.

No harm, Timmy says.

Fair dues.

I put out the word you went to England.

We drink in silence for a bit. Then Timmy says: Why don't you go to England?

I can't tell them that I already emigrated once. Home is a different language.

You're in trouble all right.

I'm in trouble.

It's not the guards anyway? Otherwise I'd have a summons for shooting that car.

I tell them they kidnapped my mother and they whistle through their teeth. Everyone knows the story by now, it's on the telly every night. She's been gone three weeks. It's the topic of every conversation seemingly. Who kidnapped the drunk?

I never made the connection, Pierce says. I didn't know that was your mother, of course.

What are you going to do?

I tell them she can look after herself.

I respect women, but my mother started to take care of herself long before she stopped taking care of me. She got in the habit of promising more than she could give. Come home early, we'll cook something nice. Let's go away for a few days, someplace nice, Tramore, Rosslare, with a beach. A nice caravan. I'm thinking: My mother is more trouble to them. They won't keep her long. They won't be able to stick her and they can't afford to pay for her habit. Which is Hussar vodka. But it's three weeks now. The clock is ticking.

What I didn't think was that they might just do her and fuck the body into the sea to be washed up around a pier in this ferry terminal. People to look over the rail of a ferry going to England and see this hole in the head looking up at them between the empty plastic bottles and the seaweed and the shit. I didn't realise how big Pat Baker was, how serious he was. If I did I would have turned myself in. But first I'd have put my daughter and my girlfriend on the boat, get them the hell out of this shithole of a country to someplace where the air was clean. By the time I found out, it was too late for all of that. Too late to make anything good.

So I tell Timmy and Pierce about my theory. She'll drive them round the twist, I say. They'll be tearing their hair out before the end of it. They'll pay *me* to take her back.

They don't laugh.

But she's your own mother, Timmy says. When he got tired of weddings he used to show me old home movies of the happy family playing on the beach, going to people's communions, singing happy birthday. That's my dear mother, he'd always say. Just there. Look. God rest her.

Pierce reverses his car up to the back of mine. I have a present for you, he says. He looks around the car park of the Halfway Inn, very mysterious. There's no one else there. I had to wait till Timmy left. I thought he'd never go. He opens the boot and there's something long wrapped in blanket. He takes a box of something I can't see and pops it into the back of the van. Number twos, he says. I think there's about thirty. Then he lifts the blanket out. It was my father's old gun, he says, it's old, but it's better than the one I use myself, only heavier. He lays it gently down on the floor of the van.

Keep it oiled up. It won't let you down.

I'm staring at him. Jesus Christ, Pierce, I say, if ever you want someone to think you're selling drugs or something, you went the right way about it. Backing the car up. Looking over your shoulder. You're like a fucking cartoon.

Well, I couldn't just hand you a gun in front of everyone, could I?

He looks mad about it.

Why not? You have a licence. You're entitled to.

Well, no.

I shake my head. You're some fucking Protestant, I say. No licence. I thought you were all honest.

We laugh about that.

Then I say: You were expecting something?

I was expecting something.

Thanks, Pierce.

Get lost someplace where they can't find you.

I'll try.

We shake hands. I feel his strength. All the loneliness, missing his son Hally and his wife, the empty farm rich in useless blackberries, and still this hero handshake like the war isn't over yet, the last battle. I hold on to it as long as I can, hoping some will come my way.

In the Glass Eye

Max's brother is a serious man. He was the first person ever heard of in our estate that smoked ice. He got the habit in Boston, Mass. Crystal meth gives me dreams, he used to say, like he never had dreams before. It also gave him hallucinations which years later returned to electrify him. He once saw a ship parked at the corner by the Spar. He was trying to buy chewing gum. People said he put his hands up and ran them along the sides to see if it was real. His very words were: It feels true but I'm fucked if this isn't that ice ship.

Max remembered the time before he went away. He used to look after me at school, Max used to say. Nobody pushed me around.

When he came back from the States he got a job as a heavy, pumping people for money and slamming meth. Max said he might have had a gun at one point. Not long afterwards he did six months for offences against the person. When he made his move he was like a loose piece of a machine. Every part of him was twisting, swinging. Short artificial movements. He went through people. Anything in his way broke.

Why he reminded me of the blackbird is he had one dead eye made of glass. Nobody knows how it happened. He went to the States with two eyes and he came back with one. He told various tales. In one he gets it shot out, but there's no scar for the exit wound. In another he loses it in a knife scatter. Nobody believes that either.

The best one is a car accident. This is how he told it to Max and me one night when he was feeling on top of the world.

I'm tearing over the Tappen Zee Bridge out of Westchester, New York, he says. Well downriver I lamp the George Washington Bridge, sucking the shit out of Manhattan Island. There's a speed trap the far side of the Tappen Zee, we see it coming up in the windshield like the end of the world, and we know we can't stop. Jesus, fuck me, we were flying, flying, boy. We go through and they take off. We're flashing along the Hudson. Up the New York State Thruway, left into Nyack. South Delaware Drive, Sunset View, Broom's Boulevard. We thought we lost them but there they are, flashing lights in the rear-view. All these houses with lawns and people walking dachshunds. Fuck this, I say to my buddy, step on the gas. I'm all stepped, man, he says to me, it's through the floor. Once or twice we nearly kill someone. We finish up swinging into this multi-storey mall, The Palisades, I think, like it's the second biggest in the world or something and there's nowhere to go except straight. We were well stoked. What we hit I don't know. A slice of plate glass tipped through the windscreen and pierced my buddy right here. (He indicates his chest area.) He's dying in the seat and I hear the sirens. He's smiling at this piece of glass like it was a toy and just gently touching it here and there so as not to cut his finger. There's pink bubbles blowing at the entry wound. I'm like: At least he's going out on a high. There's four fat people looking in what should be the windscreen. A woman on a mobile calling 911 or maybe the talk show. There's two kids holding flashlights still clipped on to the cardboard. I'm like: Give us a little light here. There's three or four dummies in bits and one plastic head on the dashboard. It still has a baseball cap. That fucking dummy was smiling. They had a display right inside the door looking out but the dummies never saw us coming. I take off. I'm gone a long ways before I notice I'm blind in one eye. Later I see a doctor in the ER and he takes this small splinter out, not much bigger than a nail-clipping. Better come back for tests, he says, how you get this? I'm in remodelling, I tell him. Plate-glass window fell on me.

Think about this one, he says then. I come out some exit door, attempting to make good my escape, and all of a sudden I'm looking up at this green sign, trying to read it with one eye. It says, this burial ground for coloured people was deeded in 1854 or something. Like I thought I was undergoing some kind of chemical thing. A burial ground for homies in a fucking shopping mall? But another time I went back and it was there all right. It'd never happen over here.

This story was told to me and Max in something like those very words and it's about the only credible thing I ever heard out of him. I believe it.

So when they put out the word that a body has been found, the first person I think about is Max's brother did the hit. I never heard of Pat being violent except for breaking legs and stuff. But Max's brother had a certain reputation as I already said.

Timmy and Pierce come looking for me. I meet them in Cassidy's Halfway Inn by prior arrangement. They have a Chinese barman now. I'm there an hour ahead, getting tanked up and upsetting the clientele. I'm emotional. I know what's coming. I heard the news too. The latest in the kidnap story. A body of a woman has been found. The police are not naming the deceased until all the family have been notified. However, sources suggest that it is the body of the kidnap victim and that she has been shot. Cut to camera talking to the same bitch as last time. What she's not saying is that my mother was a wagon and they hated each other's guts, they were fighting all the time, complaints to the Corpo, knocking on the wall, throwing things into our garden. Instead of all that she's lying through her teeth, enjoying being famous: *She was a good neighbour, a decent woman, she never had anything to do with drugs.*

Prescription only. And booze. She never had anything else to do, in fact.

I'm wised up before they come. I go through the shaking hands part and the sympathy. I tell them we didn't get on. Pierce says something about blood, I'm not entirely clear what. But they're working on me.

If she's not identified . . .

Someone'll do it. That old bat they keep interviewing. If she knew her so well, let her go down and look at her. See how she likes that. After all, what are neighbours for.

She's your own mother, Timmy said.

So I heard, I said. Why don't they go after my fucking father. He might still recognise her.

Get off my back, Pierce, I said. And I felt it too, at the time, like there was someone on my back riding me into The Baker's hands. I could feel the rush.

I was not sober. We all got in Pierce's car after the

management expressed an opinion on me, and drove out to Jazz. She was asleep on the couch. I noticed that since we moved to the seaside she was inclined to take a nap in the day even if she wasn't working nights, which she didn't have to for some time now. I was doing well enough for the two of us. Kaylie was on the floor making Happy Meals out of Play-Doh and a few plastic moulds.

Somebody whacked my mother, I said. It must've been your lousy fucking brother.

Pierce said: Easy now, easy now.

Timmy said: No language.

She was only half awake.

I said: This stinks. They're trying to flush me out. They're using her body as a bait.

She looked at Timmy and Pierce. She looked at me very cool. Nobody is that important, she said. Tell me what's after happening. Get out into the kitchen. I'll be out in a minute. I was just asleep.

She got herself straight and came out. She made tea. We all sat down around the kitchen table. Kaylie gave Timmy a Happy Meal and he looked at it like he wondered if he should eat it. She showed him her Barbie. Timmy was not into kids.

About a mile away was the sea. There were boats out there with engines that I fixed. The engine on a trawler is the same as the engine on a tractor and sometimes they even use tractor engines, or compressor engines. They get them marinised. Every old guy in a boat has a favourite engine that was built for something else. I knew if I went to identify my mother this would all go. No more house on winter rent all year round. No more walking down for a pint. No more waiting for Kaylie outside the school and

93

listening to her stories. They whacked my mother to get me to come out of hiding. This whole meeting was to make me walk into their hands. Nobody knew it but that's what they were doing. My friends were trying to get me to commit suicide.

I won't do it, I said. I'm nervous about Kaylie. What if they come after her?

They don't know where we are.

They will if I do the ID.

Jazz looked at me. She undoes me again like she did before. I'm going to save you, boy, she said.

No way can one life add to another. My mother thought she could add my life on to her own. When she found out it wouldn't work she gave up. If you add or subtract nothing, nothing changes. What was added was nothing, what was taken away was nothing. I suppose I broke her heart.

One time Max discovered Buckfast Tonic Wine. Look at all the alkies, he said, sleeping out, twisted out of their skulls morning, noon and night. How do they do it? Buckie. It's like you know a tonic, boy. Made to a secret recipe by the Benedictine monks of Buckfast Abbey.

There's no old alkies, I said.

They're all fucking old, he said.

I'm not touching that crap.

Fucking langer dan, he said. You'll drink what's good for you. This is class stuff.

He had a bottle of Buckie in a brown paper bag.

Know what a tangent is, boy?

Max was top of the class in maths, not that there was a gang of geniuses behind him or anything, but when he went to school he was good. If he had a decent family background or an old man with a steady job he might've turned into something. And Pat Baker might've turned his attention to ripping off legitimate customers and becoming an insurance agent or the owner of a chain of DIY stores. But everyone gets into whatever is handy and Pat is the only success.

A tangent is a line that touches a circle in one place. Just one place.

He put his hand up and touched my face and I pulled away fast. No fucking gay shit, I said. I told you before.

Like I'm a tangent, he said. When I'm dead and gone you won't even remember me.

He was pale and thin that time. His hand, I remember, was cold but soft, and light like a girl's. He was always chancing, always trying one on. But inside he was cutting back, downsizing, selling out. And I knew what he was talking about, that one place. I could still feel it, something invisible, invincible, containing pain and memory and I forget what else. Which I was unable to forget even though I tried.

And Jazz said something like that too once. Nobody makes an impression on you, she said. You're so cool, if I dropped dead tomorrow you'd be the same as ever. You're shatterproof.

As the insurance ad on the telly says, before we're born we're able to hear but it takes years to learn how to listen.

Time was when I knew the magicians who had the secret of eternal life on a first-name basis. Two friends meeting on a busy street. They shake hands and in that magical transaction a twenty goes one way and a paper twist of powder goes the other. Their word is their bond. Their good name.

Where do they all come from, everyone different in their own way? Reaching back from the dead, reaching out of life. Is the baby the start? Where did the number one soul come from? What's the engine that drives the whole thing? Not love, never mind what they say. Maybe loss. Maybe anger. Maybe need. The whole system powered by what's missing, everything coming and going, everything changing because nothing is ever enough.

Down at the pier I watch them shifting boxes into the co-op truck. There's the smell of refrigeration and fish and cold cold air. Someone tells me their troubles. Sounds like the wet-liner, I say. Maybe the seals. It's automatic, but I'm thinking about something else.

Old Friends

I ring Micko and ask him to set up a meeting at a neutral venue with Max's brother. I want to negotiate. He has the contacts.

How are you, boy, he says to me. We all thought you were dead.

I'm not.

Am I talking to a ghost or not? Jesus, lad, there's people screaming for your blood. Sorry about the mother.

Thanks, Micko.

Fucking animals, whacking a woman.

I miss her.

She was your own mother, boy.

If they wanted to get at me . . .

No need for that kind of thing.

I was wondering if you could do me a favour.

Ask me. I know what you're after. Just ask me.

I tell him I need to see Max's brother and he whistles. He says he doesn't think it's a good idea. I say for old times' sake and he says it might be a bad move. Be wide, boy, he says, don't get sentimental on me. These are animals we're dealing with.

I notice the we.

Max was my mate, I say. We were close.

Max was a fucking stoner, boy.

He was great.

Great out. A lunatic. The best.

He agrees to talk to Max's brother. It's a delicate situation, he says, and will involve negotiation. I hear the club manager in him, the man used to dealing with people. He's an executive now. I bet he never even touches a nodge. A long time ago he took the first steps to regain control.

Thanks, Micko.

A thing of nothing, boy. Anything I can do. Like I said, sorry about the mother.

Thanks, Micko.

Fucking wankers, whacking a woman.

He sends a driver down which, according to Micko, tells Pat Baker he's sponsoring the meet. Is there a foreign language school for gangsters, or do they all watch *The Godfather* first? He picks me up at a neutral venue about twenty miles from home. I never saw this guy before. He's a cold crazy that I know would eat me without salt. He must be fifty. He sings these loopy songs he makes up as he goes along. If I were a lobster I'd whistle and sing and I'd follow the ship my true love sails in. Nine hundred children and a crop in the fields. But me arse is at home in old Ireland in the county of Armagh. He has this one to the tune of 'God Save the Queen'. Send her uproarious, happy and snorious. I don't remember half of it. He's watching me in the rear-view to see how I'm taking it. Then he tells me he has trouble with foreigners. The fucking fujies, he says, they say: Take me to such and such a place. Then, I left me money at home. Hang on and I'll get it. Know what I mean? Fucking Nigerians and foreigners. Like we're paying them to take taxis. He has a photograph of Elvis on the dash, and a ring on every finger.

We pull into the car park of this pub. There's a huge bridge, maybe a hundred feet high, like a railway bridge. The driver gets out. He walks spread out like he has things under his arms and between his legs. He opens my door and says: Get in the pub. I'll send him in when he arrives. Stay with the crowd.

I notice that autumn is here, definite. There's leaves blowing around and my sweater feels thin. I am aware that I haven't put on weight since I gave up abusing my metabolism.

There's no crowd. Only an old guy drinking stout. He nods and I wonder if he's expecting me. I order a whiskey. The old guy gets up and goes out a side door. In three minutes he's back, still jerking his zip the last two inches, both hands down, one holding the lower part, the other jerking. I see there's a piece of shirt caught in the top. No way am I going to tell him. I can see myself trying to get that piece of shirt out while the old guy flips the zip, and Max's brother walking in.

The barman gives me the whiskey and I pay. There's ice in it. I hate ice but I'm too nervous to complain. The door opens behind me and in walks Max's brother. I think I'll shit myself. I can't see if he's tooled up. I look at his armpits and his waistband but I can't tell. This is all new to me. He walks up and shakes my hand.

Sorry about your mother, he says.

Is he sorry he did it, or sorry it happened, or sorry it happened to me or to her? I don't ask. I say: Thanks.

What're you having, he asks.

I notice that the barman has trouble deciding which

eye is looking at him. He keeps looking from one to the other. Max's brother has a new better eye than the old piece of stone he came from America with.

Two whiskeys, Max's brother says. He turns to me. For old times' sake, he says.

We talk about my mother for a bit. Then we talk about Max. Then we talk about Max's father. Max never talked about him, I say.

He never knew him like I did.

Suddenly I see there's this thing between us, a kind of understanding about the fact that both our fathers fucked off – his to prison, mine probably to his wife and kids for all I know. I never knew who he was. Like we're both bereaved after some tragic accident.

What you think, Max's brother says, would we have turned out different if they stayed the course?

I shrug my shoulders. I'm trying, I say. I'm in a steady relationship. I got a beautiful daughter. I got my own place. I'm working. I got a life now.

He says nothing. He turns his whiskey around slowly in his fists.

You should see my daughter Kaylie, I say. Want to see her picture?

I brought a picture on purpose. I take it out of my back pocket. It's creased and a little curved where it took up the shape of my ass. He places it on the bar. He straightens it with the edge of his hand, slow and deliberate, and he looks long and hard. I realise, with a sick feeling, that she's standing at the edge of the pier and there's a boat in the background. You can tell from a boat's number what port it's registered in. Is he looking at the number? Maybe he doesn't know these things.

She's a little darling, he says after a bit. I got a daughter of my own, you know. The situation is a bit dodgy at the moment. I might finish up in the family court.

That'll be a change, I say. I'm thinking it's usually the circuit court he's in. Or the central criminal. He has charges outstanding, Micko told me. Offences against the person.

He doesn't laugh. Her mother is a bitch, he says. A right bitch beor.

Unlucky. My girlfriend is mint.

Again he says nothing. His delicacy of feeling is making it difficult for me to come to the point. His good manners.

I try a different tack. How's Pat?

He swings around and looks at me with the good eye.

His sister is asking for him, I say.

She is like fun.

She is. She's like family oriented, you know. She said to pass on the word. She hopes he's keeping well. And her own sister Stacey and the family. Any new additions since we took off?

If I was you I'd leave her back. If I was you I'd leave her back to her brother and I'd do a runner myself. Take my advice.

That's what I wanted to talk to you about. I can't do it, you know. I'm crazy about her. She has me sorted. I'd die if I left her.

Die with her, die without her. Same difference.

I can't do it.

He shrugs. I'm starting to panic.

You don't have to do it, I say. Just because Pat Baker says, it doesn't mean you have to do it. I'm not holding it against you about my mother. She probably drove you cracked. She'd drive me cracked any day. I wouldn't have kidnapped her in a fit. But you could leave us alone. Jazz and me, we're not doing Pat Baker any harm. Tell him you won't do it.

He's staring at me.

What are you talking about? I never touched your mother. You're losing the run of yourself.

You work for Pat.

I work for Pat.

Who did it so?

Haven't a clue. None of my business. Sorry about it all the same.

He lifts his glass towards the barman and shakes it. It's empty.

Same again, he says. Two whiskeys.

This one is mine, I say automatically.

Score, he says. Mint. So what are you doing with yourself these days?

He shifts on the seat so I have the benefit of both eyes. He's settling down. I can see this is going to be a long one. Outside the autumn night is falling fast, full of leaves and stars and the big black skeleton of the bridge.

Old Times

All Max's brother wanted to talk about was old times. I
never talk business, he said. He wanted to tell me about
this time he took Max on a train trip to someplace. They
were going to see a zoo. He had this very clear memory of
the railway carriage and he wanted to tell me every detail.
He was particularly good on the toilet, which he said was
very clean. He had memorised the notices. He said the
notices in Irish were poetry but the ones in English were
just plain English. They started out early in the morning
and there were rabbits in the fields, and a fox, and they
saw a couple of hares just waking up. This was some
kind of heaven he was telling me about – just Max and
Max's brother in the early morning going to the zoo.

Jesus, I miss him, he said. What happened to him? He
was well intelligent. The whole family was intelligent.
Listen to this. *Chun uisce d'fháil ón steallaire, brúigh ar
an troitheán.* I haven't seen that in sixteen years maybe
but I still remember it exact. It was over the sink in the
toilet in the train. There was another one, I'll think of it in
a minute. Or how about: out out brief candle life's but a
walking shadow a poor player that struts and frets his
hour upon the stage and then is heard no more it is a tale
told by an idiot full of sound and fury signifying nothing.
They made me learn that at school and I never forgot it.

There's a worrying sound to this particular quote, but I

don't say anything. I'm hypnotised by this one-eyed hit man quoting poetry and trying to convince me that he loved his brother.

This is about the fifth round. We've moved on to pints by now, the bright whiskey burning inside us like ice.

Will I tell you something you don't know about my brother Max? Max used to steal books from the library. He used to read them. *Ten Great Works of Philosophy*. He had seven. He was going after the other three but they took them off the shelf. *The Poems of John Keats*. Season of mists and mellow fruitfulness, close bosom friend of the maturing sun.

I never knew he was into books. I knew he knocked them off but that was business.

Ná caitear tabac. That was the other one.

In the toilet?

No smoking. It doesn't sound the same in English. The Irish has a poetry to it.

Say it again.

Ná caitear tabac.

It has. Same again?

Max's brother nods. I wave to the barman. He puts a glass under the tap and pulls back on the lever. He has that perfect lean that barmen have, like they're pulling the levers of the world and a river is flowing out.

Know why Max moved out?

He didn't get on with your mother?

Max's brother shakes his head. He takes three deep gulps from his new pint. As he raises his head after each gulp his lips have a cream moustache that increases until he wipes it with the flat of his hand.

My mother. God rest her. Was a decent woman. A saint for all I know. That was only a story Max had. He had a victim complex.

Why, so?

We all have it. You have it yourself.

Why?

Because we fucking are victims. Ever seen a youngster after being driven to school in a jeep by a woman with blonde hair and a designer tracksuit? In the meantime you're going to school yourself with a rat-arsed fucking Adidas with the knees worn out like some old wacker. Well, if you did you'd know who the fucking victim is meant to be.

Why did Max move out?

I threw him out. I can't stand queers.

Max wasn't queer.

I caught him.

Fuck.

Not a word of a lie. He was my brother but no way was I having that. The mother wasn't well at the time. The heart was bad. As you know she passed away the time you were in hospital.

I missed the funeral . . .

You had your own troubles.

His face is sorrowing. I recognise the stillness. I think of my mother in the water, what she might look like now, in the morgue. If Max was alive he might have kept her company.

He was turning tricks, you know. Bringing them home. Paying for his habit. My mother thought he had a lot of friends. If she found out it'd kill her. So I fucked him out. He never told you?

He said the old lady was an alcoholic.

God rest her, she was total abstinence. The father was fond of the gatt all right.

But you . . .

Sure, I'm fucked.

Are you still on the ice?

I'm off the ice. I smoke a bit. The odd nodge, you know. But I'm fucked. I'm not well at all.

Nothing too bad, I hope.

Hep C. At least I never got fucking Aids. I came close enough a few times. I tell you, a blood test can scare the shit out of you. The ex tested positive but the kid is clean. We parted on those terms. Know what I mean?

So now you're working for Pat.

I'm working for Pat. It's steady. Before that I did personal security for this ex-millionaire. No names. He had a saying. He used to say: Ambition took me to the top, cocaine made me want to jump, but a whore took me down. Well, he was just another rich asshole. I met the whore. She was OK. All these millionaires are the same. I prefer Pat.

Enforcing?

He shook his head at me. I never talk business.

What I want to know is, are you coming after me?

Have to take a piss, he said. Maybe he didn't hear me.

When he came back he was unsteady. He was zipping his fly in the same old way that the other guy had and there was something stuck in the zipper too. He was sort of folded in and his left hand was holding down the bottom of the zip, an awkward twisted stand. I could see the hepatitis in his face, a yellow that was nothing to do with sun. A yellow in the whites of his eye too, though the false one was clear as water.

No offence, he said. But Pat wants to nut you. He wants his sister back. Now she's damaged goods he wants to fucking wipe you out. If he gets you it won't be quick. His reputation is on the line here. If I was you I'd take off.

I was shaking badly.

Are you going to do it?

He shrugged.

Pat gets these ideas in his head.

Asperger's Syndrome, I said. That's what Max said it was.

Max's brother looked at me out of his eye, full of pain and loss. He didn't say anything for a time, then he said: If Max said it . . .

He said, Lookit, for old times' sake, do us all a favour and fuck off to Australia or someplace.

Will I tell you something, boy, he said. He put his finger to my forehead, slow and soft. He looked at the spot he was touching for a second. Then he said: Max fucked you up bad, boy. It's all in there. You're well lucky you got away this far.

My driver is gone. I feel like calling Micko and telling him what I think of his service. I call a taxi instead. Before I tell him where to collect me I check what kind of a car he uses. Toyota Corolla, he says. Nice one, I say. I'm at the Old Bridge Tavern. I'll wait out front. I'm a thin guy in a grey hoodie.

Not that there's anyone else but me here.

*   *   *

I hear Pat Baker on the TV and I notice his voice is OK. He's denying that he's a criminal. I call for Jazz to come in, to see her famous brother. She stands at the door, maybe thinking some kind of family thoughts, maybe not. Whoever he's with, she says, he's a disgrace, look at the get-up. This reporter is walking along beside him and I guess the camera must be walking in front, looking back. I try to imagine what the whole circus looks like. Pat wears this tracksuit that doesn't hold his belly. You can see his vest tucked in. He looks like a piece of shit. The reporter asks him about his criminal record and Pat says he was fitted up by the guards, but he's on good terms with them now. He's preparing a civil case, he says, he's been studying law. He smiles. His smile is soft. The reporter asks him about his involvement with the heroin trade and Pat laughs. Do I look like a heroin dealer, he says. Only the junkie knows that he does. To the rest of the world he looks like someone you'd see in a supermarket car park with a shitload of frozen pizzas on his trolley.

I tell Jazz the news. Max's brother says run.

We talk it over but whatever way we look at it we need money. We start to figure out ways of making more. I mention several scams I used to be good at but Jazz won't even listen. These people are neighbours, she says. You can't go robbing their cards. Get a grip.

The truth is I was never too skilful anyway.

Jazz says I'm not sleeping at night. I'm talking in my sleep. She says I have terrible dreams. I'm getting thin, she says, like I ever had something to lose. She's worried about me.

*   *   *

I tell the doctor about my nightmares but he doesn't want to prescribe anything. I tell him how my mother was whacked and it's like the penny drops. I can almost hear the click. I've been writing scripts for a drug addict. Now that I've gone this far I tell him the truth about my broken legs. He can't get the door open fast enough.

The Ark of Gopher Wood

I think we're living in the end-time all right, Carey the scrap says. The alternator is on the counter between us. A price has been named and negotiations are on. The weather is first on the list. All this old rain, he says, and thunder and lightning. And the flooding. The sea is going to rise up and drown all the cities. Except the high-up ones, of course. The fountains of the great deep and the windows of heaven will be opened. Ever hear of Christina Gallagher? The holy woman of Achill. I'm into her these days. The end-time, hah? Jaysus, it's staring us straight in the face if we only had eyes to see.

I'll give you forty for the alternator, I say.

I'd be giving it away, what.

Forty-five.

The vehicle this came out of was ninety-nine per cent perfect. It was a Honda Civic.

A waaboy?

A what?

A boy-racer?

He shrugs. Maybe.

Anyone killed?

The driver. Heart attack brought on by a blow to the chest.

Seat belts?

Air bag. He had a weakness he didn't know about.

Amazing when you think about it. Fifty.

I'd want seventy to make anything on it.

Ah Jesus, sixty so.

Done.

You're a hard bastard.

Israel shall rise up and smite her enemies. Where did I read that? The promised land has to come first, before the end. The promised land is Israel.

I seen it on the news, I say, it looks like a shithouse in a gale of wind to me.

It's the promised land according to prophecy, what.

I'll take the ammeter too.

Ten. Then the flood. It's all coming true. This is the third secret of Fatima. The pope knows it but he can't tell anyone in case he'd start a panic. Time enough for that.

All I can say is, if the flood comes there's a couple a fellas here I hope'll remember I fixed their engines for them.

He laughs. He shoves the alternator at me and puts the ammeter in a Tesco plastic bag and takes my seventy. He catches one of the retaining bolts and turns it slowly between his thumb and a finger. It revolves without coming out or going in. A pivot. The light has gone out of his face.

You'll be taken by surprise, he says. You're one of the wicked. The end of all flesh is come before me; for the earth is filled with violence through them; and, behold, I will destroy them with the earth.

Jesus, Carey, where did that come from?

Make thee an ark of gopher wood.

What the fuck is gopher wood?

A man came in here two weeks ago, Carey says. He had maybe a dodgy eye, what? He was asking for you.

Never heard of him, I say, and I know all the mechanics around here.

This guy is not really a mechanic, he said. He might be something legal. I asked for ID and he just laughed. He said you only see that on television. If you see him, tell him I'm asking for him, he said. You'll know how to describe me and he'll know who I am.

Thanks, Carey. It's this bastard that wants to settle an old score.

I'm playing it cool but I'm worried. Is this Max's brother following down the clues, or someone else? Or maybe it's someone who wants his engine fixed on the QT. But deeper down I'm confident that if it's someone with malicious intent he's in a different country where he doesn't know the rules. He thinks he's smarter because he's a city boy.

I say: If he comes back don't tell him anything.

Revenge is mine, saith the Lord.

Amen.

Don't mock me.

I'm not mocking, I say. I'm dead serious.

Mocking is catching.

I ask Carey what the flood will be like. He turns his eyes away from me. Outside his window the cars rust away in the rain. Cats prowl along the stretch-velour seat covers. There are dark stains on the dashboards, the upholstery, the carpets. Sudden death is everywhere. He says: All in whose nostrils was the breath of life, of all that was in the dry land, died. And every living substance was destroyed which was upon the face of the ground, both man, and cattle, and the creeping things, and the fowl of the heaven; and they were destroyed from the earth. Genesis seven.

You have it off the top of your head? How do you remember all this shit?

He leans forward and I smell Silvermints on his breath. All his teeth are bad. His skin is dark grained and oil or dust has long settled in the lines. There is something crazy in his eye that I have only seen in Max. I wonder if he uses. In back, where the internal organs of cars are laid out in perfect order like spare parts in a hospital, does he keep also a store of pharmaceuticals or grow herb?

He says: The imagination of man's heart is evil from his youth.

I pick up the alternator. What are you telling me here, Carey?

He straightens up and puts his right palm to the small of his back. The back gives him trouble, I heard, since he was in an accident himself. Don't forget to bond that, he says. Do you want wire for the earth? The green and white?

I have plenty.

Stick to the colour code, what? Don't leave a trail of confusion for the next man in.

I will.

I'll have a leaflet for you next week. About the holy woman of Achill.

Thanks.

She does the end of the world brilliant. She'll explain everything.

The one-eyed man will be back, he says. It won't take him long to find you. All he has to do is ask at the co-op.

Over his head is a hand-drawn sign that says: REPENT IN TIME BUT SETTLE YOUR ACCOUNT BEFORE YOU GO. NO CREDIT.

I'm fitting the alternator to a yacht. I'm upside down in the engine compartment inhaling bilge water and diesel when my daughter walks over the side. I hear a little cry and a little splash, and first I think she threw something in. Then I hear her voice again. Later this will become one of my nightmares, with dreams of my mother drowning off some dark beach or looking at me with a hole in her head, and Max on my back, and other things.

I graze my head getting out of the engine. Even before I straighten my back I feel blood. I scramble up the steps into the cockpit. Her dolls are on the floor looking up at me. The half-closed eyes of the Barbie with her long lashes. I run to the side and look down. She's not there. Where was she standing when she fell in? There's a man high up on the pier. I see it's Pete The Who. He's working on a yacht on the dry, screwing everything up probably, as usual. I see he's looking down laughing. I have a spanner in my hand but he's too far away. For the first time ever I hate someone. Then he's pointing at the other side of the boat.

She's swimming. I can't believe it. She's doing a steady breaststroke. Her little head is high out of the water and I can see her trainers kicking out behind, white through the green water. She's headed for the steps. Her hair is wet.

Swimming in the Oily Waste

I hold her in my arms. She's so small. How's my great girl, I keep saying, my champion swimmer. How's my great girl. And she says: I'm all right, Daddy. I fell in. I'm wondering what has happened to me that I never noticed that my little girl has learned to swim. It's like years have passed and I never noticed. I stand her up and I rub her arms as if she's cold, but she's not. How old are you, pet? She gives me that dead look that's supposed to make me feel suicidal. Daddy! It's my birthday next week!

But how old is she? Five? Six?

It's like I've been on the longest trip in the history of the world. The drug of all time that has kept me out of my tree for years.

Mammy knows, she says.

I shake my head sadly. Mammy knows everything, I say.

The funny thing is she agrees. Since when does Jazz The Kid become The Mammy Who Knows? Something has been happening.

Hop in the van, pet, I'm taking you back to The Mammy Who Knows.

Pete The Who arrives and sticks his head in the window. Jesus, he says, that was something. How's herself?

I don't hate him any more. In fact it is possible that I

love him. I want to put my arms around him and say:
Peter Townsend, I love you. What I actually say is: Don't
forget to connect the seacock this time. A recent boat he
worked on sank the night after it was launched. He tells
me to fuck off in a whisper. Then he winks at Kaylie.
You'll swim the Channel, he tells her. You're a great girl.

She laughs all the way back. The Mammy Who
Knows, she says over and over again. When Jazz comes
to the door she says: Hi, Mammy Who Knows. She holds
up her hand, palm out like some Indian greeting.

What happened to you, Jazz says. She's talking to our
daughter but she's looking at me.

She fell in.

I fell off the boat. I went right down, Mam, but then I
remembered I was able to swim.

She swam to the steps.

Oh my God.

I'm sorry, Jazz.

It wasn't Daddy's fault, Kaylie says. I was supposed to
be playing with Barbie and Ken.

I was fitting an alternator, I said.

Jesus Christ, come in and get warm. Off with those
clothes and into the shower.

We listen to the humming of the electric shower. Jazz
Baker, I say, you're a beautiful woman, know?

Fuck off, she says out of habit.

No. I mean it. You used to be a kid but you turned into
a beautiful woman. I couldn't tell what you're like.

She's looking at me now, not knowing whether to
laugh or sneer. But I catch her by the waist and I kiss her.
I pull her into the kitchen and I sit her down. I pull my

chair up so I can sit with my knees against hers. I hold her hand. Listen, I say. We have to make a life for ourselves. We can't keep running away from your brother. Let's get the hell out. Max's brother was looking for me.

She shivers.

Carey the spare parts guy told me. A guy with one eye, he said. Who else could it be.

I miss my sister, she says. Kaylie should be able to see her auntie.

She wants to go home. I see it in her. Right now she wants to be back where she knew everyone. Just now because she almost lost her daughter she wants to crawl back into the poisoned hole where she knows the dangers. As the ad on the radio says, her heart is aching for a change of address. But we can't go back. I know that, I just can't tell her.

Maybe we could negotiate.

With Pat?

Maybe he'd see sense.

The shower stops and we hear the door open. In a few seconds Kaylie comes in, wearing her pyjamas. She wants jelly. She knows there's some in the fridge.

I'll put out the word, I say.

No, Jazz says. This time leave it to me. I'll fix it.

The radio news says that Pat has been served with a demand from the Revenue. Developments in the fight against drugs, they say. The Criminal Assets Bureau are on his case. The reporter refers to him as Patrick The Baker Baker. I also hear that another acquaintance has died of shotgun wounds. First I think it's an internal hit, then I hear that his own sawn-off did it, at point-blank range. It deleted his liver. I hear that he was on his way to a job. He had a prosperous career as a counter-jumper and general blagger behind him. They say the gun went off by mistake. That the bastards in the car dumped him someplace so he could bleed to death in peace. This guy used to play football on The Lawn. It looks like our estate has the highest mortality rate in the country or up there with the best of them anyway.

When we were growing up we didn't know we were growing up to die heroes, that we'd be shooting each other and dying of Hep C and Aids and fuck-acting about with cars. We thought we were just going to grow up and be men like everyone else in the place. Pull women, get our hole, get a baby, get married, get a job maybe. The Corpo or the brewery or the carpet factory. We imagined the usual future. But only the Corporation is left. The carpet is in Poland. The brewery downsized when the Danes or the Norwegians took it over. And long before that we were fucked anyway.

Afterwards I found out, as part of criminal proceedings, The State V The Langer, that she was writing begging letters for me. She thought she could melt his heart because she was his favourite sister. She believed in letters the way people believed in God, like he has to be there because you need him. She had the one true faith. But his favourite sister was the worst thing she could say.

Something got into the air when I was about ten. Some mad dust. Something blew in our eyes and up our noses and messed with normal and put real instead. Something turned Pat Baker's Asperger's Syndrome into an international import and distribution business and made Micko The Thicko the Knight of the Clubs. And it turned me and Jazz into fugitives with retribution on our tails and a tendency to ignore facts.

White Socks, Tennis Shoes

The first time I saw Jazz, there was maybe ten girls. Max and I were going for chips. Max had acquired some cash, possibly from working in the service industry, possibly by knocking off somebody's wallet. He certainly had an Animal wallet that day with someone's student ID and a ratty orange bus timetable which he was studying and trying to decide if we should take a bus somewhere after the chips. And he also had a blue folder under his arm which he showed me. It was some kind of homework, belong to a student maybe. As we walked along Max was reading, in this teacher's voice he could do, bits out of the folder and bits out of the timetable. Tails will be on the 0920 dep arr Connolly pl 0955 Herr Kleits dep 504 BC arr 1025 man's character is his fate. Then he saw the girls. That's Stacey Baker, he said, ex-whore and sister of our Pat. She's some goer, boy.

Stacey is a few years older than Jazz but they look like twins.

Which one?

He pointed Stacey out but I was watching Jazz. She was practising some steps in a dance with another girl. They were joined at the hip and shoulder, arms around each other's waists, watching their feet, doing every step exact and identical. I still had a thing for the surgeon's daughter at that time but suddenly I was electric for this blonde, brown-eyed, untouchable queen. She had a tight black top and some kind of tight pants and I could see the shape of the panties she was wearing and her toenails were painted black, and there was something in the way she danced and watched her feet that made me hold my breath for her.

Look at the sister, I said.

Jacintha Baker? Don't even think about it, boy. He will pulp your testicles with a claw hammer. She's Pat's pet.

I laughed. Max could do all our teachers. It wasn't like he spent much time in school but he had them down. He could talk in algebra. He will pulp them with a hammer, he said again, in the same solemn voice.

Remember, boy, he said, man's character is his fate, as the old saying goes.

He started to giggle. She's a little Shetland pony, he said.

We tried to light a fire in the back of the orbital bus that night. We started by emptying onto the seat an ashtray that was full of cigarette ends because we heard that cigarettes contain a chemical to make them continue burning. Max said a cigarette was better than a fire-lighter. This ashtray was directly under a NO SMOKING sign. It didn't work. We had to get out by the rear emergency door because the driver called for back-up. We found ourselves out in the country, in the dark except for those weird yellow lights. Nobody stops on that road. First Max was crazy with happiness. We nearly fucking did it, he shouted. He started to sing. He was dancing around the road, holding his prick, and singing at the headlights of people going home to the late-night movie. He was singing: I'm a little teapot small and stout here's my handle and here's my spout. Then everything got quiet and he changed his tune. He swore there were animals in the trees. He wanted to hold my hand because he said he was afraid. He revealed to me exclusively that he could read people's minds and that what he saw in mine was encouraging about the future.

About two o'clock the waaboys came out. They balled up the road and down the road with no lights on, and after half an hour the shades came after them. We sat on the embankment and watched the fun and when there was a little more light we walked home. Max was shaken. I'm never going out the country again, he said, the fucking boggers are welcome to it.

Jazz told me her sister was on the game for a while. Down the docks and Parnell Place. Every fucking line in the country is called after a patriot. Pearse Street is another line. Her boyfriend of the time got her into it. Do a few turns, Scoby Kiely said, and get us straight, get us set up, a deposit on a place of our own. He had a gambling problem, especially dogs. He was convinced he knew the form of every dog. He was convinced he knew who was holding one back or who was nobbled. He was always talking to doggy people, fellows out walking greyhounds with soft caps and wellington boots. He'd do a few lines of coke, dress himself up real smart and go down the track with whatever Stacey made the night before. I'll double your money, was always his parting shot. She was making a lot to start with because she was a new face and she was only sixteen. She did this thing. She wore a tennis skirt and white socks and tennis shoes. She looked like she could play tennis and all.

None of the Bakers did drugs.

The trouble about the doggy people was they were straight and Scoby was a crooked bastard. They didn't trust him. They talked to him all right, but they never told him anything. Doggy people are a secret society. They come along with four greyhounds on a leather leash and if you look in their eyes they all look like they know something. They talk to the dogs and they talk to each other. They have this softness in them that living with animals gives you. If they saw a hurt bird they'd stop. No way did they want to have anything to do with Scoby.

Jazz said to me once: If ever I get like paralysed from the neck down or murdered or something, go with my sister Stacey.

She stayed on the game two years, give or take a couple of months. Jacintha, Stacey said, I seen the way the girls all went. They're all doing drugs and they're all getting cut by their pimps in places the client don't see until it's too late, and they all have babies in care, and they all wind up doing kinky stuff to keep going and dropping their prices, and they look sixty when they're only forty. The game is no place to get old.

She said all she could remember of the two years was standing on street corners with a cold wind blowing up the tennis skirt, arguing about money with clients and just wishing she could get into the car with the heater on. She said Jazz was haunted lucky because she got a baby and got out. A baby is a family, she used to say, but a man is just a man. Which is what happened to her when she finally got married. She got her babies, one a year for two years, and the man fucked off. She was nineteen.

Scoby Kiely never saved a penny. He graduated from

the dogs to horses with machines as a hobby on the side. He divvied up her takings: notes for the ponies, coins for the slots. He said he was spending so much on the machines in The Garden of Oriental Pleasure that he should have shares. The crazy thing is, after she dumped him he ended up working there.

What made Stacey's mind up was when she got into a Hiace with a nice looker and it turned out there were four more in the back. They drove her out the country and took her one after the other in the back of the van. Then they drove her back to the line at 4 a.m. when it was a waste of time. What killed her was they only paid her for one. That's what we agreed, the driver said. A deal is a deal. They were in a rugby team. The driver was the tight-head prop. She was sore for a week and she stayed home and did a lot of thinking. When she told the other girls they said it was a gang rape and she should go to the cops. Then they said she should get a real pimp who'd look after her interests. Scoby went after the team, thinking it was his duty. He slashed the tyres on the team bus and spray-painted RAPERS on both sides. He put sugar in the diesel tank. But the girls called him a coward so he gave up and took off. He was gone for a few weeks and when he came back, Stacey was after getting herself together. She had a job. She approached her brother Pat, who staked her for a flat. Pat read Scoby Kiely his rights. I thought you were for real, Scoby, he is reputed to have said, but you're only a fucking waster. Get your ass out of here or I'll nail you to the fucking dog-track.

Stacey said she was the one who drew Pat's attention to the money the women were making. After that he ran two girls himself. He used to pick them up in his Merc and drive them down to the line. After a while he set them up in business flats and moved them on to high-class clients. He even provided a pick-up service. The kind of clients that he wanted appreciated being picked up in a good car with tinted windows, they were high-profile people with low-profile business arrangements. He might have had a few girls working the clubs.

Once I asked Jazz what exactly her sister did to make so much money. She must be good at something, I said. I wonder, is it a family thing? It was just a game like we often played, I was slagging her, but she kneed me in the tacks hard, which was a surprise, and I had to get out and sit on the side of the bed and catch my breath. There were these glow-in-the-dark worms on the inside of my eyelids and I felt like puking for about five minutes. It was a similar experience to what I once had after mixing Ponstan and Distalgesic and a couple of cans of maybe Budweiser. But afterwards she said to me, very serious: If I die, go with Stace. She never said terms and conditions apply.

You think kids don't hear things. Two days later Kaylie says: Mam, what sport does my auntie Stacey play? Jazz said she didn't know. She didn't think Stacey played any sport. But I catch what she's saying. I wink at Jazz. Jazz looks at me for about thirty seconds, then she blushes. Tennis, she says to Kaylie. She plays tennis, but she's no good.

One of the yachts I service, the owner has a dog called Trotsky. The dog likes sailing. He sits on the coach-roof coming into the harbour and barks at seagulls. The dog dearly wants to fly. And Neilus Carey keeps a Doberman in the scrapyard but he has no feeling for him. He's just security. What's his name, I asked him. Doberman, he said.

Who ever heard of a Doberman called Doberman?

So after Kaylie fell off the boat I got her a dog. He looks like a pure-bred terrier, but he's a cross between a border terrier and a Jack Russell, I'm told. Mongrels are more intelligent and they're grateful for being respected. She decides to call him Wayne. Wayne Dog. Now when I'm minding her and working on a boat I tell her to walk the dog. But stay away from the scrapyard, I tell her, or Doberman will eat him up. When she gets back she has these stories about what the dog said to her and who he met and whose door he pissed. I have to stop whatever I'm doing and listen. She cracks me up with her stories, I could write a book.

A Rabbit Teddy Bear

One thing I dream about is my father. It's always the same dream. I'm sitting with my feet through the banisters, looking down at the hall, and there's a man wheeling a bicycle in. I never see his face. Sometimes I think that there's this genetic programme in me that makes me dream about him, like he left me a bad snapshot. Sometimes I think if I met him I'd recognise him. And then I think I probably met him a hundred times. Most likely he lived near us. My mother would never say. All she said was he was the nicest man she ever met, which is good for a child to hear, but a bit hard for a teenager. If he was so nice why didn't he stick around?

There was a time that I thought if I ever found out who fathered me I'd kill him, but I got over that too.

Jazz dreams about living in Australia. She never has nightmares. She watches *Home and Away* and *Neighbours*. She thinks about having barbecues and wearing shorts. The sunshine looks electric to her, the way everything just is itself. She looks out at this place we're actually living in, a town of maybe sixteen thousand inhabitants; a small fishing harbour; a summer-tripper tourist trade that died when global warming made us colder and wetter and windier, and Spain cheaper; an amusement park; a couple of caravan sites; a yacht club and a golf club, several bridge clubs, a driving range, a successful hurling team; a queered-up, middle-class place that was once held together by fishermen; nets and glass buoys in the pubs; a crooked harpoon in The Ship; a crusty anchor painted with Hammerite at the entrance of Phelan's car park; photographs of hookers and yawls in The Anchor; every fifth property for sale and being looked at by select clients who will occupy it for three weeks of the summer; plans for a shopping centre, a bypass, a state-of-the-art sewerage system. Up the hill the property holders build their quiet houses. They own the sea view. When they flush their toilets everything ends up lower down, where the fishermen used to be, where the houses still flood occasionally, where almost everything now is a desirable summer residence. The fishermen and boatmen and yard-workers moved out to the housing estates.

She sees that it loses its shape in the rain, that sea fog freezes between the lights. That sometimes gales blow seaweed through the streets.

What would we be doing in Australia, I say.

But I don't tell her how far away from home I feel already, like I'm living on the other side of the world. I'm afraid to move in case I break something.

Why don't you practise with that shotgun, she started saying to me. Take the dog out, maybe he could hunt. Why don't you shoot something we could eat.

Like another fucking blackbird? One time I went out with Pierce and this bird got up in front of us and I let him have it with both barrels. Pierce said I was a crack shot. There was enough left to identify the remains.

I took the gun out and cleaned it. Kaylie watched me.

She was playing with her dolls on the floor and watching me with sheep's eyes. Wayne was asleep with his head on his paws and his two hind legs stretched out behind him. Every couple of minutes he opened his eyes without moving his head to check on Kaylie.

Who are you going to shoot, she said.

I was going to say: Your uncle Pat, but I didn't. I'm going hunting, I said.

Are you going to shoot bears?

There's no bears here. If I'm lucky I might get a rabbit for the dinner.

Oh Dad, don't shoot a rabbit.

She had a rabbit teddy bear.

What are you thinking about, Jazz? I said.

I'm thinking I don't want to leave.

She was looking out at a wet night, leaning against the jamb of the front door. Down the hill I could hear a foghorn sounding and the rumble of a big engine.

Wayne dreams about catching large animals that don't fight back. I hear him sometimes deep in the chase or snuffling around at the entrance to rat-holes. His dreams are not complicated by memories.

Kaylie dreams about Wayne having babies. She likes the thought of having puppies to nurse and clean up after. She thinks Wayne should get a partner or maybe get married. Sometimes she points out other dogs as possibilities and she likes it when he sniffs them over. We don't have the heart to tell her. Another thing she dreams about is that there's a strange old woman sitting on the end of her bed. But her worst dream is that she goes downstairs and out to the kitchen and the back door is open and it's dark outside. In her dreams she just stands there and screams. Nothing ever comes through that door. She screams until we wake her up. Nobody knows why a happy child has nightmares. It's one of the mysteries, like maybe she was antisocial in a previous life.

Dreaming of Evening

Her hair is tied back loosely. How she organises it keeps it bunched around her head like it has been inflated. She is slight. She wears white trousers and a white shirt. She has freckles now. She climbs onto the boat and the boat almost doesn't move. A different arrangement of gravity and she might slip into the sky.

Dan Kelleher looks at her. He's talking to me but he is regarding her with his cold detachment. There's still a few posters from the last election that say: DAN IS THE MAN, VOTE NO. 1 DANIEL KELLEHER. He buys and sells this town, he values rising damp like pornography. But he missed out by a hundred votes and I probably know the hundred.

So you changed the oil and what then? he says.

I changed the fuel filter.

And?

The filter was fucked, I say. Like it was jelly.

Jelly? In the fuel filter?

Water in the tank. Somebody put water in your diesel tank.

Fuck.

I drained it. I think I have it out. I show him three barrels and a handpump lying further down the pontoon. You should drain the sighting filter, the glass bowl. Check it out after every hour's running. If she starts to cough, the same. Ninety-eight litres, I tell him. You could serve the filter up for dinner. New fuel filter. A gallon of oil. New oil filter. Three hours' work. I filled the tank. Three hundred even for everything.

Jesus Christ.

You shouldn't let anyone fill your diesel except yourself.

I don't.

Well, read what it says on the cap.

I have to get cash. Are you finished here?

Two minutes and I'm done.

I'll be back. Don't forget to take those fucking rags.

When he leaves, the boat rocks gently. I turn around and she's sitting on the push-pit rail. She is capable of a steady warm gaze that unsteadies people from a considerable distance. I gather the scraps of paper towel and the rags and throw them into a cardboard box. I saw her around. I made the connection a long time back.

I was at your wedding, I say.

She raises an eyebrow.

I was the second video camera.

She blushes. She says: I don't remember. That seems like years ago.

Three years ago.

I stop working and look at her. She looks away.

Then a flaw in the light makes everything uncertain. A thin layer of cloud. The sun is a polished disc on the cream satin of a dress. The breeze dies completely and the water turns to bright iron. I hear my feet moving on the fibreglass, the bunched paper towels falling into cardboard, her breathing. She breathes through her nose in an easy quiet action.

The boat rocks again, Dan Kelleher leaving the relative certainty of the floating pontoon. He has three hundred in crisp ATM notes. Even so he looks poor as dirt and his skin is not healthy.

No offence, he says, but I hope I don't see you again until November.

Suits me fine, I say. I take my cardboard box containing the light rolled-up paper towels and discoloured rags. My shoes leave smudges on the fibreglass. It is a beautiful calm evening in here, inside the breakwater. The water looks oily even where there is no oil. Two men talk quietly on the stern of a trawler ten feet above. A row of eleven seagulls of various denominations disapproves of everything. An engine rumbles on the outside, about to make the entrance. A big marinised Kubota, I guess. Not one of mine but I have seen them in my time.

Grace says: None of that turned up on the wedding video.

I see she remembers, that she saw the camera, that she was dancing for me, or for the public anyway.

I'm standing on the side-deck. I look at her and wink. Waste not, want not, I say.

The engine starts first turn. Dan Kelleher takes the wheel and Grace steps ashore. She undoes the bowline from the cleat and I pass her the stern-line. She holds them in her hands like reins. She is ready to hand them over and walk away, I can see that. She is pierced by a deep wound. Every way she turns hurts.

She is ashore one time. Next she is on deck and the boat is pulling away. The slightness is dazzling. She can do no wrong. The seagulls lift off and return. At the tip of the breakwater a cormorant dreams about something nice for the evening. They pass the lobster-potter with the Kubota, a man emptying water over the side ignores them. The pots in the stern, with pieces of flesh and weed suspended inside, gleam like dry sand. There is a slight swell against the stony seaward face of the town. There is no wind. The light is brown but it will be over an hour before the first thunder.

I'm a Careful Man

How I got my first delivery trip, I'm hanging out with a stainless-steel welder who's supposed to do a job on the pulpit of this piece of shit motor boat with a ninety-horsepower outboard and places to keep drink cans. And I'm minding the dog. The welder is edgy because the owner doesn't show. No way am I touching it unless he tells me, he says. How do I know he won't change his mind. Welding stainless is a specialised job.

I'm temporarily broke as it turns out. I'm thinking over the situation and wondering if I could revert to my old cash-machine system. It was simple enough. You cut out a piece of thin plastic the shape of the card-slot on the machine, then you glued a loop of tape to it. You went along by night and slotted the tape into the machine and you masticked the piece of plastic over the face. Someone came along, put the card in the slot and nothing happened. They went away cursing because the machine had swallowed their card. It has to be a Saturday or a Sunday so they can't just walk into the bank. As soon as they're out of sight you tear the plastic off and out comes the card caught in the loop. I did it twenty, thirty times before the banks started to put out warnings.

I'm thinking things over, not really listening to the pain in the ass stainless welder, when this stranger comes up to me and introduces himself as Skipper Something. I look at him. Everything he wears is Musto. Special water-resistant deck shoes, a Musto shirt, a watch with four dials in it. Wayne Dog doesn't like him. I feel like saying we've real skippers around here. I'm thinking about this old bastard who lays pots along the rocky side of the harbour, maybe eighty, eighty-five years old. He goes out every morning with a heron on the stern. This fucking mad heron that just sits there like he's a paid-up passenger on a ferry.

Skipper Something says he has injector trouble. He doesn't want to touch it himself. It's a delivery. Would I take it out and clean it. Send it up to Eurodiesel, I say. You need sterile conditions. I just need it to get me to Falmouth, he says. Same difference, I say. It will or it won't, nothing got to do with how far.

But I look at it for him. He's right. He hands me a beer from this, like, tank of beer in a fibreglass case moulded under the cockpit table. After another beer I offer to drive him to Eurodiesel. I'm going up anyway, I say. The dog is tied to a cleat and it looks like he's going to commit suicide by jumping in after a seagull. I know for a fact that all dogs wish they could fly.

We talk about the yacht delivery business.

Kaylie comes down in her school uniform and takes Wayne. He's happy to see her. He celebrates on the bollards and the ice plant and thinks of a cunning plan to surprise a seagull, which already expected him and is in the air before he breaks cover. When they're gone it's like the day is running down.

Nice kid you have there, Skipper Something says. I'm not married myself.

He suggests to me doing yacht deliveries. He says with

the bigger boats it's nice to have an engineer. The bigger the boat the bigger the money. I say I'll think about it. I'll talk it over.

When I get home Jazz is sitting beside Kaylie. They're doing spellings out of the *Fallons Spelling Book*. Answer sponsor plaster faster nonsense. The teacher likes them learning across the columns in case it gets easy. Behind them, silent as a snake, Wayne is waiting for a fly to lose altitude. When they get to nonsense he appears suddenly in mid-air and snaps. Afterwards the look on his face says: Did I or did I not eat that fly?

Normal is Perfect

Times normal is perfect. Like walking along the Pier Road of an evening, Jazz and Kaylie and Wayne and me. We're walking into the sunset, which is warm on our faces. There's a high tide slopping up the stones. Out on our left the yachts are crowding around a buoy, you hear them shouting *Water!* at each other. And normal families walking children or dogs. No surprises. No carbon monoxide. Seaweed and seawater smells. Kaylie is talking about school. She likes her teacher. She gets regular as clockwork ten out of ten for spellings. Neilus Carey's plastic sandwich board is on the end of the prom just before the locked gates of the funfair. REPENT OF THIS EVIL AGAINST THY PEOPLE, the front says. ALL THIS LAND WILL I GIVE UNTO YOUR SEED is on the back. Everyone knows he's talking about Dan Kelleher who bought his cottage for a song and sold it as a holiday home. Jazz saw the ad in the window when we were looking for something to rent when we got here first. A picturesque two-up two-down fisherman's cottage with room for extensions and an acre of ground with development potential, a good view of the sea. In the Christmas hurricane the sea came in the front door and out the back. But it turns out the council is reinforcing the breakwater, which Neilus Carey didn't know before he sold. Kelleher is on the council. Neilus is sitting in his car, drinking tea from a yellow flask, hoping that his sandwich board is striking fear into the godless. The dead Ferris wheel looms through his front windscreen. Kaylie always wants to get in the funfair. She wants me to open the gate, but I have no key. She thinks it's possible to just turn everything on. I point to the trespassing notices. Then we go down the sand and skim stones and throw a stick for Wayne.

On our way home we meet Pete The Who standing outside the Harbour Lights Lounge Bar. He's listening to the sound of a three-piece combo. It's a Saturday night in summertime and they need whatever pull they can get. His head is tilted so he can hear better. He tells us they're slaughtering 'Knights in White Satin'. Fucking demolishing it, like, he says. Listen. Just listen to that.

He can't stop himself fingering the imaginary strings as he listens. His left hand working through spasms up and down the frets.

I tell him we're looking for a house.

Cool, he says. Good move. He shakes the neck of the air-guitar, his fingers strained against the frets. He's bending those notes, it's in his head as clear as clear can be.

We buy fish and chips and take them home and spread the newspaper out on the kitchen table. Kaylie drinks Coke and feeds chips to the dog, and Jazz and me have a beer each. The sun is gone now but the night is so warm the windows are all open. I can hear the TV in four or five different houses. A radio somewhere is asking if it's my ambition to wake up in a queen-size sleigh bed. Everything is steady and calm. Normal is perfect. I carry Kaylie up to bed piggyback and dump her backwards onto the quilt. No glasses of water tonight, I say, I'll bring one up later on. When I get down, Jazz is watching some chat show. The kettle is boiled, she says. Look at this.

A man is trying to make contact with the dead. He says: I'm getting something about a death, a dead mother, this is a very young spirit who wants to talk to someone called Mary, is there a Mary? Three Marys stand up in the audience. One looks unsteady. Jesus, Jazz says, he's talking to a fucking spirit. The Marys look a bit unhappy about this unexpected comeback. One of them keeps trying to sit down but the man beside her pushes her back up every time. People around her are getting annoyed. If her mother wants to make contact from the dead she should have the decency to listen. Children should be obedient.

I'm getting something about an operation, maybe a stomach operation, the man says. Oh Jesus, the unsteady woman says. Is it someone belonging to you, dear? the man says, someone close to you? It's my mother, the girl says. She says to tell you it's all right, the man says, she has no pain now, she's happy, the only thing she's worried about is you because you haven't let go, you see, your mother says you must let go. Let go, dear.

I will.

She's happy now.

OK.

She says there's someone here called Frank or Francis or Frankie.

That's my father.

He sends his love. He says he's happy too. They're in a happy place with a lot of light. He says he misses you but he wants you to let go too. He says he sends his love.

The unsteady woman looks suddenly cool and deadly. She looks at the man. Tell him to fuck off, she says. She doesn't blink.

Later there's a *Crimeline* special and I'm surprised to see all the old places are justly famous. They tell me that a certain acquaintance of mine was stabbed to death. The crime took place in full view of the CCTV on the side of the street. The shades were looking down from thirty feet up like God. They never trouble themselves. They pick up the pieces afterwards. I saw threads of blood on my hand one day and I wondered if God plans the colour of blood and the colour of skin and the shape. I thought about this acquaintance lying on the street with God's square eye watching him bleed to death. Did he think it was the end of the world or just his own single death? Or is it the same thing? As always he died for a woman. A knife for a woman, a gun is for drugs. It's a question of the right implement. A woman pierces you with a fine point, a long wound that screams coming in and going out. A deep wound with a fine entry is the most dangerous. For drugs they shoot you in the head.

Kids Go Fast

The Lawn was the first respectable working-class area in the city to get into drugs. The houses were all Corporation. Most of the men that got them worked on them, so everybody had a hand in building their own home. My grandfather was a mason, the last person in our family to have an honest trade until me. He laid the back wall with his own hands. He built the pantry. What we used to call the pantry. I remember his bronchitis. When I was four we moved in to look after him. He used to give me a drag on his John Players and laugh at the coughing and he used to give me a suck of his pint. He liked the face I made. I'll make a man of you, me lad, he used to say, but he died instead. He was three weeks in hospital. If he'd only give up the fags, the nun said. They're going to give me up instead, sister, he said. He called them coffin-nails. Later Max brought me up to show me the same ward. All the old men asleep in white sheets, the drips and the bags of piss and the smell. This might have been a dream. This is the smell of old age, boy, Max says, who needs it? This is where my Pops was, I say. How did you know? I know everything, boy, he says. This is where they bring the terminals.

I walk along the ends of the beds. This old man calls me and asks me for a glass of water. I take his glass and I fill it at the ward tap. He puts his bones around my hand to hold the glass and he drinks it very shaky. Then he drops back on the pillow and says: God bless you. A sign over the next bed says NIL BY MOUTH. He looks dead. His lips have white or grey powder around the edges. All old men look the same. He doesn't ask me for water; maybe he knows he can't get it, maybe it's because he doesn't ask for anything at all. This is what it's like to be dead, I think, or maybe I think it later when I'm going back over the incident in my head. This is what it's like to be dead, not needing or wanting anything. Suddenly I'm happy for my pops. No more cursing the fags are gone, go down the Spar and get me a packet of John Players and a pint of milk. He never noticed when we moved to litres. No more sucking air and not getting exactly enough. No more waiting until two or three o'clock for his daughter to come home and take me off his hands. I'm meant to have a life too, she says, no kid is going to stop me having a life. My pops was a mason and he built our wall with his own hands. He didn't build it high enough.

Fuck me, I heard Max whispering, I do believe it's Mogadon.

He had a little plastic spoon with two pills on it. It was on a bedside locker. He put his thumb on one pill and snapped the other into his mouth, a swift and critical movement. When I refused the offer of the capsule under his thumb he flicked that in as well. Later he slept the sleep on a pile of laundry bags in some room down below the hospital. This was before he moved into the morgue. I left him there.

Pops' funeral was massive. One old guy told me there was no block laid on any site in ten miles that day. All the old men with bad backs and bad knees and lame legs.

Frizz-haired women with big handbags. The kind of people that never talked about pain. It was the last big funeral; I remember little crowds waiting for coffins later on, family, friends, maybe twenty, thirty people, a good half strung out one way or the other. Death from complications. It was letting the side down. Junkies don't go to funerals much. Angry mothers, telling radio chat shows: Why did he do it? What did he see in them drugs? He was a nice boy. Or maybe: God forgive me, if I had a gun I'd murder that fucking X. This was after people from The Lawn started to deal in their home turf, when people knew names. X might be Pat Baker after he started to deal in The Lawn, which fair dues he didn't do at first, but it pissed him off to see bastards from across town supplying on his patch.

See kids on the edge of mourning crowds talking like big men about how this poor bastard OD'd or fell out of a window or got Aids or bad gear or set fire to himself, like this was a hero's death. Like he died for Ireland. Wondering when they'll be old enough to do the same.

See kids racing to get hammered out of their heads. To go fast. To be able to talk the talk. This is here I'm talking about. Who cared? Nobody gave a shit. A teacher said to me once: You're bright kid but you're going to go the way of the rest of them if you're not on it already, you're never here, you never do a stroke of work, why don't you make use of your brains instead of burning them? He was wasting his time.

There's a pool of something under the extractor fan at the back of the basement of the hospital. Piss or water or oil. And in the middle of the pool is a half-rotten cardboard box that says UHT MILK 100 CARTONS NEVER BE WITHOUT MILK AGAIN. A sign overhead says this is an emergency assembly-point. I start to cry. Fuck you, Max, I say, fuck you for bringing me here.

I Hear the Wake-up Call

The shooting of Micko is a wake-up call. I don't need another one. It's all over the papers and all of a sudden I know who killed my mother, who actually pulled the trigger. Not Max's brother but The Baker himself. Max's brother would never do a woman. I always thought Pat'd farm it out, that he couldn't do the business on an old neighbour himself, that he'd need to call in the professionals. Now I see him differently. I panic. I go home. I tell her to get packed. I tell her we're off. I tell her the form on her psycho brother.

So we're on the run again, she says. She has one hand on her hip. I'm not afraid of my brother Pat.

He done my mother. He's a fucking mad psycho.

Somebody else done your mother. Some pervy guy. They arrested someone, remember.

They had a guy in for questioning. They released him, remember. The DNA didn't match.

Fuck DNA. I know my brother didn't do it.

So how do you know, like?

He's my fucking brother.

He's coming after me, Jazz. He's back in business. Look.

I give her the paper. There's a picture of Micko in the full of his health, front teeth like a toothpaste ad. He's wearing a nice suit, Armani probably or a very good rip-off, and there's a blonde on his arm with tits the size of turnips. Some kind of lights behind and above him, a chandelier maybe. The blonde is his current (now former) partner. They both have a tan.

Fuck, she says, reading with her lips moving. He was tortured.

She spreads the page out on the worktop.

He was beaten with a claw hammer, she says. Oh my sweet Jesus.

What I'm talking about.

She looks up at me. He won't come for us, she says. He has bigger things to do.

It'll be soon, I tell her. It has to be. After this. Know what I mean?

She shakes her head. I explain how the distribution trade works, the territories and the mutual agreements and the fluctuating supply and demand and the pressure of turnover.

The investors'll come after him straight away, Jazz. They'll know this is a turf war. Everyone in the business knows who organised this one. Someone'll grass him up sooner or later. He has to come for us now. He'll be too busy later.

He doesn't want me back.

But he wants to get me. I crossed him first. I took you. He was going to marry you off to someone respectable. Get the family respectable.

You are respectable.

I fucking wasn't when I made you. I was fucking mad.

What are we going to do? I'm not leaving. Go if you want, I'm staying here. I'm not running.

I give her the worst look. What happened to your

dreams of fucking off to Australia, Jazz? What about put another steak on the barbie, Bruce? What about *Home and Away*?

What would we be doing in Australia?

I'm a marine engineer.

Where's your fucking papers? You never even were an apprentice.

We could go to England.

I'm not going to England.

I cave in. I sit down hard on the kitchen chair. All of a sudden it hits me. We have a life now. We have friends. I have a business. I even pay tax on non-cash transactions. I'm straight and I'm clean.

I'll call Max's brother, I say. He's the only one left. I'll fix things up.

I'm thinking, what would it cost to put a contract on Pat. I'm thinking maybe just to put the frighteners on him might be a special offer.

Max's brother is a psycho.

They're all fucking psychos, I say, but Max's brother is a friendly psycho.

How are you going to call him? Like, do you know his number or what?

I have his business card.

You have in your arse.

It's in the drawer with the receipts. At the back.

I go upstairs and come down with Max's brother's business card. Jack of all trades, the card says, any work considered. It's a fucking joke, I say, he's an enforcer for the distribution trade.

There is a landline number. I ring it and get an answering machine that tells me to ring a mobile. The mobile switches to voice-mail and I'm told to leave a message after the tone.

This is Max's friend, I say. My number is oh-eight-seven-seven-four-five-four-three-nine-oh.

Jazz looks at me. What are we doing? she says.

I shrug my shoulders.

Are we going to be able to afford this?

We have a bit put aside.

Are we going to kill my brother Pat? Max's brother is a psycho. I don't want him hurt. He's still my brother, you know.

Maybe scare the shit out of him, I say.

The mobile starts to groan. It's switched to vibrate. It's moving on the worktop and we're looking at it, she doesn't want to pick it up, I don't want to pick it up. Any second now it's going to vibrate over the edge. I pick it up and it's Max's brother.

What do you want, he says.

I have a job for you.

Score, he says, I'm freelancing these days. My former employer is a nutcase.

How much?

Depends. What?

I want someone done over.

For you, a special price. Five hundred. Is it who I think it is?

Our old friend.

Score.

Cool with you?

Cool. I'd do it for nothing only I have responsibilities.

So?

I'll meet you. Same place. Five o'clock.

Not today. Tomorrow.

Talk to you then.

I hang up and put the mobile back on the worktop. Before we can say anything it's moving again. We look at each other. I pick it up.

I have a job for you, someone says.

Who's this?

It's Pete, Pete The Who. I have two engines and I'm fucked.

I look at Jazz and I start to laugh. It's just Pete, I say. He's fucked. She laughs too.

Fuck you, Pete, I say. You scared the shit out of me.

Pete has this reputation to protect. Everybody knows he's cool. Once upon a time he was a little boy who knew about rock and could do the air-guitar and look like he had something real under his fingers, an important skill for fourteen years of age. He knew pop was shit first. When he was sixteen he was working the summer holidays in the caravan park and he discovered cannabis resin. He was detained once or twice for possession but he was never charged. He invented new recipes for mushrooms, once or twice causing severe diarrhoea, when he picked the wrong fungus. Later he was taken into custody for his own protection. Someone saw him in the graveyard, bollocks naked except for a motorbike helmet. When they picked him up he told them he was looking for Finn MacCool. It turned out he had mushrooms for tea. He couldn't remember why he thought this guy would be in there, but he thought maybe he was dead. Keep off the mushies, he said to me, you never know what's in them. And the judge asked him what he was doing with the helmet, did he think he was Flash Gordon?

A long time later when I'm working in the yacht delivery business, when everything is different and I'm all sentimental about the past, we're delivering this seventy-footer, stereo speakers in the head, power winches, microwave. The skipper is an asshole. Who did this fucking engine? he says to me suspiciously, like it was me.

Not me, I say.

Who fixed it? he says again with steely determination.

Exactly, I say. Who fixed it.

I happen to know that Pete The Who was out of his tree when he put it together. I can still see him holding an injector in one hand, which is supposed to be kept, like, sterile clean, and a toke in the other, smiling at me and talking very cool. I may be pushing this a bit, but in memory I seem to see a NO SMOKING sign on the bulkhead behind his back. I forgot all that when I signed on for the delivery.

Because at that time we were five hundred miles out of home, bound for the Azores and it's totally calm, and we're two days behind. I'm hanging arse in the air over the engine, I'm digging what looks like ash out of the heat exchanger and I can't touch anything because the metal is white hot.

The penny drops with the skipper. Very funny, he says, and he fucks off below to look at the charts again and make sure we're still in the same place.

What happened to Pete in the end was he took a bend too fast in the old Golf van and finished up attached to a Hymac. He wasn't even stoned when he died. He was deadly when he was sober, but a gentleman when he was high. I'm doing this baby for you, Pete, I say. I'm still picking up your pieces.

Stories always find their way. I hear the details later, from a man in a bar who tells me he was the one who knocked on my mother's door. The way he tells it sounds right.

Micko is walking his five-year-old son by his second relationship. It is a fine day in May and in the park on their left there are people lying on the grass. A Mercedes S-Class comes to a halt just ahead of them and Pat The Baker makes his appearance.

How are you, Pat? When did you get out?

Two weeks ago, Pat says. What the fuck did you do with my business, you cunt?

Pat, he says, the patch was vacant. I just stepped in to keep the supply up.

You took my dealers.

Somebody had to do it.

By Jesus you won't fucking do it for long, you cunt.

Three nights later Pat arranges for Micko to be picked up by one of his dealers who tells him that there's been a problem with the last delivery he shifted. The previous winter and spring a number of people died from bad gear, though not on his patch, and Micko is anxious not to have any quality-control problems that might bring trouble on him. They chat about holidays as they drive to an industrial estate where the dealer keeps a small lock-up warehouse. The dealer recommends a caravan park he has stayed in recently, but Micko is beyond all that. His holidays are in Marbella where he puts his two families in a five-star hotel to eat seafood and swim in the pool. He follows the Germans, he says. Wherever the Germans go the finish is tasty and the place is quiet. He goes for that kind of thing. When they open the ware-house door Pat Baker steps out. His Merc is parked behind him. He is holding a police-issue Smith and Wesson 59.

Hands up, Micko. This is judgement day.

At least this is what the man in the bar says. How he knew everything only occurs to me later. Then he tells me he knew my mother. I thought I recognised your face, I say, but he shakes his head.

No way you know me, he says. You might of seen me in the paper, though. I'm the face of defiance, 'member?

I remember all right.

The Lonesome Whistle

I'm dreaming of Micko inside that lock-up. He's kicking the door. I'm trying to hold him back but someone else is pulling me down. It's Pat Baker, I know. If he pulls me down he'll kill me. Then I see that it's Kaylie. Wake up, Dad, she says. Mam is downstairs. She said to get you. I only wanted a drink of water.

I go down and Jazz is standing in the dark, looking out.
What's up?
There's three men in a car.
Good for them.
They're after driving around three times. They keep stopping outside different houses.
I'm awake all right now. I look out. There's nothing there.
There's nothing there.
They might be gone.
Mam, can I have a glass of water?
Jazz fills Kaylie a glass of water and while she's filling it I see the lights of a car turning slowly onto the road. Now the dog is awake too. Kaylie is slapping her knees and calling: Wayne! Wayne!
Is it a Merc? Jazz asks.
Kaylie is going upstairs. Wayne is following her. He's not allowed in her bed but I don't have time to say so. He takes advantage of emergencies.

I can't see.

Nighty night, Dad.

Nighty night, sweetheart. There's three guys in it. It's only a fucking Honda Civic. They're stopping.

I hear Kaylie's door close. The car is stopped outside our neighbour's house. The lights go out. A small thin guy with a number-one haircut gets out. He goes down to the start of the street and he walks up. I can see him pointing. He's counting. He stops outside our door. Then he gets back into the car.

Get the shotgun, Jazz.

Jazz gets the shotgun. I break it open.

Get the cartridges.

Where the fuck are the cartridges?

How the fuck would I know?

It's your gun.

Fuck.

Two guys get out. They start counting again, one on each side of the street. There's only one house left with a number on the door. Number twenty-three. It's on the other side. I can see they're trying to work out how the street is numbered. If I look sideways I can see the deck lights of the trawler I've been working on all day. They're probably loading cans of Campbell's Soup. They'll leave before first light. I think it would be so easy to sign on a boat and take off. Maybe one of the Spanish factory ships. Jazz could too. But there's Kaylie.

The two guys get back in the car. One was the small guy, the other was an older man. They drive the car down to the end of the street. I can hear the engine ticking over real quiet. The two men come up the street.

I close the shotgun. I'm going to have to pretend.

They stop outside my neighbour's house and the small guy puts his hand on the waistband of his trousers under his tracksuit top. They walk up the path. They look in the windows. Maybe they see his GAA trophies or maybe they see the wheelchair. They go around the back. I run upstairs and look down from our bedroom. The thin guy climbs up on the roof of my neighbour's back shed and looks in the bedroom window – the boys sleep up there; they converted a ground-floor room after the accident. The old guy stands at the bottom keeping sketch. The thin guy gets down again. A loose slate breaks. They go round the front and take a peek at the trophies. They get back in the car and drive away.

Next morning I sleep late. I meet my neighbour sunning himself in his wheelchair on his front path.

What a day, he says.

I'm glad at least that he appreciates it. If I knew two men almost put a bullet in him and he didn't appreciate a sunny morning I'd feel let down.

How are things, Jerry?

The way it is, he says, is things could be worse. I spent a long time cursing this fecking chair, but the way it is is I have to live with it. I'd be worse if they never invented the wheel.

We have a quiet laugh about that.

The compo is coming, he says, so my solicitor says. Tell me this, boy, he says, how is it you can be arrested for soliciting but you'll get a solicitor on free legal aid? When the compo comes I'm going to get a motorised chair. I'm thinking of starting a racing club down the clinic. Formula One Cripples. How's that for a title? Foc for short.

It's a runner all right, I say and he starts to wheeze, laughing.

A fecking runner, he says. Dead right, boy.

He says Wayne is shitting in his garden. I say I know it but I can't catch him at it. If you see him, hunt him, I say.

His son John comes out of the house with his level sticking out of a green rucksack. I'm off, Dad, are you all right? he says. Perfect, my neighbour says. Don't do anything I wouldn't do.

He's in college, Jerry says, learning to be a bricklayer. Believe it or believe it not.

Jazz and I stayed talking until we were sure they were gone. Jazz was shaking. They were after us, she says. He got three heads to come after us. I know the old guy – he runs a couple of brassers. He's only a fucking pimp, he's a gutless wonder. Wee Willy Connell. But who's the thin guy? Did you see the way he had his hand under his top? Did he have a gun?

Max's brother wasn't there, I say.

Unless he was the driver.

I got a good look at the driver.

You don't think they were after Jerry?

What? Like because he missed the penalty in the '92 final? The only harm Jerry ever did was get stuck into a concrete pillar.

They saw his trophies.

They knew I never won any trophies.

They'll come back. There must be a contract.

The house was cold. Jazz made tea but we never drank

it. I held her hands and tried to rub them warm but the cold was inside. In the end we went to bed. I put the empty gun on the floor beside me but I didn't sleep until first light. Just before I drifted off I heard the trawler hooting the foghorn once, twice. The skipper had a signal for his wife, two lonesome whistles when the lines were clear.

The Blackbird Watches from the Shadows

The blackbird eye is watching me from the shadows. He has a Nike bag on the seat beside him but it doesn't look heavy. Sometimes a bag looks heavy, sometimes it doesn't. How are you, boy? he says. I thought you were in America.

I order pints and ask the barman to send them down.
Well, I say.
Well is right, he says. How's things with you?
Mint, I say, apart from that fucker trying to nut me.
Into each life some rain must fall. How's the beor?
She's mint.
You're looking at a married man.
I look at him. He's staring at the mirror behind the bar which reflects the back of the bottles and part of the ceiling. He looks proud. The barman is humming and looking at the telly which is on mute and not visible from our seats. He has his arms folded and his back to the lift-up counter.
Jesus, man, congratulations. How long?
Six months. We have a kid. A boy.
Congratulations. Jesus. That's good news.
Long-time partner. We tied the knot. The kid is two years old.
Score. Half reared so?
This is where all the trouble starts.

You're telling me. Our Kaylie was mad. I remember when she was small.

We talk about children when they start to walk, that weird few years when everything that can be moved or picked up becomes a deadly weapon. He says if you want to stop any army let a two-year-old loose on them. He'll drive everyone round the twist, screw up all the machinery and piss off the generals. We have a good laugh at that one.

Still, he says, a daughter is well easier than a son.

I look the other way at it. Didn't you have a daughter in another relationship? Any news of her?

Fucked off, her mother did, boy. Took my little girl with her. I miss her.

Unlucky.

The mother was a wagon. My present relationship is better all round. What's up? You had work for me?

I swill the stout slowly around the inside of the glass, swilling the white stuff up onto the edge. I'm drinking slow because I want to keep my head clean. He's already halfway through the one I bought him.

We discuss the possibility of frightening Pat Baker. Max's brother tells me that Pat is gone psycho altogether. Then he tells me about a small-time counter-jumper he worked over for a client. Money, boy, he says, it's always over money. My client was owed for a few items of hardware. Be careful, he says, one of the things he owes me for is a sawed-off.

He leans forward and lowers his voice.

I cornered him in the car park of The Dukes but he hadn't a piece on him. He was a small man without the fucking piece, know what I mean. He paid up under pressure. That's the way, boy, the only way.

I look at the blackbird eye which is not looking at me. It is looking at something on the floor about five feet away. Following something. I look, expecting a beetle or an ant, but there's nothing there. He's trying to tell me he's not funking anything.

You heard about Micko?

I nod.

He was destroyed altogether. Ruined. If he lived he would never walk again. No surgeon'd be able to give him a face, there wasn't enough left. So I heard. Some say he was buried alive.

Fuck.

Pat has this kid working for him. Jesus, he's some langer. Pure fucking psycho, know what I mean, like? Pure mental.

You worried about him?

Nah! Not me, boy. I'm well tooled up.

He pats the Nike bag. I get the feeling he's not telling the whole story.

Watch out for this langer though. If he sends someone for you it'll be him.

Max's brother suggests that we get together and kill him. The way he tells it we'd be doing everyone a favour including the cops. I know, as sure as I know my own name, that Max's brother is in the shits about Patrick Harold The Baker Baker. Like everyone else around. I think about the chain-grip with some regret. I'm thinking maybe I'm underestimating this man's connections, that even now I haven't a clear idea of how big the situation is. I try to think of someone really big but I can't make Pat fit. The trouble is he was a neighbour, I grew up with him, I'm with his sister.

No, he says, shaking his head, very sad, there's only one thing to do. We have to nut him ourselves. We'd be heroes, know what I mean. Even the fucking shades.

Can't do it, I say. The girlfriend is pure set on it. No way can we kill him. We just have to fix him up right.

Can't do it so, he says. He don't frighten. It's all or nothing, boy. You're in or you're out, which?

Out.

So be it. Can't be done so.

Then we talk about Max and he tells me that Max's father is in the building trade now. He's out of the Joy and he's legitimate.

I get these dreams, I say.

I'm thinking about certain dreams I get about times when I was living with my mother, even before Max became a big part in my life. One of them is that I'm working in the building trade but I get walled into a cavity wall by mistake. Max's brother thinks about that one. Jesus, he says. Walled into a cavity wall, hah?

It's because I'm thin, I say. I'm weedy. I'd probably fit in the cavity all right.

The head is well fucked, he says, pointing one finger at his own forehead. All that crystal I did over in the States. There was a time when I was a real memory man. Dates, poetry, telephone numbers, I had it all. At least I never got Aids.

How's the Hep C?

Misdiagnosis. Max had it though. He was knackered.

Max had tetanus.

I decide not to believe him. I try to keep focused. I try to remember exactly the way things happened. Certainty is the only protection.

We talk engines for a bit. It seems he's driving a diesel Golf. He describes her ailments to me. I tell him she's burning oil. Probably the oil scrapers. I tell him to bring her down to me, I'll give him a free service. We shake hands. It turns out the eye I was looking at was the dead one. When he turns full face to me I see life on the other side, fear maybe, the yellow of hepatitis certainly. The dead eye is shiny pure, like a wet stone.

I'm thinking, what kind of fathers will we all make? There's none of us normal. One story Max told me was when the brother came home from America, Max found him curled up in the toilet covered in puke. Max asked him was he all right. He got up and hit Max one in the nose. Then he shoved Max's head into the toilet bowl. He was shouting: Drink! Drink, you cunt! Max's shoulders wouldn't fit through the toilet seat otherwise he would have drunk just to get him to stop. What kind of a lousy brother is that? Max used to say.

I never saw Max's brother again. He went down in the world. He was doing compensation scams, driving into council property and claiming whiplash. First they paid out, then they started fighting the cases. By the time he died they had a fraud pending on him. He drove into the wrong hole and broke a gas main. Max's father is the only one left. The mortality rate among my friends and relations.

Last thing I said to him was: About the langer . . . ?

Small feen, he said. A pure cunt. Number-one haircut. Small tash. You'll know him when you see him. White hair, probably bleached, I'd say. Dangerous, well dangerous. No fucking cop-on, know what I mean.

I said I'd watch out for him. Max's brother waved his car keys at me. He stumbled against the door. I'm fairly hammered, boy, he said. A couple of pints is my limit these days. The liver is knackered. If I run into the force on the way home I'm fucked altogether.

Arriving and Departing

I try to figure out what would give me the courage to kill Pat Baker. I go through the drugs I had over the years. Maybe coke, I think. Maybe temazepam if I stayed awake. I take a train back to town. The ads were all different in the station. Don't see a good night wasted, says Diageo. Roughage is out. And I walk down to the Tandoori Queen. I look around me at the queue and I wonder if anyone here knows. If someone has magic in his pocket, something wrapped up small in paper or tinfoil, the magic bullet. I look close at the faces but I seem to have lost the trick. All I see is hunger.

Two, three hours I walk around trying to pose a threat to society until I start to feel well stupid. For a while I wish I brought the gun even. It takes a while to hit me that I didn't talk the language any more, if I ever did understand it properly. Like maybe something else was happening all the time and I didn't understand the words so I never knew what I was doing. Not guilty because I hadn't a clue.

But I get a buzz out of walking the old streets, knowing every car that passes might be the fatal Merc. I'm in your yard, Pat, I'm thinking. I'm walking your patch. He won't know me now. He still thinks of a weedy kid who put a chain-grip on him, not a marine engineer. I'm wearing deck shoes and Levis and a leather jacket. I see the people I used to be waiting on corners in tracksuits in the cold of a winter night. I want to go home. When I see a Merc stopped at a traffic lights I try to see in. There's a businessman and his wife inside. I still hate them even though they're not Pat Baker. They own the country, the rich cunts and the dealers.

The strange thing is that my legs start to act up. I notice it going down a hill, where the screws went in and under the ball of my left foot. I start to think they're going to give out on me. Then I start to worry that if I have to leg it they won't hold me up.

I'm sitting by the river and it's like glass with ripples and the church spire from the other side is reflected in it. There's a corrugated man coming down the outside on some kind of strong corrugated cable, he's holding himself off and gently walking backwards down into a blue sky, which when you think about it is this filthy river spitting up the mucus of a thousand years or so. I'm thinking, what if that cable broke? I think of falling down on my back from that spire. There's gravestones some-where below, I think, maybe slabs, maybe crosses. I walk on. I don't know how I found myself back in the estates, no way did I want to be there. This is my nightmare, to wake up at home again.

All of a sudden I need to go to the jakes. I walk up into the houses and turn into someone's garden and have a quiet crap in the shrubbery. I think too. I think about my legs and I come to the conclusion that they're the same as always. The pain has never fully gone, maybe I have a touch of arthritis already. The lights come on in the house and I hear the noise of the telly coming out the window. Daddy Bear is reading the paper in the blue light and Baby Bear is running in and out and Mammy Bear is cooking something nice, not porridge anyway. And I'm crapping in their garden. I feel a little ashamed that in the morning they'll come out and wonder is it dogs or does it look human. I didn't come back for this.

As I'm leaving I bump into this woman. I stand back and apologise and she fucks me out of it and then she stops and sort of peers at me. Jesus, she says, long time no see. She's a kid I used to know in The Lawn. What are you doing now, she says, if The Baker finds out you're here . . .

I tell her I'm home from England. I'm also thinking I didn't know I was this famous. I'm doing well, I tell her. Working for a company that services Audi trucks. I think fast but the only place that comes to me is Dagenham. Where the batteries come from, I say.

Cool, she says. You probably heard I'm on the game.

No, I say, I didn't.

I'm not ashamed of it, she says.

Dead right, I say. It's an honest trade.

The way I see it, she says, there'd be no marriages left if it wasn't for us brassers.

I agree. I'm seeing this anger in her, like I charged her with something. Like she's giving a press release. All the innocent guys get to give a press release from the court steps. At the same time I'm hoping she doesn't decide to grass me up.

I don't do drugs and I don't do bondage.

Dead right.

So, she says, you know the Wallaces? He's a customer.

Who?

She points to the house.

No, I say, I just took a crap in the bushes. I was taken short.

Jesus Christ, she says. You fucking animal. But she's grinning. Come for a drink, love, she says, for old times' sake. I'm just after me walk and me tongue is hanging out for a wet.

Sharon, I can't, I say. You know the way it is with me and Pat. Issues, you know. I only came back to see what the old place was like. If I show my face in a pub I'm a dead man.

She gives me a sweet look. You're homesick, she says. You came back to see the old place. Home is where the heart is.

Except for you-know-who.

He's on remand, she says. One of his girls told me the other night. He's up for offences against the person. He went for Willy Connell and Willy says he'll testify. Everyone says he'll chicken out at the last minute. Nobody testifies against The Baker. He's a mad fucker, that Pat Baker. How's Jacintha?

I tell her Jacintha is mint, we have our own place now in a nice estate outside Dagenham, Kaylie is going to the local school, work is OK, we're happy. I start to enjoy the story. English people are different than us, I say. You can't talk to them, you know? Not like I'm talking to you. No community, know what I mean? But we have a nice house, a council house, and the work is steady.

Everything worked out for you, she says. She squeezes my arm before she says goodbye. Tell Jacintha I said hi and kiss what's-her-name Kaylie for me.

Goodbye, Sharon, stay wide.

She's wearing stretch denims and a leather jacket, a

perfect body, a serene perfect face. Blue eyes and full lips. She looks a million. Her hair is short and she walks like a tall animal. I remember when she was a little kid in a school pinafore coming home from the convent and teasing the boys.

As I head back I'm thinking Dagenham sounds good. I could turn around now and walk back to the station. I could get that old boat-train. Everything would be simple.

I'm having a quiet pint on the way home watching the telly on mute. I see Grace Kelleher dancing in her wedding dress. She dances loose and fetching, shaking herself. Leaning a little backwards she is like a tree bent by the wind, quivering with strain and strength. She stands spread-legged before a light and I see the shape of her legs and the divide at the top. I look around and no one else is watching. She is dancing for me. I think some crazy god is wrecking my head. Then a fat woman is talking and the programme's title comes up. *You've Been Framed*, it says. There are other wedding videos. What the fuck are you doing, Timmy Stuart?

It occurs to me that a couple of weeks back I heard the day job put him on protective notice.

I recognise another one.

The barman is using a very fine screwdriver to interfere with something just out of sight. Three office girls are telling each other an important story. I am the only one who knows Grace's secret. The barman straightens and puts his glasses on. Good as new, he says. Look, he says, holding up a plastic box containing the screwdriver and several tiny steel screws. A spectacle repair kit, who thought that one up? Brilliant when you think about it.

Next day I start my first delivery trip. It's the same skipper that had the injector trouble, different boat. I overhauled the engine on this one, too. Owners, he says, they don't give a fuck. Jazz comes down to the pontoon to say goodbye. Take care for Christ's sake, she says, no hero stuff. No hero stuff, I agree. Just bring the fucking boat over and come back, she says.

The engine is sweet. I listen as he cranks it up. I hear the water spitting out the back. I watch the rev counter and the oil pressure, the temp and the ammeter. So far so good. This is the first time I ever had to depend on my own work. I'm thinking of that hot injector in there pumping juice into the head at a billion-bar pressure, a nice clean injector, not like the last one, and I'm whispering to it like a baby. I'm listening for a miss but all I hear is happiness.

There's a light sea running outside and a north-easterly.

There's a magical five seconds when Jazz and Pete The Who are holding the lines and we're still attached. Then Pete coils his line and drops it onto the bow and only Jazz is holding us. She's looking at me with her big dark seal's eyes and I know I'm coming back, not death or doom or anything could resist that lure. Then she passes me the line and the skipper puts the wheel hard over and nudges the throttle and the bow drifts off and then we're moving sideways. Arrivals and departures.

If you're going to puke, puke in the bucket, the skipper says as I'm waving goodbye. But he's the one who uses it.

I discover I'm genetically immune to seasickness. I think my circulatory system is so full of the leftovers of assorted pharmaceuticals that I'm immune to half the diseases in the world. Where did the fine day go? We're thirty miles out and it's the Arctic already. My nose and lips and ears are numb. My eyes are dry and scratching in the sockets. I wish I owned warm clothes.

It takes me a long time to work out what he's doing with the sails, but later, after he starts looking down into the bucket, he puts me on the wheel and gives me the basics, and like magic I see how everything fits. I'm not Popeye the Sailor Man but I can keep the whole job moving. I don't believe it. All the shit I heard around the boatyard and what it comes down to is: don't let the sails flap.

I steer like crazy, trying to hold the bow from turning up into the wind, as directed, while we're screaming up and down waves like a mad hyperactive pinball and the skipper keeps his head very far down in the bucket. It's the highest buzz I ever had, a pure wailing high. I'm fucked if I ever thought of this before.

But there at the point of departure everything was cool. The blue sky was a kind of blessing. Jazz waved until we cleared the breakwater. I coiled the lines down lazy and slow and I watched until she was hidden by the stone.

While We Sleep

The boatyard in winter is a strange place. All the hulls laid up, some with masts, some without, some covered, some naked to the winds. Pete is working on a big Perkins; I hear things falling. Some owners like to do things themselves. Others pay. There's a man of eighty-four stripping the varnish off his toerail with pieces of picture-frame glass. He works over every inch like time doesn't matter to him. Who knows what he did before he got old but whatever it was he was good at it. The halyards whip in the breeze, they batter on the hollow masts and sometimes the masts or blocks ring like bells. On a misty morning I find the gate open before me and two or three people in overalls are walking around sizing things up and getting ready to change something important. We blow on our hands and talk of wood, metal or plastic. We have theories. Today they're craning the engine out of the belly of a sixty-foot monster. Tomorrow they're sandblasting fibreglass; the manager shows me the cancerous lumps all along the waterline, osmosis, the old age of fibreglass. When they're finished the hull will be poxy and tired looking. Emergency plastic surgery. From time to time we call on each other and swap something – time or tools or parts.

Jazz comes down and sits in the cabin while I fit a new

impeller. She boils a kettle on the cooker and we drink the owner's tea. I eat my sandwiches.

Jazz, I say, we should get married.

Fuck off.

No, serious.

Why?

Well. There's money in it. Tax stuff. So I hear anyway.

There is like fun. Who's going to pay someone to get married?

Well, for fuck's sake will you or won't you.

She drinks her tea. I wait. I have the old impeller on a piece of kitchen towel on the table. I have the new one beside it. The new one isn't keyed. I think they sent me the wrong part. I'm going to offer it up, just in case, but I'm pretty sure I'm right. I'm going to phone the distributors and fuck them out of it. This is a morning's work wasted. The trouble is nobody gives a shit any more. The guy on the phone thinks any Volvo part will do. Like Volvo only ever built one engine. Like if it has Volvo on it, it must be the job. What's a nought or a one more or less on a part-number, a nought is such a small thing. I'm going to go ballistic.

Jazz laughs suddenly.

I might as well, in case you think of someone else.

Right so?

It's cool with me.

I give her the eye. Like the ad says, Jazz, you're sitting on a treasure chest and I have the key.

Not here, she says.

She has this dread that we'll be fucking in a boatyard sometime and the shores that hold the boat up are going to work loose with the vibration and the boat'll go over and knock down all the others one by one. Twenty, thirty boats with unplanned holes, or masts snapped at the spreaders.

There's this thing everyone does when they're kids. You hold your hands out and someone puts pressure on them, trying to close them up. You count to a hundred. Then they take the pressure off, take their hands away, and it's like you're holding something. You can't close your hands. All that's there is air. You look down and what you see is emptiness that you can't go through. For a long time there's nothing you can do about it. This thing I had for Jazz and my daughter.

Jazz often wonders where things went wrong. Her daddy was in the building trade, a plasterer, she thinks. He died of a heart attack when she was small. She thinks maybe the stepfather started it all. He was hard on Pat. He used to clatter Pat and Stacey too, but never Jazz because Jazz was his favourite. She used to sit on his lap. Then the mother died too. Jazz was nine.

What did she die of? Something complicated, Jazz says. She smoked a lot. Jazz thinks the actual cause of death might have been pneumonia, but it started as something else. Not cancer but something in the lungs. Nobody actually told her. Every morning she coughed for a long time and Jazz used to worry that she was catching a cold. Sometimes she got what she called a weakness. Then she was in bed for a while and she went into hospital and died. So that left Jazz and Stacey and Pat and the stepfather.

I gave up sitting on his lap when Mam died, she says, I

got suspicious. Then he started clattering me too. Pat made him go.

How did he make him go?

I don't know. He told us he was going to make him go, that's all.

What did he do? Did he put the frighteners on him?

He was only sixteen.

Did he get a gun?

Jazz looks away. She knows.

What about Social? Didn't they come after a family of kids?

Pat had it sorted.

How?

He sorted someone to keep drawing his cheques.

Dole fraud.

Well, at least they didn't take us into care. We stuck together.

I point out that maybe if they were taken into care Pat mightn't be going around with a claw hammer. Jazz says the family has to stick together. There's no changing her mind on this point. And about the fact that Pat put bread on the table by stealing car radios, graduating to mugging and a little small-time blagging once he got his hands on a piece. Whatever didn't require brains, if it was criminal, Pat sussed it. Then she loses track of him. Somewhere around the time Max and I met, Pat Baker went into business in a big way. He was like one of those inventors whose time has come. Nobody knows what the scam was, but he was acquiring status and power like one of those magic land deals the politicians do and abracadabra they have a stud farm and a helicopter and respect. It was a magical flowering of commerce and creativity.

Nobody in our family was ever in business before, Jazz says.

She says he was very protective. He spent a lot of time conspiring about how to pervert the course of justice. He made sure they got no hassle from anybody, especially the shades. He went after a teacher's car with a length of chain once. Another time he sent her down to the post office with about twenty letters. After a couple of weeks letters started to come back with money in them. Then they had some kind of credit with the local Spar. She thinks they were respectable at that time.

Protection racket, I say.

Pat settled the bill every month.

But she remembers the time he was away for the assault and things got hard. That's when her Stace was going with Scoby. No way would he come near Stace if Pat was out, she says, but Scoby was OK. He used to buy me a box of chocolates. The only thing is I always thought he was too old. He was nice to Stacey too. But he had no head for money. And he was a crap pimp, no guts. A good pimp, people have to be afraid of him.

Jesus, Jazz, you have one fucked-up family, know that?

Look who's talking.

My mother had the nerves, I say. You can't hold that against her.

I have to have my sister Stace, she says. No way am I getting married without a bridesmaid if you're having a best man. I'm not getting married without her.

176

She turns away and punches the pillow into the crook of her neck. In three minutes she's asleep. I hear her steady breathing. I listen to the noise of the street in case some langer is driving up and down practising his counting. I listen for the sound of my daughter breathing in the next room but I can't hear it, any more than I ever can, but just listening makes me feel like I'm gliding through the wall and looking down on her. She has her fist under her cheek. I smell the warm bed smell, a milky goodnight kissing smell. We're all in the same place when we're awake, but we turn aside into our own world when we go to sleep.

I think about Pat keeping accounts.

So I tell Pete not to book the monkey suit yet. The marriage is on hold, pending investigation, I say. But I don't tell him why because Pete talks, especially when he's toked up. He rambles. I tell him Jazz is having doubts. He puts his arms around me and gives me a hug. He gets emotional. Jesus, boy, tough shit, he says. Sorry 'bout that. Jazz is OK, she'll get her head straight.

I know, I know, Pete. But until then the whole thing is on ice.

Cool by me, cool by me, he says. Tough shit all the same though.

I watch her close. I know her moods. But I soon see she won't change her mind. She's carrying on like nothing ever happened. Who'd think I made her a proposal of marriage? Even Kaylie is in on it. She was all excited first, now she's like her mother, the ice-queen. Last week she was colouring a picture of a bride and groom and playing Happy Families with

Barbie and the girl next door. Today her crayons are black and green and she's doing dragons and ponies. Her teacher is reading *Black Beauty*, which is about a horse. Her teacher knows nothing about the wedding but she's on their side by instinct. Women have this thing. They just know. I see the women are against me and I'm old enough to know that I'm lost.

Something is getting ready, getting coiled up. There's a spring winding somewhere.

Kaylie's eyes are not like her mother's. Jazz has deep dark eyes that you don't look into for long for fear of drowning, but my daughter's eyes are like old brown copper, worn down and comfortable. Like a good sunset. And she smiles at everything. If there was no sun it would be night, never mind the stars.

Kaylie notices that Wayne is not too good. Dad, she says, Wayne is bleeding. Her face is serious and her eyes study me very carefully. She wants to know if I really have all the answers. She shows me two watery pools of blood on the concrete path out back. The dog is standing looking at them and just shivering a little bit. I see a necklace of slightly darker spots marking the route he took. His eyes look dead and his hair is hard as wire. After a bit he starts to cough. It's a deep cough, he looks like he's trying to drag something up out of his interior.

He's pissing it, I say. He's not too good. It looks to me like he ingested something bad.

We take him to the vet and the vet thinks about it for a bit. He diagnoses rat bait.

It's an anticoagulant, he says. It's stored in the liver

and gets recycled. It thins the blood out. His lungs are filling up. I can hear that. He has maybe a few hours, a day or two at the most. Do you want me to give him the antidote?

He looks at me like I was some kind of pusher, or I was trying to exterminate Wayne, like I gave him the stuff on purpose, maybe just to see what would happen, or because I didn't like dogs. It was my fault.

There was a rat holed up under the wall at the end of the garden so I bought a box of poison and stuffed the little blue blocks as far down as I could get them, but one morning Jerry called me out to look at his hedge. Just on the other side of the hole that Wayne made to get in and out of the garden, I see a luminous blue dog-shit. Then I saw where Wayne was digging out the rat-hole to get at the bait. All the blocks were gone. It looked like he inherited my interest in chemicals.

I watched him close and for three weeks nothing happened, except maybe he got a bit lame at times. But I could see no symptoms. He didn't look like a poisoned rat to me.

So when Kaylie sees him bleeding I don't make the connection. I put him in the back of the van on a sheet of plastic and Kaylie sits in there with him and we all drive to the vet. The vet gives him a couple of injections and says he'll most likely be fine but he's keeping him in overnight. Then we all go home and sit around talking about him like we just lost a close relative. It's like we came so close to this loss that we never knew we'd feel, and at the same time I'm thinking how easily solved a dog's problems are, but not for us, there was no antidote for Max. Jazz tells Kaylie the story of survival, like Lassie coming home after all, the way Wayne will too. Kaylie believes in it like in the ad where the dog's covered by Direct Line pet insurance. She cries but she has the faith and she trusts in the legend.

A Happy Family

We're walking home after a few scoops. Black Silk played Phelan's and there was a full house. The usual crap. 'The Boys from the County Armagh', 'Stand by Your Man', 'One Day at a Time', 'Four Green Fields', 'Four Country Roads'. Kaylie loved it. She kept pulling us up to jive and getting her mother to teach her how to waltz. It's mostly families, the women at the tables with the kids, the men at the bar talking football or quotas or engines. They are all obsessed by engines. The grandparents always dance the slow dances, every step perfect, covering the floor in some secret pattern. A lot of dark faces and torn hands. People who know each other well enough to keep out of each other's way. The number of men lame in one leg is above average. We leave just before closing time, into the crisp clean air. We don't smoke, Jazz and me, because smoking ruins your health.

We're happy and we have money in our pockets now that the deliveries are coming through steady. Jazz says they're the icing on the cake. I explain how a sailboat works and she laughs and says: You'll never get me into one of them. But I can't tell her how much I love it, the way the wind takes hold and the boat sits into a groove and all the moving and the noise. I'm trying to lean over as if the sails were full and I'm making a swooshing for the water, and Kaylie is laughing at me.

Then as we turn onto Quay Street, out of the bright lights, I tell Jazz what I heard.

Good news, I say. Your brother is down for larceny and receiver of stolen goods. A mate of Micko's is out at the caravan park for the last fortnight keeping his head down. That was who I stood a pint. He says it's freezing out there. The caravans are all damp. He hates the seaside.

Jazz stops. We're standing at the beginning of the pier. Kaylie is holding Wayne's lead and Wayne is pissing against a crate. Everything feels unreal like an American TV show where everyone ends up wiser at the end.

He's my brother, she says.

But at least he's off our back.

What did he get?

Two years.

Starting when?

Then, below us in the black water of the harbour we see Dan Kelleher's Mitsubishi Pajero. The rising tide is just beginning to lap over the roof and the driver's door is open.

Sweet Jesus, Jazz says. Wayne starts to yap.

Kaylie says: Look at the car in the water.

Is there someone in it?

I take my trousers off and walk down the steps into the October sea. There's a dead dogfish floating against the tail-light. I can see its guts hanging like a frayed string. There's a plastic cup and an empty tube of Wurth high-bonding sealant, favourite in all the yards. It looks like a mutant syringe. I hold my sweatshirt and vest as high as I can. I reach the hatchback and look in. A sticker on the back window says: WHOA THERE FAST CARS FRIGHTEN

HORSES. I pull off the clothes, bundle them together and toss them onto the pier. Wayne goes ballistic. He doesn't like cars in the water or he doesn't like me getting into a car in the water. He's barking his head off.

Call the fire brigade, I shout.

The fire brigade? Kaylie says. It's not on fire.

I duck forward to check the passenger seat.

The Pajero is empty. I come up spitting, I know what goes into this harbour. I'm thinking, I hope my tetanus is up to date. I see Jazz and Kaylie looking down anxiously. I wave to them. I realise I'm holding a woman's handbag. I hold it higher but they can't see in the dark.

Did you call the fire brigade, I say when I reach the steps.

The mobile is at home, Jazz says.

Cool so. There's no one in it.

Where the fuck is your man? she says.

Your woman, I say. I give her the bag. What's-her-name, Grace.

Jazz hands me my clothes one by one and I pull them on over wet skin.

Is she dead?

She's not in it, I said.

Kaylie says: Who, Dad?

I jump up and down and flap my hands. Wayne tries to lick the salt off my shins. He's having trouble because of the jumping. I'll tell you one thing, I say, it's fucking cold.

Jazz grins at me. I'll have to warm you up, she says.

I'll tell you something else, I say, that fucking piece of shit jeep is totally fucked. That engine will never start again.

Mind your language, Jazz says.

We walk up to the barracks. By now I'm chattering like a tappet. There's a little light on the button of the voice-box. I press the button and say hello. After a bit a voice comes back to me to tell me to go ahead. The dog growls. He has his head on one side looking suspiciously at the voice box.

I'm reporting a jeep in the harbour, I say.

Which harbour is that?

I tell him where to find it. The voice is coming from twenty miles away, very soft and airy like a lover whispering. They don't man this place by night. He asks me for my name and address. I give him a false one. I'm tempted to say, Patrick Harold Baker. But I resist in case his fame has spread.

Any casualties?

I tell him I looked in and there was no one there. I tell him I'm fucking freezing. I ask him does he have any idea what the temperature of sea water is in October.

You did good, sonny, he says. Stay there. I'll have a car down in ten minutes.

I tell him it belongs to Dan Kelleher, the auctioneer at the top of Ship Street. No, I don't know where his private house is. Why don't they try the telephone directory.

And how did he know he should call me sonny? Is there a class in training school for how to address people like me? Every bogger cop I ever met called me sonny or sonny boy.

When we get home Jazz makes me take a hot shower. I stand in the warm stream and feel the heat coming back slowly. I remember hearing that a shower can kill someone with hypothermia by causing the blood to rush to the skin and away from the brain. By the time I think of it I reckon I must be safe. I'm leaning against the back wall and the water is like tiny gentle needles or some unheard-of drug that makes everything feel. Where is Grace Kelleher? Did she miss the bend for home? Did she drive straight in and change her mind? Or, seeing it was her husband's jeep, did she drive and jump and head for the hills? I like the last idea. If there's one thing I hate it's an auctioneer in a Pajero.

Jazz has the handbag open on the table.

We forgot this, she says. I shrug. Kaylie has lipstick on and a gold earring and she has this little mirror in a silver case open and she's studying the way the light catches the gold in her ear. There's a rough crown on the lid of the box and the words CLARENCE HOUSE. She has a plastic mug of hot milk with the word CREW. Jazz is reading a letter.

Don't worry about your brother Pat, I tell Jazz. He's used to the Joy. He'll fly it.

Listen to this, she says. I never loved you anyway, I only married you because my father said I had to, if I had half the courage I have now I'd have said no, it's not too late for me to make a new start, I'm getting a job and I won't be a burden to you any more like you were always saying, you won't have to pay for my fancy clothes any more, don't worry about me I can look after myself. Yours faithfully Grace. PS By the time you find this I'll be far away.

She looks up at me.

I say: She didn't plan to drive it in the sea?

That's what I think.

An accident?

Or she got a rush of blood to the head.

Revenge?

We both laugh. Kaylie wants to know what we're laughing at.

The lady drove her husband's car in the sea, I say.

Why?

To get rid of it.

Why?

Because she hates jeeps.

Repentance, Love

Jazz decided to visit Pat Baker in prison. What harm, she said, he's behind bars, he's not going to kill me in front of the guards and all the witnesses. She wanted a real wedding. All I have to do is talk to him, she said. He'll see I'm happy. I'll tell him you went straight, that you're working, that we're doing fine. He'll leave us alone.

I kept Max's diagnosis in mind and tried to convince her. In the end I said: What will happen to our daughter if you're gone, and she just laughed. But the night before she was nervous. She started the same thing about Stacey again. Look after Stace if I don't come back. And she said to me that Stacey would make a good mother. I saw her off to the bus with a packet of photos from the One-Hour Photo. She was going to show him the snaps.

She said: I'm going to say, This is your niece, Pat. And this is her communion dress. If you weren't trying to kill us you could a come to her holy communion.

I drove her to town and she got the train to Dublin. Don't leave the station, I say. You'd never know who you'd run into. Just get on the train and go.

When she came back two days later it was all sorted. Pat forgave us. He swore he never put out a contract. He wished us well. He was hoping to get parole for the wedding to give her away, and Stacey was to be the bridesmaid. It was the sacrament of reconciliation. From the safe confines of Mountjoy Gaol, Pat Baker touched our family and healed all.

She brought a copy of a newspaper she picked up at the station. There she saw the photograph of an associate of her brother, looking straight at camera and giving the world the two fingers. Face of defiance, the headline called it. His trial collapsed due to the total amnesia suffered by five separate witnesses who once claimed to know something about the unhappy death of Micko Casey. They were out of their tree at the time, they said, beer and E affected their memory, and a couple of pages further on there's some rock star saying the same thing about his history. He's not giving us the finger though, he's asking for respect.

As it happens we had a delivery to Lézardrieux in France. I'm making good money out of this, I said. I hate leaving you on your own. Don't worry about us, she said. There's no fear of us. Meaning I was the one with the price on my head. I left her practising that same dance with Kaylie, the dance she was doing the time I first saw her, Kaylie and her locked at the waist, their arms around each other, watching their feet. They barely looked up when I left although I kissed the pair of them. The list of people who were invited to the wedding was on the worktop behind her. Maybe twenty names. I'm leaving you the mobile, I said, in case Kelleher calls about the house. I'll be out of coverage anyway. I could be gone a week, ten days, depends on the weather. And I saw Pete The Who before I left and told him the monkey suit was on again. He gave me the V for victory.

*　　*　　*

What happened to Dan Kelleher's Pajero was Neilus Carey got it for scrap. Kelleher bought a new one, exactly the same model Pajero, and he probably bought a new sticker about horses for the back window too. He barely had it a week when it was stolen. I'm thinking too about what Jazz thought when she saw the brand-new jeep outside our house. Did she think Dan Kelleher was calling about our offer? Coming to tell us that the deal was on or off? Because the day after she came back from Mountjoy, we made a bid for the house we were renting. We walked up to Dan Kelleher's office and laid our cards on the table and he agreed to think about it. Jazz thought he looked like Dirty Den only a bit bigger. She never saw him without his jacket before. It seemed to me that he had no interest in anything at that time. Grace was disappeared, I don't know if they were in touch. He looked to me like he wasn't really listening to us. He was staring at something, and when it came to the details of our offer he didn't haggle. I'll think it over, he said. I'm inclined to go with it. When we were leaving he said: All right? Leave it with me. Talk to you soon. But one thought occurred to him before we left that showed he was all there. Could we pay any of it in cash up front? He could do us a special.

He never said anything about screwing more money out of us. He didn't give us the usual auctioneer's talk about how valuable the property was and the resale value and the location. He didn't get up when we came in or went out. There was inertia in him that made him want whatever was happening to keep happening for a while. A flywheel of idleness just spinning quietly between things he had to do to stay alive.

So when the Pajero stopped outside our door – no counting houses this time – it must have seemed to her that Dan Kelleher was calling to finalise the details, even though it was after ten o'clock at night. She probably wished I was there and cursed me for taking off on this delivery trip. She probably saw the car, put two and two together, and rushed around to get the room tidy. I saw her do that before when someone called unexpectedly. She probably never saw her assailants. Not, at least, until she opened the door.

Everything that happened afterwards is what you would expect and what I know about it I heard at the trial, mostly forensic stuff. I watched him closely as he sat there in the box taking a personal interest in the prosecution witnesses, and I saw that, in addition to the features I noticed the night he looked in and saw my neighbour's trophies and decided not to kill him, he had the big facial structure and bright dead eyes of a pure-bred setter.

The day I came back from the delivery trip was bright and windy, a brittle shaky afternoon, full of uncertainty and change. There was a metal sign at the pier head that spun in the wind. It said on one side REPENT, and on the other LOVE. I remember we joked about it, the skipper and me, as we tied up the little wooden yacht we were after bringing back. We said that Neilus Carey was moving into the big time, and what kind of a car was suitable to carry the word of God, because we could see that the sign was made of scrap metal and that it was welded in several places with beady thick seams. Skipper worked out it was a Bentley, but I know it had to be a Merc. I remember thinking that God had a manky sense of humour, sending dead people's cars to Neilus Carey so he could turn them into bible quotes. When I got home the house was closed up and I knew right off that something terrible happened. Even before I noticed the tape. The worst thing I imagined was that she met someone else and ran off and took Kaylie with her.

But then my neighbour's door opened and Jerry came out. Then his wife Amanda came and formally took charge of his chair and guided it down their path, out onto the street and up to where I was standing. She was crying and Jerry was staring at me. When they got to three feet away she halted the chair and stepped down on the brake to lock it. Then she came round from the back of the chair and held out both her hands and took mine in them.

I'm so sorry, she said. Jerry and me are so sorry for your trouble.

What is it? I said. What's after happening?

They looked at each other. It was a you-tell-him look, one to the other and back again. It was like one of those cartoons where they pass the bomb to each other until it finally explodes in the hands of the person who invented it.

A Long Way Down the Track

But I want to tell about that day she came back from visiting her brother Pat in Mountjoy Gaol. That was a fine dry day in early autumn. I had a tricky piece of work aligning a new engine and every time I tested the alignment I was microns out and I knew if I started it, although I couldn't really run it fast because she was on the hard standing, it would run rough and maybe damage the shaft or the p-bracket or the box. So I didn't think about Jazz all morning. Pete was there to help because I needed someone to move it with me and work the chain-lift. It is one of those cursed jobs that simply will not come right until they come right. But by noon we were winning. The curious thing was, and I saw this before, when the engine was perfectly true it looked crooked. That is the way with physical things very often. The eye is a fool to the hands. About half past twelve we started it and ran it for a few minutes until I saw the engine temperature indicator begin to climb rapidly and it seemed to me that the alignment was sweet and true and quiet as a child. I told Pete to get the gear off for me and phone the owner and I went home and scrubbed myself, threw the overalls in the washing machine. That was the last time that the feel of Jazz was in the place, the last time it felt like home to me. Kaylie was at school. I picked her up in the van and she was all excited to be going to town. How long will it take, Dad? A couple of hours. Are we there yet? Not yet. She wrote a poem for her mother and that very day she got ten out of ten in a spelling test. Another red-letter day. I told her she got the brains from my side. So we sang songs as we drove along. We counted the number of white cars we met. We waved to complete strangers to see if they would wave back. We beeped the horn at traffic lights and counted the people who gave us the finger, we even made one man drive through a red light after which we stopped that particular game.

When we came to town I got quiet. We drove through the industrial estates with their green lawns and shiny trees and space. Then we drove through the housing estates. We came to the streets I knew so well. We passed the Tandoori Queen and other places. Once we saw a Mercedes with BAKER KAB on the sign. I said: That company belongs to your uncle Pat. I didn't mention that he was in prison at that moment or that he was a psychopath with Asperger's Syndrome. Children don't need to know everything, though if they knew a bit more than we're prepared to tell them it might set them up better for what happens, the trouble is knowing which bits to tell at the time. Should I have revealed Pat's legal standing to Kaylie? I might have been thinking about all the things I did. Or about Max dying of tetanus or whatever. Or about how the place I grew up in got fucked up. Or about my mother. In fact, I was probably thinking about all of them at one time or another, but when you have a child in a car you have to talk too, and explain, and remember names of places, so I don't believe I was thinking anything very clear, just drifting from thought to thought and getting a bit sad and missing people that I couldn't mention or didn't want to talk to my daughter about.

We drove into the station car park and found a place between a Range Rover and an Opel Astra. The Astra had a large gash in its side, like someone used a can-opener to get a passenger out. Then someone tapped the sharp edges flat. I never saw a wound like that before and I didn't like to see it. I held Kaylie's hand on the platform. The train arrived on time and two hundred people flowed out of it and Jazz was not one of them. I waited until the man started to close the doors and then I went back out. Jazz was sitting on a bench in front of the ticket office. How did I miss her? She looked tired and happy. Kaylie flew to her – I swear she did not touch the marble tiled floor – and was swept up into the air with her legs swinging. There were kisses for the two of us. I had to tell myself that she was only away two nights. How did I miss you, I said. You didn't. I wasn't on that train. Later she told me she thought about pretending, but she knew she couldn't do it. She was afraid. It turned out that instead of staying in a B&B in Dublin as agreed, she came down in the late train the same day and stayed the two nights with her sister Stacey back in Devonshire Street Lower three doors up from where Jazz lived when I went back to get her, and now it was all arranged about the bridesmaid's dress. It was arranged too that Pat Baker would apply for parole to go to his sister's big day. He swore to Jazz he never touched my mother. It seems he forgave me long ago for everything I perpetrated on him. Whatever I heard was part of the weird rumours that surrounded him. I was family now and he would like to be the one to walk her up the aisle, to give her away. He felt, in a way, like her father, the only father she had left in the world. He would write to her as soon as he knew that they would grant the parole.

As I said, it was the sacrament of reconciliation. I didn't like the thought of Pat Baker walking down the aisle towards me.

But she had terrible news too. Stacey's children were gone. They were taken into care. Jazz wasn't too clear why, but it seems Stacey got into trouble, maybe for possession, maybe for something else. She got six months. When she came out she was in the Women's Refuge for a bit. She wasn't too good.

She wouldn't tell me why they took the girls, Jazz said. She just kept saying it wasn't her fault. Jazz thought maybe she was hiding something for someone, maybe one of Pat's crowd.

It all came out in a rush. Then she told how she decided we should buy our own house, not move someplace else. It's time to belong someplace, she said. Everything is settled now. We don't have to be watching our backs. I'm sick of paying rent to Kelleher and never having something to call our own. I'll go back to cleaning if I have to.

I think about the ad for the mortgage that knows what you want before you want it. The bank is just waiting for us to come in so they can tell us exactly what we didn't know we desired. Like I got the same feeling from people I had a commercial relationship with before. Everybody has their drug of choice.

But Jazz is the one with the head for money and so I agree to everything. I say, yes, yes, of course we can pay the mortgage. Of course we have the down payment.

We'll maybe get a county council mortgage if they still have them and end up paying next to no interest. The car was hot with her happiness.

We were mad to forget. And maybe at first we didn't think it would ever happen. But it was all worth it for that couple of hours, dreaming. Every minute of thinking that we were bulletproof and perfect was worth a million hours of everything else. This was what I thought it was all about, like love, the three of us in the car making up fairy stories, living happy ever after for a while.

There was a burning sky. On our right-hand side it seems like something catastrophic was happening just over the hill. And when the sun finally vanished there was rust or blood on the bellies of clouds. Small flocks of birds moved across it. The track of a contrail fell down into the sea; high up it was coming apart but closer to the edge it was straight and thin and concentrated. And only one bad thing came in our way and that was just a dead cartoon rabbit stretched out in the road with his pink see-through ears sticking up.

That's pure magic, Jazz said. That sky.

Then she told Kaylie that *she* was to be a flower girl and she would get a special dress and she would have to hold things for her and stand at the altar. The car was suddenly full of memories of flowers and music. Everybody smiled.

Jazz, I said for no good reason except maybe that I was happy, I'd be lost without you.

And the last thing she said to me before we turned into our own road was: Don't you worry about that, boy, you're stuck with me whether you like it or not.

*   *   *

A long time afterwards, we're waiting for an owner and four or five days in a row the skipper gets the call on the mobile. Not today. Maybe tomorrow. He's this top businessman, the kind that doesn't even bother wearing the clothes. He flies his wife down but he likes to make the long trip himself. We're sitting in this twenty-metre yacht with everything from stereo to microwave. Satellite telephone. We're crewing it to the Med where he will pick up local help cheaper. This morning the call comes that he won't be down for three days. Right, the skipper says to me, I'm not sitting here on this fucking anchor any longer. So we move out. He takes us into these islands, this group of reefs really, reefs with grass on top, so small no one has ever lived there, this lonesome empty kind of place. When I go ashore I find there isn't even a rabbit track or a sheep track. Just birds. The tide comes in through this narrow entrance about thirty feet wide and barrels out the other side. You better be sure of the anchor and the holding in a tide like that. The holding is good and the anchor stays where it's put. The skipper doesn't make mistakes. So that night we smoke a little and he turns in early. I sit in the cockpit watching the moon rising over the sea and listening to the swell falling on the reef outside. Where am I, I ask myself, fuck. The mackerel are breaking all round the anchorage, herding sprat into the little rocky bays and going crazy. The air is warm. About eleven I see this black shape working slowly in from the entrance, looping along the surface, a kind of oily looping movement. I can see the head and the roll of the body. It's a seal hoovering up the shoals. When he moves into the moonlight he looks up at me the way seals do. They are curious creatures. Somehow I get it into my head that this is the soul of Jazz, her big eyes looking up at me from the water. It was the dope maybe. I kneel on the seat on that side and I look down and she looks back. I see the black night water and I see these big black eyes on it. It's like I'm looking down a long tunnel.

Then the skipper comes on deck in a rush.

What the fuck is up, he says.

I just look at him.

You're fucking crying, man, he says. I heard you below. What's up? Get a grip, will you. No more dope for you, Jesus Christ, you scared the shit out of me.

He looks over the side and sees nothing. He turns the spotlight on and the seal disappears.

There's nothing out there, man, he says. Look. Just rocks and water.

He's furious. He glares at me. Look at you, he says.

My face is wet. I might have been making sounds.

Hit the sack, he tells me. And shut the fuck up.

And all night I'm listening to the seabirds and wondering where souls go. Some connections that just don't give. Like strong cables that hold in the crazy tides, the springs that fizz down narrow channels in the dark.

We were anchored in the Carthy Islands, hanging in there on thirty metres of chain and a CQR anchor – as I said, they were no more than reefs with bits of grass on top but we were sick of harbours – and I cried myself to sleep, and after I fell asleep I had this nightmare. I dreamed we were anchored in the Carthy Islands and the anchor was dragging. I don't know why because I knew the holding was hard sand, which, next to mud, is the best. I saw the bone-coloured rock with the scruff of heather shading down into black stone and black water.

When an anchor drags first it's slow. It jumps a bit along the bottom, snagging on things. You can hear that if you're awake and if you're listening. After a long time you learn to distinguish it from other sounds, especially the noise the chain makes shifting on the bottom. I dreamed I could hear the anchor moving, but for some reason I couldn't do anything about it. Then it started to gather speed and I could feel the difference in the boat, in the lie of the boat to the tide or something. I dreamed I looked out, though I had no cabin window that looked sideways, only one that looked up like a hole in the head into the dark. I dreamed I saw the reef slipping past. We weren't headed for the sea but down towards a danger called the Sharrav Rocks. Then I *felt* the anchor catch on something hard, and I *felt* the chain parting, a thing that must be nearly impossible. At the time, even while I was having it, I understood all of it.

A Pool of Tea, Islands of Broken Cup

What happened to Wayne is he barked at the intruders. The first one to hear him was Kaylie. She went to the top of the stairs and called him but he wouldn't come. When Jazz opened the door she was holding his collar and saying: It's only Mr Kelleher about the house. When she saw the langer outside she tried to close the door. The langer came in very fast and Kaylie saw her mother stumbling and falling backwards into the hall. She saw him kick Wayne. She heard the sound of something breaking in Wayne and his voice changed. Kaylie moved back into her bedroom then and closed the door and sat down on her bed with her hands over her ears. When the noise stopped she went downstairs. She says she thinks she pressed her hands so hard to her ears that she blocked them. As she was going down she heard nothing at all. She could see that the kitchen was messed, but she didn't go in there to tidy it up. She thought her mother would be cross because she's supposed to help around the house. She stood at the door and she saw that the chairs were on the floor. One of them had a broken stretcher in the back. There was a pool of tea on the tiles with islands of broken cup. One of the drawers was open. In the sitting room the telly was still going. The light changed to different shades of blue. She didn't go in to turn it off. The dog was lying on his side in the hall beside my boots. His chest was moving very fast and silent. He lifted his head to look at her but he didn't say anything. She talked to him. She called him Wayne Dog. Then there was a light outside on the road and in a few seconds a guard was standing at the door. He looked at her. Then he picked up his radio and talked into it for a few seconds. Then he stepped inside very carefully.

There is a radio at the station. It drives me crazy with talk. Trying to sell me things. People with fake voices. Who invents this shit. They want to eliminate me from their enquiries, they say. They say they believe me but they don't. They bring the skipper in and he shows them the paperwork. They ring the harbourmaster at Lézar-drieux. They can't work out the French accent but they believe him. There's a poster of a missing person, something printed off a computer, I think she looks like Jazz. For maybe an hour I'm thinking she's not dead. She's kidnapped and if they act fast enough they'll find her. Like all they have to do is care. Nobody cared about my mother, not even me, and she finished up with a hole in her head. If I took responsibility then. Then I figure out she's dead all right. I look closely at the poster and I see that the girl is not as beautiful as Jazz. Maybe to her mother she was, or whoever loved her, but not to me. To me there was only Jazz. Now I get the shakes. Until then you could hand me a glass and there wouldn't be a ripple. A steady hand, like all this happened before. But when I start to shake I'm shit. I have to sit down. I let it happen, I say. It was me because I wasn't there. He was after me and he got her instead. She was only second best but he didn't give a fuck. Who are we talking about, sonny? the cop says. I say: The feen The Baker sent. The mad fucking langer. Someone warned me about him.

What fucking baker?

They're not up to speed at this time. Later they make all the connections, but at this time the way they look at it is a domestic violence incident. They think I'm on the run. They're surprised when I turn up.

I go in to find out what's the story and I discover, all of a sudden, I'm helping police with their enquiries.

But even in my hour of need I don't name Max's brother. Watch out for that mad langer, he said. I can see the future as clear as glass. Jazz is gone. I'm shaking like a sick dog. I know I'm guilty too, but I have all my old skills at not grassing friends and neighbours. The only name I say is Patrick Harold Baker.

The brother of the deceased? one cop says.

Who happens to be in Mountjoy Gaol, the other says.

You know who he is, I say.

Oh we know all right.

Well, ask him.

This station is maybe a hundred years old. The walls are the colour of mastic. There's plastic chairs. There's a district map behind the desk. I see the harbour and the beach. I see where we live. Where we used to live. Now it's only Kaylie and me, but they won't draw a new map because she's gone. People die every day. Their names come up here in this room but not for long. Only guilty people remember. Innocent people talk themselves into trouble, but the man that did the deed is happy with his memories. He keeps his peace.

Then about four o'clock I have this perfect vision like I used to have from time to time when I was using. The sun is coming in the window like a spotlight and I see myself sitting in that plastic chair. I see that I'm crying like a child. I hear the name I'm saying, and it's a painful name. I hear the hard dry cough but there's nothing wrong with my chest. I'm surprised to see I'm still a fucking weedy kid, like I never grew up, like all my hormones are fucked since way back. And I'm not looking through my own eyes. I hear her say: Get a grip, boy. I'm going to save you, boy. She never did. Life-saving is not our best. But I straighten up. I wipe my eyes with my sleeve. I breathe slowly for maybe two minutes. Then this kid I am, sitting in the plastic chair, tells the story straight. And the man writes it down. And I'm fucked if it makes any sense, but I sign my name and they let me go. They're putting two and two together, things my neighbour Jerry said, things they got out of Kaylie before she stopped talking, missing vehicle reports. Now they're looking for a burned-out Pajero somewhere on the edge of some estate where nobody ever heard of a car on fire. They're following a definite line of enquiry.

Jerry showed me where they buried him, down his own garden because ours was all taped off for the forensics boys and the pathologist. Who gave the dog into his care? He couldn't remember. But down at the back of his garden is a little bump with Wayne in it. It's the only thing planted in that garden. I don't think it will grow.

The two of us waited for a few minutes, looking down in silence. I couldn't get the idea out of my head that what I was looking at was the grave of a child. Then Amanda called that the tea was wet and we wheeled about and went back inside.

*　　*　　*

They worked it all out easy enough. I was away. I was number one suspect. The next of kin were Pat The Baker and Stacey, and Stacey was back on the game. They got a care order. I know what they said. I heard it all before. My mother used to say: If you don't behave yourself they'll take you into care. And when she was desperate and sorrowful she would say: Don't think I'd be able to stand up in court for you; they know all about me. But the family courts are a secret. What happens there nobody knows, except that what goes in and what comes out are two different things. By the time I got back, Kaylie was somebody else's business.

I feel something painful rising in me but I know it won't do me any good. I'll only prove they're right. Never give anything away. But they took my daughter and I feel like they broke one side of me. I'm falling down drunk with pain already. I can't touch things or even hear things sometimes. I feel I'm in shrink-wrap, looking out. Everything is fuzzy and crooked and I can't touch anything, or I can't get near anything real. Then times I feel unreal myself, like my past finally caught up with me and passed me out. Like I can walk through walls, eat glass, drink poison and it makes no difference. Like I belong in a different galaxy. Like Jazz was all that kept me from exploding into a billion very small things, leaving no forensics. Not a hair of my head.

I write to Pat Baker in prison. I tell him the bad news. His sister has been killed by some drug-crazed feen from our own country. His niece, my daughter, has been taken into care. I tell him I mourn with him the loss of his sister and, in a way, his niece. I ask him to get parole for his sister's funeral, to come down and pay his respects. I don't mention I'm going to kill him, but I have conceived a plan to get his escort away from him and I have a chain-grip ready. Nights I spend working out the details of how to get him someplace convenient and what I'm going to do. I take the most trouble over the things I'm going to say to him before I break his neck. I feel the shape of the words, the way each one goes home, and how much of a blow it might be. I forget that Pat was never a good listener, that anything I say would be wasted, that any-way he expects people to lie. In my crazy plans I think Pete is going to help, that he'll agree to commit murder with me for old times' sake. Jerry too in his wheelchair.

My lock-up workshop is in each story. I think about borrowing welding gear and a rivet gun and various other useful tools. I think about that chain-grip. The vice. Various ideas to do with compressed air. I invent choices for him, different ways he could suffer. I give him ten minutes to make up his mind. I plan to live with him for maybe twenty-four hours or death, whichever comes first. When death happens in my story it's always a disappointment. I start again. The beginning is the same as the end. Somebody dies, somebody pays – somebody pays, somebody dies. After a while I figure out I'm more interested in the stories. I never thought I had a good imagination until I started on a suitable compensation for Pat The Baker.

But anyway he doesn't come to the funeral, possibly because they wouldn't give him parole, possibly because of a guilty conscience, possibly because he wasn't sure of his welcome. But he writes back. He says that he was shocked when he heard the news, which a prison officer broke to him. He cannot express his sorrow. He feels lonely without his favourite Jacintha. He writes a bit about the good times they used to have in the old days. Shit about playing Snap and watching telly.

Like when exactly?

This was back when you didn't need a criminal record to make friends and influence people. The thought of him sitting in the Joy inventing a happy family makes me puke.

So I initiate widespread enquiries and I make plans for a while and then one morning I wake up in Pete's place, like he invited me to stay until I got my head together, and I realise I won't kill the fucker. I'm out of my league. I didn't do it when I could and I'm never going to get another chance. The way I see it the world is divided into two kinds of people, the ones who could kill somebody and the rest of us. I'll be lucky if he doesn't turn his Asperger's on me again. Then I start to think about Kaylie and make different plans.

What can be said about the funeral? I try not to remember it. Pierce and Pete The Who and Dan Kelleher and my neighbour Jerry in his chair trying to get between the gravestones, graveyards not being wheelchair friendly. People who own boats with engine trouble. Half the town. Stacey Baker represents the family. She's strung out, I see, crying and sweating and catching my hand and letting it go all the time. She looks like someone that has trouble swallowing. Neilus Carey knows the prayers by heart. His voice can be heard everywhere, coming in a split second late on every word. Ashes to ashes ashes, dust to dust dust, I know that my redeemer will come come. Like an echo from some other country where nothing much changes. I ask Pierce where Timmy is and he just shakes his head and puts his finger to his lip. Maybe the protective notice didn't work. He points to the priest who is counting down the prayers on his rosary beads. I try to hear the words. There were strangers there – a woman with dyed blonde hair, a bald man. They have kind faces but they don't like what they see. I think they don't like Pete crying openly and clenching his fist over and over again. They don't know his circulation is bad from smoking too much shit and his fingers go dead if he doesn't keep them moving. They maybe think he's a violent person with a plan to commit something. The box is lowered down and people throw things in after it. I have nothing to throw. I just watch the things that people drop in graves and wonder what they turn out to be in the next life, what way they're changed by passing over. I think it's like a boat going down, settling gently and taking its own dead air to the bottom, pulling bits and pieces of floating stuff down too. The last time I saw Jazz she had money in her pocket and she was going to buy a house. I feel like I'm nailed to the floor of some river bed and the water is howling through. Except people shake my hand. The touch that keeps me from bending over backwards or breaking in two.

After the prayers, when people are talking about going someplace for a drink and a bite to eat, Stacey comes over to me and she kisses me. It's meant to be a sympathy kiss but it's like maybe she lost the knack or old habits die hard because it's a wet one on the mouth. A second, maybe two or three it lasts, taking me by surprise. People are looking. I have to turn my head away. In one blind touch I think I'm touching Jazz, the way that happens.

For just one second I'm comfortable and happy and I have a positive outlook on life. And then I'm fucked again. She tells me Jazz was her only sister and she doesn't know what she'll do. She's so lonely, she tells me. She tells *me*. I can see she's not together. The two of us are drowning but she wants to pull me down, like if we're drowning in the same sea we're not alone. I slip away for a while.

First I'm only walking away from the other mourners, trying to get some headroom. Then I find this pair of walking boots outside the door of a Rent-A-Cottage. They're stuffed with newspapers to dry out. I try them on and they fit. So I head first along the coast then back into the hills. I walk for three days until my money runs out. I'm sleeping wherever I can find someplace dry. The first day I'm living on Mars bars. Then hunger makes me high and weak, everything important and useless at the same time. I eat raw stuff and green blackberries. Once I find an orchard and I eat so many apples I'm doubled up with cramps for about four hours. Once or twice I seriously consider ways of dying. I'm walking these narrow roads with dark bushes on either side, specks of red on everything like something has been sacrificed, and I come across this blackbird, I seen you before, I say. I know who you are. He looks up at me and he says: I am the angel of death.

And No Going Back

The social worker tells me that Kaylie is withdrawn. Her hearing is affected, probably psychosomatic, and she has nightmares, she's frightened of dogs and loud noises. She is troublesome at school though the teachers make allowances and the summer holidays are coming any day now and time is a great healer. She tells me that the foster-parents are very experienced and Kaylie is lucky to have them. She will not discuss the court order. She will not discuss me getting my daughter back. You're not even living at home, she says, where are you living now? She looks at me like she knows the answer and is only waiting for me to lie. She wants to hear, she says, that I have entered counselling. She tells me that she wasn't born yesterday, that she knows more about me than I think, that I need to get a steady job. Have I tried for work in a garage? I explain to her that I am a self-employed marine engineer and that I also do yacht deliveries, and she says what kind of an environment do I think I can give a fragile child like Kaylie with no steady job and the kind of friends I hang out with? Later again she calls it a seasonal job. Your brother-in-law, she calls Pat Baker, even though I tell her three times he's no relation of mine.

She tells me there's no quick fix.

I think she's maybe hostile or something.

I call on Stacey in Devonshire Street Lower about three o'clock in the day. She's lying down and kind of dreamy. She wants to comfort me but she doesn't have the energy. Lie down, she says. Stay for a few hours. I'll be all right then. I tell her she's fucking up my chances of getting my daughter back and she says: I can't take this now, I'm not able for it, please why can't we just talk, I'll be all right in an hour. She won't tell me who's pimping for her now. She says her sister would never forgive her. Your sister is dead, I say, she can't forgive anybody. Stacey starts to cry. If I tell you, you'll go after him, she says, and he'll hammer you, he's a crazy bastard.

Where does she get these ideas about me?

I only want you to stop long enough for me to get my daughter back, I say.

It won't make any difference, she says. They know all about us. Where do you think my babies are gone? They're not here, are they?

Jazz wanted me to take care of you, I say.

So get into the bed will you. Come on.

The traffic lights outside her door make a clicking sound when they change. In the quiet of the night you hear it. And the pedestrian light bleeps like a long-distance alarm. Cars stop outside all night. They're waiting for the lights to change, but it seems like there's a million people thinking about calling. Then about six o'clock the city rumbles into life and Stacey comes home tired and silent. Beside her bed she has a double photograph frame with pictures of her kids they sent one Christmas. At least they're together, she said.

I wonder if I could get one of Kaylie.

*   *   *

I get the call to say they picked him up. They have DNA. I don't want to go into the details. He'll be remanded, they say. No judge in his right mind would give him bail. They mention the gravity of the charge and the fact that the fucker would probably abscond. They want me to come in and do a parade. They have half a dozen likely men lined up. All I have to do is say the word.

I hear it on the news. When arrested he replied: Nothing to say. Surprise, surprise. Like they think maybe this time he'll own up like a decent man. Nobody says they did it unless they're innocent, the perpetrators of a tragic accident.

Mostly the accident is some kind of love they believed in. Something that wasn't true.

And then it's like this closed door that I should go through but there's no following her. I know even if I did go through that the door would be to a different place. We'd be in the same hole in the ground but we'd never be together. I work out that I lost her for good. Who believes in the next life? Like even if there was a heaven I'd finish up there, no way. This is the way it is and always will be; some bastard cut her off, I'll never touch her again.

I'm just drifting day to day. I know it. I can feel the set of the tide that's pushing me along. I'm window-shopping. I'm a tourist. I remember the feeling from before, just moving through places, waiting for something interesting to turn up, not really believing it, not even hoping, not seeing straight, not making connections. A little bit invisible.

Now when I go back it's always like the first time. I

should go home and start up my life again, start making a home, but I never slept here once since I came back, hiding out at Pete's, sleeping on his couch, on the floor when the couch starts to feel short, not sleeping much as a matter of fact, or sleeping at Stacey's where at least there's a bed. Walking in my own gate I feel like a professional intruder. I open the door and the first thing I smell is disinfectant. There's no stains on the floor. Light falls down the stairs when I throw the switch. I don't want to delay down here with the dead and the child. I feel them: Jazz lying crooked in the kitchen surrounded by stuff from the sink and a broken chair, Kaylie sitting by the dog with her hands over her ears. I feel like silence has only just fallen. I smell blood. I rush upstairs and throw myself down on our bed. It feels warm under me like someone has just left. I smell her Yardley on the pillow. I'm sweating. I go into each room and turn the lights on. I don't draw the curtains because I think if the neighbours can see in nothing terrible can happen. After a while I calm down and go round to each room and turn the lights off. I go down and look into the kitchen which is normal, although there's one chair missing. Jazz isn't waiting for me there. I look in the hall, then I go out and close the door quietly behind me. I drive into town to visit Stacey.

Way Up Over Everything

Stacey is gone to work. I see the new Pajero is parked outside a flat in Devonshire Street. So this is where he is when he's not at home. I wonder if this is why Grace left him? Maybe he was doing a little door-to-door canvassing. Or maybe he's showing a des res to someone? Unlikely. It's viewing by appointment only this time of night. Since the video of his ex-wife came out the party dropped him from the ticket, nobody wants a politician if his wife starred on *You've Been Framed*. Neilus Carey told me his father tried sixteen years to get a proper sewage system but Kelleher and friends fucked it all up at the planning. They built four or five hundred houses and handed the shit over to the Sanitary Section to deal with as they saw fit. The pipes drop a hundred feet to outflows that stick out of the harbour wall. The fall keeps everything moving nicely. Solids come down like projectiles heading for the wild blue. Now they're talking about a state-of-the-art sewage works and guess who owns the land? Politicians, he says, I could write the book.

But when they come cold calling nobody says I'm not buying any of that shit. What they're pushing is pure toxic but everybody buys, and they end up on a trolley instead of a bed, or queuing for a living, or being watched by interested rats in some shithole flat. They sign away their life like it's their duty to vote for one wide bastard over the other. Like guess who closed down the centre where the NA meetings were held, but they built some kind of a racecourse for the mates? Like what the country needs is more fucking horses and a tad less people? Once when I was a kid a politician came round The Lawn with his bits of paper. When he was leaving he got stuck in a junction with a man in a Hiace van. He rolled down the window and told the van about the right of way he had and how he had a meeting somewhere, but the Hiace man didn't move. He was one cool Hiace van driver. He just sat there with his fists on the wheel, looking. When he had enough from the politician he got out. Fuck you, boy, he said. He pulled out a knife. He pressed the magic button and a blade came out. The politician stopped complaining. He went round the car and stuck each tyre and the politician's car sat down on the rims. I forget the make, maybe a Volvo. Then the Hiace man made the blade vanish. Don't go away, he said to the politician sitting there on the rims in the junction, there's people here hoping to see you.

But when I stand at the bar in The Bailey, there's Dan Kelleher standing beside me. We look at each other and we both know we're sleeping with whores and there's this instant camaraderie like people from different football clubs meeting unexpectedly in a foreign city. We recognise the coloured shirts. We want to be nice to each other so nobody will feel it necessary to cast aspersions. We take our pints to a table under a silent screen. The Sky News ticker casts a blush on the far wall. I see by his eyes that it is not his first of the night.

Hard times, he says to me. And I agree.

She was a lovely girl, he says. Even though I really only

saw her the once. In the office that time, you know. A smasher.

I agree.

Jesus, that was incredible luck.

That wasn't luck, I say. Her fucking pusher brother was trying to kill me. Even from inside. That was a contract that backfired.

He shakes his head and sucks on his pint. This is a new way of seeing things. He looks at me with what might be respect. He's maybe thinking he should be nicer to me.

I tell him my daughter was taken into care and the bastard kicked the shit out of my dog.

Oh Jesus, he says. I didn't know.

Well, there you are.

Jesus.

They won't give her back.

He looks at me and shakes his head. I notice he has a limited line in body language.

I'm a working man. I'm clean, more or less. I have money in the bank. What the fuck is wrong with me?

He shrugs like he knows something.

Do they know something I don't about me? She's my daughter. How the fuck do they know I'm not a fit person? What is it?

He shrugs again.

Look, I say, if it was you?

If it was me, if I had a child, which I don't, the child would go to Grace, my ex, anyway. Women always get the child. Ever hear of Parental Alienation Syndrome?

I shake my head. But I'm remembering Grace. If I was a judge I'd give the child to her.

That's what I have, he says, Parental Alienation Syndrome. Your man in *The Times* has it too. What's his name. I read him about it the other day.

I ask if he's getting anything for it, but he ignores me. He sits looking down into his pint for a bit, then he says he should have more fight in him, but he hasn't.

But if I was you, I'd lose the child anyway, he says. Why?

He shrugs his knowledgeable shrug again. You don't sell yourself, he says. You look like shit and you act like shit, no offence.

Now he gives me a lecture about houses. He explains why rich people live on hills and own the view. He tells me marketing is a kind of religion and you have to think about converts all the time. About making people see things differently. He tells me if I can't tell the sucker at the poker table, it's me. He tells me that when he's selling a house he's selling an identity. Which in the end of the day is something I do not have. If I was a property owner everything would be different. He takes out his wallet and he puts a credit card on the table. He puts a beer mat beside it. He puts an ashtray beside that. There's cigarette butts and a spill of some kind of liquid in the ashtray. Maybe beer. He asks me which belongs with the ashtray. I look at the shiny American Express card and the beer mat. I'm a judge, he says, I need to decide where I'm going to place a child that has come into my court with a question of care. I look at the beer mat. I look at the credit card. The credit card is a decent middle-class person with a track record in foster care. The beer mat is the natural father. The ashtray is what the judge thinks is the cause of all our social ills. If he's a good judge he thinks the ashtray just means the poverty trap. If he's a bad one he thinks the people who live in it invented it. He just wants to know where to send the child.

I shrug.

Dead fucking right, he says. The Amex gets it every time. No way the judge'll give it to the beer mat.

Look, he says, in business we estimate that it costs us eight times as much to get a new customer as it does to keep an existing one. Think of the care system like that. It's cheaper for them to give your baby to a foster-care family than it is to fix whatever is wrong with you.

So?

So, you have to atone for your sins. You have to make it cheap for them. Know the price or pay it, as the man says.

I have to look like a fucking credit card.

That's the way I see it.

Stacey comes in about four and all she wants to do is sleep. I'd be happy to sleep the rest of my days as long as there was a body beside me. I dream things that wake me up. I wonder what Jazz would say. And nothing feels the same. I get up at eight and make her a cup of tea the way I did for Jazz, but the pills drag her down again before she finishes it. She doesn't talk. She never dreams. She sleeps that dead sleep that has no way in or out. She doesn't just close her eyes. She goes blind for six hours. Right in the middle it feels like she'll never come back, and when she does she looks let down, like she had high hopes. I don't like to be around when she finally wakes.

I call on Pete and we talk engines. Or I go straight to the yard. I keep busy but I can't stop thinking.

*   *   *

Stacey helps me buy the suit. She takes me to a place businessmen go. She brings Joey Meehan, her pimp along, because he has a legitimate operation on the side and because she knows I'm not going to attack him like she was talking about at first. There's a long mahogany counter. Soft sweaters folded on racks with little logos of men playing golf. Yachting caps, pictures of racing boats. The place smells like wool and leather and polish. The flunkies wear double-breasted jackets. They pick out a nice double-breasted suit with a very fine stripe. They buy me a blue tie and a white shirt. Joey himself chooses the tie. Joey likes me. He says I'm doing Stacey a power of good. He doesn't see me as a commercial prospect, he says, because I'm family. As long as I don't interfere in her work. He drops a tenner on the counter as a tip. Stacey says he's a big spender. She tells me all the girls on the line call him Flash Joey, but he never lets his girls do heroin and he pays for the doctor. There's worse than him, she says.

He drives us home in his jeep. We're way up over everything. We can see down on people and through windows.

I'm all upset for you, he says. I don't know what I'd do if I lost my daughter.

He shows me pictures of his family while Stacey makes us tea. He tells me that his daughter does gym-khana. He shows me a picture of her on a horse. She has big dead eyes. The horse is not looking at the camera. His other daughter works in insurance, a tall thin blonde, I see her sitting beside a computer wearing a fake smile and a college cap and gown. When I look closely I see that the computer is a fake too, just there for the photograph. Graduation day, he says, the proudest day of my life.

Stacey says he has a lovely family.

He sips his tea. He drinks it the same way I learned – the saucer in one hand, the cup in the other, the little finger sticking out. He looks dainty and well brought up.

Now, he says, you need a business address.

I tell him I have a workshop and he says I should get a card printed.

Stacey smiles at him. He smiles at me. It's like he has conferred my child on me just by not hating me.

He holds his cup and saucer out and Stacey puts a little milk in and pours the tea again. His spoon, stirring the sugar in, makes no sound. The liquid swirls around and the spoon follows it, but it makes no noise.

Joey is a delicate man. He leaves politely at half past ten, and when he's gone Stacey tells me he did six years for killing a man with his fist by mistake. Nobody touches his girls. Before he left he shook my hand and patted Stacey on the shoulder. There's my good girl, he said. See you tomorrow.

Then Stacey shows me her collection of postcards of the seaside. She looks at them like they were broken promises, or the boy next door who fucked off. There's two of the amusements in full swing, one of the Ferris wheel going round in the dark, just a circle of small lights. There's the prom. There's the town from the air, the trawlers, the yachts, the boatyard.

I tell her I tried to stop Jazz keeping in touch with Pat.

He was her brother, she says. Blood is thicker than water.

When Stacey goes out to work I try the suit. I'm

standing in front of the mirror where ten minutes before she pulled her miniskirt straight and checked her make-up. I'm wearing a blue pinstripe suit, a white shirt and a blue tie.

What do I look like? Maybe an auctioneer.

A Place of Safety

After the social worker messes me around a second time I figure out that this is the slow virus that never dies. People drop out of sight. Shit happens. What you think is a good day is really the start of the worst day of your life, what you think is the end is only the beginning. When you're down they kick you in the gullet and your teeth fall out. Max died and my mother turned into a bicycle and Max's brother collided with a gas main and Jazz stood for me. This pain. This empty place. It works from the inside out and certain people have just an incredible diagnostic power like an echo-sounder. To them you're as empty as a drum.

So I start to make enquiries. I put the word out. I walk the streets and for the time being I'm untouchable because of my pain. People shake my hand and say they're sorry for my trouble. I have no enemies. I'm in mourning. I find out where the people live and I go and look at the house where they're keeping Kaylie, which, it turns out, is no bigger than ours. There's a window downstairs with a heavy brown curtain. There's a teddy bear in one window upstairs. I don't recognise that bear, maybe something the foster-parents gave her. There's no dog. The strange thing is it's in the same estate where I hid out from the posse. One of those places where the second wave of children is coming, little groups of kids smoking in out of the way corners, a new generation moving up from their starter houses, a temporary rest in the merry-go-round where everybody owes somebody something until they die. Also known as The Property Ladder.

There's a FOR SALE sign at the old guy's gate. I can see the window I used to look out of. Now I'm standing in the place I could see then, with the green behind me. Out of habit I look up and down but it's not a Mercedes-type estate.

I ring up and ask them for a viewing, not that I could afford it, but I'd like to see inside, back where I was that time. Which I tell none of it to them. They tell me all their agents are tied up at the moment but they can have someone down there next morning early and we settle for ten o'clock.

In the woman's face I see that she doesn't believe in me even though I wear my auctioneer's suit. I tell her I need a property to launder my drug takings. Her smile is a wrinkle in leather. Take your time, she says, but she checks her watch. Whenever I go in a room she goes in the previous one like she's counting the furniture. I used to know the guy, I say. Why isn't his daughter moving in? She shrugs. She does or does not know? It's hard to tell. I stand for a long time in Helen's room, my room. Even now I don't know the meaning of what happened. I open the drawers but there's nothing in them.

The furniture is separate, the auctioneer says. She's standing in the door watching me.

Would you take ninety, I say to her. She raises an eyebrow.

I have the deposit, I say. It's an offer.

She shakes her head. No chance, she says. I can't bring an offer like that to them. I'd need a substantial increase.

I'm up to my max.

Sorry.

In the kitchen the fridge door is propped open with a chair. Its sad dead air is everywhere. The chair where he used to sit is in its exact place, as if his body was extracted from it by some powerful suction force. He was my father, I tell the auctioneer. My mother was the local bicycle, but this guy was my father.

Now she laughs.

A neutral venue, the social worker says, my third try. A supervised visit. So I pick the Tandoori Queen. The waitress is Chinese. She takes our order. Kaylie doesn't ask for anything, but I know she likes curry. The social worker says she'll leave us to it. She goes out and walks up and down outside the window. Kaylie doesn't look at me. She looks at the table, the vinegar bottle, the ketch-up. She looks at the picture of some Indian woman with too many arms. I can see her trying to figure out where all the arms fit in. So I start to tell her about the boat I'm working on. I tell her how Pete is keeping. I ask her is she all right and she nods her head. I don't know what I'm seeing in her eyes. The social worker said she wasn't on any medication. She said it like I insulted her by asking. But Kaylie's eyes are secrets. The Chinese waitress has the same eyes, but she speaks a different language. She puts the plates in front of us and says: OK, OK? I say yes, everything's OK. She goes away. She doesn't smile. It's your favourite, I tell Kaylie. Curry. But she doesn't eat much. She pushes things around her plate. After a while she asks me when she's going home. I smile because this is the most she has said. Soon, I say. I have it nearly sorted. The only desserts are lychees and ice cream. The social worker comes back and sits down. I see she chain-smokes. I suppose it's no fun.

This used to be an Indian place, I say. She looks around.

Isn't it?

The dessert is lychees and ice cream.

It doesn't make an impression. She says she likes lychees. She's looking at the woman with too many arms.

Tandoori is Indian, she says.

Kaylie eats the ice cream and the social worker eats the lychees. She puts her arm around Kaylie. She's trying to be nice. It'll all work out, she says, won't it, pet?

Kaylie nods her head, her hair hanging around her face. Then she looks up at me and I see Jazz in her, like a breeze blows down on the sea and changes the surface. I remember the night Jazz was holding the newspaper over the fire and suddenly there's a brown place on the paper and then it's burning.

Kaylie's dark eyes scorching mine.

Time to go, pet, the social worker says. Say bye to Daddy.

I See a Good Day Coming

Pete tells me he fell in love once. Some kind of good manners stops him from naming the girl as she is now happily married. He sees her most days, he says, walking a baby mostly. They fell in love over a book at school. She was reading *Wuthering Heights* for her exam and so was he. He didn't know that Cathy and Heathcliff were doomed, he said. He never got that far at the time. Now he reads that book over and over again like a bible.

They caught me smoking hash in the jakes, he said. Sudden death, know what I mean? I got expelled. So I got a trade. Love, love, love, he said, it's like some fucking fast animal, no difference which way you turn you can't get away. It fucks up the two of you.

But one day I figure it out. I notice he's inclined to leave the job about eleven. I follow him. He leaves the yard and heads for the prom. At the far end he lights a spliff. The wind blows the smoke away like a gunshot. He takes the cliff path. Ahead of him is a woman with a pram. Bits of foam float up from the breaking waves. He stays thirty feet behind her and she never turns round, as if she knows he's there and is happy but doesn't want to make a thing of it. They walk the circle round the headland and back into the noise of the traffic where she turns left and Pete turns right. He stops after a

hundred yards to look back and sees me. He waits for me
to catch up.

So? I say.

You fucking followed me, he says.

She's a minter, Pete.

Fuck off.

We walk back together to the yard. He has a Volvo
Penta 35 that's losing power for no reason; I have a beat-
up old Lister-Petter to recondition. Two long-term asso-
ciations. This kind of thing takes time.

She married a blacksmith, he says. Believe it or believe it
not, there is still such a thing. When they were married
he was working for the stables and barely able to keep
body and soul together. But then he got the idea of
selling fire-irons and stuff. Make a poker with a twist in
the handle paint it black charge a small fortune, that
kind of shit. Arty-farty blacksmithy stuff. He's fucking
manky. Know the house with the round window? That's
him. Ever see that Ford Transit with MASTER BLACK-
SMITH MOBILE WELDER? That's one of his. She's not
happy at all.

I ask Pete how he knows she's not happy and he says
he just knows. I ask him if he ever talks to her and he says
he never gets the chance.

Anyway, he says, she's a married woman.

It's an evening in May sometime later, days maybe.
We're sitting on the teak deck of a Nauticat, passing the
toke around and looking at the sunset behind two
hundred aluminium masts. The yard gate is closed but
we have the combination, we come and go. We have the
place to ourselves.

He says: Someone told me if you stick a cigarette in a frog's mouth he can't breathe, so he explodes.

Cool. How do you do that?

I never saw a frog in my life.

Me neither.

He sucks deep on the toke, holds it and then talks as he breathes out. Well, he says, I was that frog.

I look at him for a minute, trying to figure out what he's saying. I have this picture of Pete when he was maybe fifteen, sucking on a toke and holding on too long. Then I think maybe he means if she kissed him he'd turn into a prince. Then I think smoking too much shit addled his brain. I let it pass.

How's the Volvo?

I'm fucked if I know. I been on to the works. They're faxing some info. I keep thinking it's compression but the heads are perfect. Brand new.

Compression rings?

Tried it all before.

How about the pump?

He looks at me. The fuel pump?

Maybe faulty.

He shakes his head. Never heard of it.

A vacuum in the lift?

He's thinking. I see the centre of his eyes get small and clear and pointed. When he's thinking he sticks his tongue into his cheek, like a child with mumps. Nobody gets mumps now. They wiped it out. One time Kaylie was sick. I walked her up and down the kitchen floor and she burned like a hot engine. I was afraid to touch her face. She had her head on my shoulder and her hot hair against my cheek and I felt her short fast breathing. The only song I knew was 'Wonderwall'. I sang it maybe forty times. I thought this simple thing, some ordinary bug maybe everybody got, would wreck everything. What will I do if she dies on me, I was thinking.

Jesus, you could have something, Pete says. I'll get them to fax the spec. It's a new engine. Maybe they never checked the spec for the tank.

We smoke for a bit. Evenings like this hurt. The air is warm. The sky is that kind of red that means a good day is coming. One star is burning through all the light, I see it between the masts.

I should have kept running, Pete.

He says nothing.

I never decided to stay. Maybe Jazz did, but I just funked it. I should have kept going when I went this far.

Don't be going over it.

Pete, I'm buying a boat.

He looks at me for a bit.

Not that heap of shit you were looking at? *Windshit* or *Birdwind* or whatever the fuck?

Songthrush.

What kind of fucking name for a boat is that?

I'm not changing the name. It's bad luck.

It's timber, man. A hole in the water to fill with money. It's for sale because the guy that owned it dropped dead. Know how old he was? He was ninety-one and he was fucking senile. He couldn't get anyone to crew because they were all afraid of the boat.

It's cheap.

There's no such thing as a cheap boat.

It's solid.

Like a rock only it leaks.

All timber boats leak.

You have it bad, man. You have it bad. You convinced yourself you needed it. Then you convinced yourself it was the right one. Then you looked at it and convinced yourself whatever was wrong was fucking historical. You're a yacht broker's dream. Get a grip.

I shake my head. I'm going to get my daughter back, I say.

They won't give her back just because you have a heap of shit historical wreck down the harbour.

He swings around so his back is to the guard-wires and his feet to the coach-roof. He's looking into my face.

Sinking at her moorings, he says.

There's things I can't tell you, Pete.

Rotting.

I'm buying it.

Well, fuck me, he says, if you go down one morning and all you can see is the top of the mast don't say I didn't warn you. I'm giving you no more dope, you can't handle it.

I see a good day coming, Pete. For the two of us maybe.

You're going to need all the good days you can get on the good ship SS *Birdshit*, he said. But I could see he was thinking maybe I was right.

But she's not as bad as that. She has a good suit of sails. A working Primus stove. Best of all a nearly new Yamaha 10hp. A long comfortable keel. I delivered boats like this. I took one to Chichester and I delivered boats twice as long that weren't half as easy. Mahogany on oak frames, the best of it, laid deck, brass ports. The main problem was she had iron pigs for extra ballast and someone concreted them in place. There was probably a certain amount of rot – timber needs to breathe – so some day I'd take the concrete out and see what was going on. She had a comfortable little cabin with enough headroom to sit up straight, oil lamps, a good compass and an echo-sounder. She had a full kit of sail including a storm trysail. The man that sailed this boat knew what he was doing. I could feel his competence everywhere, the ghost of a decent man.

Later my lawyer would regard her as a liability in my case. He would say it was no fixed abode and people with no fixed abode were naturally under a cloud of suspicion as far as normal people were concerned. People knew where they were with you if you had a house, he said. He wanted me to go back to renting.

I bought her on the last day of May. I moved my bits and pieces down and dropped the keys of the house back to Dan Kelleher's office. His secretary smiled at me. On her computer the words LOCATION LOCATION LOCATION were slowly moving around the blank screen. On the wall was a poster of a concrete building with the words: SUPERB THIRD-GENERATION SPACE, MUST BE SEEN. He won't be happy, she said. You're supposed to give a month's notice. She winked. So where are you off to?

I'm moving into a boat, I said.

Cool. I was out in Mr Kelleher's boat once. It has a hot shower.

It was a bright warm day and the halyards were ringing their bells in the harbour. I rowed out with a bagful of messages – toothbrushes, tea, a comb – and a pound of sausages and rashers. The racing boats were on their way out and one or two owners called good luck to me. Dan Kelleher passed with a crew of blond boys in fancy hi-fits. He never looked my way.

Like I didn't exist.

I Shake Hands with my Soul

I take *Songthrush* west for a few days to try her out, anchoring in the islands, lying deep in the Illen river one night of a gale, trailing a line over the stern for fish. I'm learning the ropes but I'm surprised to find I've picked most of it up already anyway – somewhere along the line my natural immunity to the sea turned into love. At night the cabin fills with the smell of burning oil and cooking. I sleep in a fog of food and carbon monoxide and I learn to think of it as the smell of comfort. I feel like a monk. They won't give me access to Kaylie, though they're not saying I won't ever have it. Just now, while she's still trauma-tised, they don't think her father is the right person. When I ask they just spell out her symptoms like the obvious diagnosis is she needs to be kept away from me.

I fix a small diesel leak into the bilges. The timbers are taking up and the cabin is becoming dry but the auto-matic bilge pump clicks in at strange times, so I wake at maybe one or four to hear something like a horse pissing over the side. I learn to come and go under sail because there is no diesel oil to be had down here and the engine is not powerful enough to push her against any kind of tide anyway. The weather is mostly kind except for one bad night. For three days I hear nothing but moving water and seabirds. One night coming along between Hare Island and the Gascanane I hear the ghost of something crying. It's a dead cold grey night, the first and only bad one. There's a hard following sea coming in from the south-west, there's no seabirds, no seals, no dolphins, the only other boat is a crazy fisherman lifting pots three miles back, and I hear this voice crying behind me. I turn around and there's nothing, only the waves. I light the navigation lights and the red glow on the sail looks like safety. I pull my hat down hard and concentrate on the failing day and the blank wall of rock ahead that the chart says will turn into a channel when I get closer. I'm frightened of the sea pushing me in, the wind scheming to get me into this bottleneck that maybe I won't get out of again, that maybe the engine won't start if I need it and the wall won't open up where it's supposed to. I never learned navigation. I usen't to worry about any of this when there was somebody else in charge. When I look back I find myself looking up at waves. They come at me in the white of the stern-light and the boat lifts gently or maybe corkscrews a little to let them pass under and away. The land is all around me, closing in and fading out at the same time. Darkness is moving out to sea. I hear it again. I'm thinking of one time she was crying, I can't remember why, one of these times of trouble that kids think will last for ever. It was maybe a bad dream that she woke from, or that I heard her dreaming. I'm wearing the T-shirt I sleep in and she's wearing her fleecy pyjamas and she's hot and sticky from the dream. I'm saying: Don't be crying, baby, don't be crying, girl. She takes no notice. Then it's like all of a sudden she starts to get interested in the noise. Like she's practising wailing. She starts to do something different. Making animal sounds or seal sounds and then listening. I hear someone moving around next door. I tap her on the bottom and say: Come on now, don't be waking the house. And suddenly I start to wonder exactly how many fathers are standing in the middle of a room at that very moment trying to get a child to go to sleep. The way I see it there could be a million or ten million. All of us with different languages saying the same thing. Go to sleep. Don't be crying. You're waking the whole house. Everything is all right. And then I start to wonder about the different things that wake them up. I think about hunger and explosions and diseases and teething and death. The one thing I don't think about is what actually happens to us.

A long time ago I remember turning into this hallway where I knew I could buy things. I don't know what I was into at the time. It was the ground-floor hallway of some block of flats. They pulled it down after; nobody gave a fuck. There I see another kid my own age. We look into each other like we know we're dying. For a long time we were lonely and desperate, days and weeks, and then I turn a corner and there is my soulmate who knew the pain I was in. I look him in the eye and I see myself. The same for him. But do we shake hands? You can't shake hands with your double, they say. The explosion would destroy the world. Did I visit his grave subsequently? When I heard that he died quietly of something bad he injected I was happy that death touched him up instead of me. No way did I want to stand on his little plot of ground that he owned all to himself and know the one true thing of my own fucked-up world. What's your own name there, I said to him. Don, he said, who are you? That was the only time we spoke. The door opened into another state and we paid our money and we spun the wheel. Back in those times I sometimes had the feeling that I was in a vehicle of some kind, maybe a train, that was forging onwards into the darkness. I felt I was close to the driver. He was out there with his hand on the throttle, looking down the line as far as the lights could show, which was not very far, and the darkness was rushing at him always the same distance away. Pushing out with always the same halo around, carrying a small patch of light in a very large shadow the size of half the world. And I sometimes thought that this driver was maybe very close to nodding off or maybe a heart attack, and that he would fall down on the stick and we would be out of control. I never had any idea what was outside the lights. Maybe we would tear into some end-of-the-line station and fuck up the lives of two hundred people waiting for their loved ones to come home. Maybe we would fall over the edge of a tight bend and roll down the embankment and come to a stop in relative peace in a boggy patch of land. Maybe the line went round in circles. Maybe there was no end and if the driver died the rest of us would be immortal. Time stood still in the crazy rush and things went by on the edge of light and vanished into the past, never to be seen again. That was how I was in those days, one fucked-up passenger on some night train.

In the Multitude of the Slain

I come home and pick up my mooring on a wet evening in June. The rain smoothes the water out. I hear a dog barking and the sound of cars waiting for the lights. I make my plans and I sleep the sleep and in the morning I row ashore with my auctioneer's suit in a shopping bag. I put it on in Phelan's gents' jakes and when I come out the barman whistles at me. Cool, dude, he says, my compliments. I ask him to mind my kit and he throws the bag behind the bar. One for the road, he says, but I shake my head. I'm off to see a solicitor, I tell him, about getting my daughter back.

He makes a pinching movement with his thumb and one finger, meaning I'm going to need money.

I stare at him. I'm wondering does he ever think about what he's saying. Does he think I wouldn't find the money to get my daughter back?

Pete was asking for you, he says. He was wondering if that heap of shit sank under you.

No fear.

Oh the hard man, he says. Fair dues. She didn't let you down?

Sound out. She's tight as a nut.

Fair dues. Listen, the best of luck.

Thanks.

He has a bald patch which he worries about. He grows

236

his hair long and pulls the threads across. It looks like someone teased out a rope. But he dresses like a looker and he goes to the city on his days off, nobody knows why. Some people say he was married before he moved here, he has a son someplace or a married daughter. He doesn't talk.

Neilus Carey comes in at that moment. He walks right up to me and says: The horseman lifteth up both the bright sword and the glittering spear.

Brutal all right, I say. I'm on my way to meet a solicitor about getting Kaylie back.

He winks at the barman. And there is a multitude of slain, and a great number of carcasses; and there is no end of their corpses.

Give it up, Carey. You're giving me the willies.

The barman puts a small whiskey on the counter and Neilus Carey picks it up and examines the colour against the light of the window. Then he puts it down again. He is a satisfied man. The barman says: Will you talk English, Neilus, and stop your fucking bible stuff. Then he says, under his breath: God forgive me.

Where are you off to dressed like a funeral director, what? Carey says.

I tell him I'm going to see a solicitor about getting my daughter back. I tell him I'm a little hopeful.

I'll say a prayer for you, he says. You could say one yourself. The man above forgets no one. You could try.

Sorry 'bout that, Neilus, I say. You know me. I'm not into that stuff.

The barman says he's not a religious man himself and Neilus Carey says there's divine mercy and God is strong on family values.

You gave up the house? he says. I hear you're after moving into a boat?

No use throwing good money after bad. I was lonely anyway, as a matter of fact, the house gave me the creeps.

A water itinerant, what?

Kelleher was fairly pissed about it, the barman said. So I heard anyway. He was taking your name in vain the other night.

Carey says: That was my father's house that bastard stole. Your man Kelleher.

You sold it to him.

I didn't know they were going to stop the flooding. I couldn't get insurance.

He did though, the barman said. He knew about the flooding. What's the point of being a politician *and* an auctioneer if you can't turn a few bob out of it.

They're buying and selling us like sheep. It's an auctioneer's republic. The fucker is running again and he'll get in. Mark my words, he'll get in. An independent.

The barman shakes his head. The boys'll take him back, mark my words. He'll be back on the ticket when they see what way the wind is blowing.

He pinches some imaginary money between his fingers again. That's all those boys understand. The law of the brown envelope.

How many auctioneers in the Dáil, tell me that, Carey says.

The barman shakes his head.

They're all fucking auctioneers.

I say I have to be going. I have an appointment.

The barman says the suit is something else.

All of a sudden I feel tears. I'm standing at the bar

looking at them and there's water coming out of my eyes and I can't lift a hand to wipe it away, like I'm paralysed or something. The barman picks up a glass and starts to examine it, then he picks up a cloth and starts to wipe it very carefully. Neilus Carey looks away. After maybe half a minute I manage to use my sleeve.

We're living in the end-time all right, Carey says. Still looking at something on the floor over near the window. I know it now.

A bright morning is turning into rain when I get out. It's coming in from the sea. Another day like yesterday, full of promise and ending in nothing. Maybe I should have had a drink. I'm nervous.

The Place I Came From

I can see where they're keeping Kaylie from the room where I used to sleep in the old guy's house. My old room is empty, someone cleaned out all the clothes, but there's still the smell of a woman in everything. The dried-plant smell of a woman who died a long time ago. That's why the letters stopped suddenly. I imagine a brutal accident for her, or at least some quick clean disease. I miss her. I miss the old guy coming up the stairs and whispering the name. I miss his loneliness. Early on the first morning I see Kaylie come out with her foster-mother. From where I am her hair looks a bit out of condition. Jazz would never stand for that. The clothes are new too, or maybe the top is not, maybe Jazz bought it in the spring sales. I'm not too sure. I try to remember her clothes but I keep thinking of when she was small. What size shoes does she take? I think I never knew.

They get into a car and two hours later they're back with a boot-load of groceries. Where do they shop? That night I slip out and bring the van back. I park it round the corner out of sight. She doesn't come out to play. I see kids kicking a football one day. Another day three girls sit on a wall. Her foster-father goes out every night. I follow him but he's going to a bridge club. He walks there and back.

What the lawyer told me was it makes no difference if I

prove these particular foster-parents are not fit – they'll only move her to someone else. Anyway, I can see they're normal and why should I try to screw up *their* lives. They're not the enemy. She holds the foster-mother's hand when they walk. I see her playing with the teddy bear in the upstairs window. I see her light go out at night, shadows on the blinds. I see everything and it doesn't add up to much except maybe kids can be happy in more ways than one.

The lawyer told me he had a Legend 426 DS with a Yanmar 56. He was wondering what I'd charge for a service. He said the Yanmar was sweet but he was thinking about replacing it with a Nanni 21 because it was dead weight in the boat. Racing was his thing, he said. I said I didn't think the Nanni would push it but I'd have to see the spec. I said there was a calculation. As he showed me in I saw photographs of big boats running behind coloured balloons, twenty, thirty boats, maybe ten million euro, charging at the same point just in front of the camera where they will all turn and go back the same way again, just for the fun of it.

I said: Why did they take her away?

He said: In the first instance because the death of your partner and the traumatic circumstances, taken together with the fact that you were missing and could not be found, and you were initially a suspect in the case, meant that there was a danger to her health or safety. Both, I should think, given the circumstances.

But I came back.

These things have a certain kind of momentum. It becomes difficult to roll back a court order. Not impossible, but difficult. They got an emergency care order in the district court. The foster-parents are very good. They'll give you visiting. I'll sort that out.

They already did, I say. But he's not listening.

The time Kaylie fell in the water and she swam to safety I held her in my arms and she was like a wet animal, everything clinging to her body. She was heavy with water. People say take off your clothes if you fall in the sea, take them off because they'll fill with water and pull you down. But water doesn't weigh in water. If you pull your clothes off you'll die of hypothermia. You'll wash up naked somewhere. Her little heart raced close to mine. Her face wet my chest. She was my brave girl. She saved herself then but she needs help now. I waited until the lawyer looked at me and then I held his eye for a long time, maybe a minute. It felt like hours. I asked him, while I was looking at him, why they wouldn't give Kaylie back to me, and he did this knowing thing. He half smiled, half shrugged. He looked away. He said:

Well . . .

I didn't stop looking at him. I want to know, I said.

So he holds up his two fine hands to me and he starts to count the reasons down, one finger at a time.

Firstly they looked for next of kin. Your brother-in-law is in prison and is known to the police. At the time of the death of your partner the local police had not connected you with him.

Fuck him. He's nothing to do with me.

Unfortunately you come from the same place, you cohabited with his sister, she had visited him in prison not long before her death, et cetera et cetera.

I'm thinking how he sees that same place I came from. He probably knows more people there than I do now. He probably knows all my old neighbours and their alibis. He knows which of them had troubled childhoods and other mitigating circumstances. Which of them had bad habits. They come in here with their tracksuits or their leather jackets, and their nicknames – Scoby Kiely, Flash Joey, Wee Willie Connell, Micko and The Baker – and he wears a pinstripe suit, and between them they invent a place for people like me to grow up in, a special kind of fucked-up world with its own law of gravity ten times stronger than anywhere else on the planet.

Next your sister-in-law.

Stacey?

Her two children are already in care. She is known to the police in her own right.

She's on the game. I know.

Apparently.

He used up one hand already. I don't know how he was counting, some special system lawyers use. There was one fist and he was tapping it with the index finger of the other hand. Two pigeons made passes at each other on the wire outside his window. We were two floors above the street. There was trouble on a roof across the way, slates missing, a rafter and some torn felt like a storm got in or birds, somebody going to wake up some morning with a hole in a formerly intact room and a night's water distributed evenly over the furnishings, someone who would see the sun before long, a little light getting in.

You and your partner are not a family under Irish law. The health board has the right to remove your daughter *ex parte* because you were missing and could not be found at the time.

Pete Townsend knew where I was. We filed a TR with the coastguard.

Peter Townsend? I represented Mr Townsend.

I understood this lawyer and I knew what he was. Not that he wouldn't do a good job for me, but I knew, even though he didn't give any sign or say anything or look at me in any kind of special way because this is the secret of success: that he had a certain view of me that I would never be able to change. Probably, to him, a Norry is always a Norry, and likely to reoffend no matter what. I had no desire to prove myself to him. The way I saw it, he wasn't worth the effort.

You have no other family.

He sifted through the papers on his desk.

I see the court ordered a psychiatric assessment. In the opinion of the social worker your daughter was severely traumatised and will need counselling at the very least. I see the phrase *known to the police* in relation to you. You've been in trouble before?

Not me. I was never convicted of anything. I never did anything wrong.

Your mother . . .

My mother was whacked by Patrick Harold Baker. He was trying to get at me.

He didn't react again. He held his thumb against the side of each page and ran it quickly down like the slide on a vernier scale. When he got to the bottom he put the page to one side and started his measuring all over again. Then he looked up.

From our point of view time is against us. The whole process is crystallising against you. First and foremost we'll be applying for access under Section thirteen.

They'll be doing a welfare assessment. We have to prepare for the day the order comes up for review. I have the date here somewhere. We need to prepare a case to the effect that you are a fit person to have custody of your child. This means showing the court that you're capable of looking after her and providing for her in moral, social and physical terms, and, since the issue of a criminal background has arisen, that you are not in any way associated with your brother-in-law or the activities for which he was committed to prison, or your sister-in-law's activities.

Does that mean I can't see Stacey?

He stared at the papers on his desk for about thirty seconds, then he straightened the papers, then he looked up at me. He did not answer.

After a time he made a joke. If you were a woman all this would be easier.

I felt like I was fucked. Like he came at me from behind and got me down. I felt sick. I got up to go and found I wasn't well enough to stand. There was a deep hole in the floor and the world was spinning me into it. It was comfortable and dark down there and I knew the locals.

For some reason Grace Kelleher came into my mind. I saw her standing on the dock with the reins of a boat in her hands. I saw the magic poise, how she was there one moment, perfectly balanced like some kind of a fine animal, and the next she was facing the other way, looking back at me from the deck of the boat.

I dream a dream about women. I'm not too sure who is who. Helen the woman whose clothes I was wearing while I was hiding out from the posse, or Stacey or Jazz.

They're making judgements. I wake up thinking I'm on the run again and I'm wearing women's clothes. I think I hear the old guy moving around. I slip out of the sleeping bag and stand to one side of the window, taking care not to be seen. It's crazy but I think I can smell someone frying rashers like the old guy used to do every morning.

Once the mobile rings. The house is like an amp, boosting the ring-tone. For five or six rings it sounds like the whole place is going. It's my solicitor to say he fixed me up with a visiting time. They're going to let me see my daughter. He told them it would be worse for Kaylie if she lost both parents. And after all, he said, the social services want the best for her too. They have her best interests at heart the same as ourselves. I don't mention that I've seen her twice in the Tandoori Queen, the same waitress each time, that the social worker's name is Christine, that she's married and has three kids of her own. That she doesn't seem to like me much. I don't mention that I'm biding my time in this piece of real estate and that I'm watching every move my daughter makes.

What can I say about this place? This housing estate where I hid out once before, where I'm still hiding out from something even though I tell myself that I am actually watching and waiting?

People sleep in the houses and dream dreams of their own making, they have no legend forced on them by circumstances outside their control. Their houses are full of little devices that make things happen. Things that turn the heat on, turn the dinner off, turn the radio or video on, timed alarms, egg-timers, timed lights and locks and water-heaters and microwaves and watches and diaries. They have breakfast TV to explain how everything works, and multi-channel and the newspaper, and *Coronation Street* as a warning. They are fully informed. Up at roof level where real gets lost in the sky they look into the universe with aerials and dishes. They have the pretty pictures and the ticker tape at the same time. Nothing escapes them. They have that smoke smell. That sky. That sound of children you can't explain. They have washing on clothes lines in backyards, different-coloured shirts and vests. Food cooking smells. Sun comes early and turns the whole place into a crystal. It warms the city to have this precious structure making and remaking in the light of each new day, throwing the way things should be onto the way things are, the fragile faces luminous and new-Windolened, the doors releasing little gusts of normal whenever someone comes or goes.

Planning a Comeback

There's a locked gate around the side of the house so I have to climb over. It's shaky under me. There's a small patio at the back and a blue plastic paddling pool with a plastic fish floating in it. The fish has a big smile. At the end of the garden there's a blue metal swing. There's flowers along the sides. There's no shed. No ladder. No chairs. Nothing to climb on. I look at the patio door and I see the little white rectangle of an alarm stuck on near the frame. I hold my torch up against the glass. The room is tidy. There's a couch, and a telly on a pine table with a video and a satellite box on top. There's a computer and a printer on a trolley. There's a picture on the wall. The kitchen window is alarmed too. There's a chicken de-frosting on the sink, I see a trail of watery blood running down the grooves. In the torchlight it looks like it has a face and two bony eyes. Stickers on the fridge held on by magnetic heads. There's a row of tiny copper pots and pans hanging above the door. One of the pictures on the fridge is a coloured-in fairy tale with KAYLIE written in blue crayon at the bottom. There's a calendar with a photograph of sailing boats and a sunset. We had one in the kitchen – Jazz used to mark off the days I was booked for deliveries in red pen. It's probably still there.

What I do is I hit the window with my fist, double glazing so there's no chance of breaking, but I want to see if they keep the alarm turned on. It's one of our old tricks. If the alarm doesn't go off you know something useful. If it does you leg it into the dark. Most alarms go off by mistake a couple of times a year.

I hear this high whining sound and a light comes on downstairs. Then a bedroom light comes on.

I slip back round the side of the house and over the gate in case I have to make a run for it. The whining stops. I hear the patio door sliding open and a man saying: It's all right, love. False alarm. Nothing here. Maybe I hear a woman's voice very distant. The door slides closed again. I step out onto the front lawn. The downstairs light goes off. Everybody expects trouble will come at them from the backyard.

No light has come on in my daughter's room. She didn't hear it? Or alarms don't frighten her? Children sleep like the dead. She never used to hear Wayne barking except maybe one time. He'd keep us and the neighbours awake all night but she slept like the dead.

But she used to wake to imaginary sounds. She sometimes thought the house was haunted or there was someone downstairs. She'd start to cry in her room and we'd hear it the way parents always hear the smallest sound a child makes, or she'd come running to us and crawl in between us in the bed, a bundle of sticks in pyjamas that took up more room than a grown-up and moved around all night.

So now I know it has to be shopping day.

Pete is down the boatyard. He's working on a stern-gland that seized onto the shaft. He has the chain-grip on one nut and a big blue Stillson on the other. He has the chain-grip jammed against a block of wood and he has his foot against the Stillson. There's a smell of WD40. I tell him he's going to fuck the threads completely. He just keeps saying: Bastard bastard bastard.

In the end he relaxes and says he's going to have cut the fucking shaft, it's welded on. I ask him if he tried heat. No go, he says. The fucking shaft is fucked. I don't think this guy knows there's a greaser. Ten to one if I got it out the shaft'll be scored.

It'll be off now anyway, I say. You were standing on it. You bent it.

It's steel, man, he says. But I can see I worried him.

Pete, I say, you're not a mechanic, you're a scrap merchant.

He grins.

What's up?

I tell him what he needs to know about my plan and he tries to talk me out of it. I tell him where I want him to be and where I want the van. He shakes my hand and says he won't let me down. He said something like that when I asked him to be best man. Then he meant he wouldn't turn up stoned or forget. I'd never let Jazz down anyway, he said, whatever about you, you bastard. He was grinning all over his face at that time.

We go below to the cabin. He has the engine open. I can see this huge Saab 60 or 80, all gleaming gunmetal. He tells me it's the first service the guy ever gave it in six years. He says it's fucking criminal. He almost cries over what the heads must look like. He's imagining what's inside the cylinders, the carbon building up in the dark like some kind of cholesterol. I have to get the heads off, he said, just to see. There's a week in this. Man, I'm fucking stressed bad. This is a big baby.

We talk about Jazz for a bit. I think this is the first time since the funeral that I let myself actually talk about her.

Pete tells me things I never knew. He tells me about when I was away on deliveries and she used to come down the yard. She said to him once that she liked the smell of diesel. I remember seeing her smelling my clothes before she washed them, kind of hugging them to her face. We all smell of the engines – WD40, waterproof grease, solvents, gasket-maker. Our hands are chased with carbon.

He says she used to bring a few sandwiches and they'd sit out on the slip and look at the sea the odd fine day. There'd be Kaylie throwing sticks for the dog.

She was always telling me I was too thin, he says. She used to say: If I was married to you I'd fatten you up.

He laughs as if the idea of being married to Jazz was crazy.

I miss her, man, he says.

Me too.

Fuck the bastarding cunt.

Fuck him.

Fucking crazy druggies. They caught him anyway? He'll get off on a technicality?

No. They have everything. DNA, the lot.

Fuck him.

He'll get life anyway.

Won't bring her back. No way. I'll do it for you. I'll be there. You have my mobile?

The old number? I have it.

The same old number. I'll be there. Want a smoke?

I'm clean. I'm staying clean until all this is over. I have to keep a clear head.

Nothing like a toke to make you see clear, Pete says. You get fifty-fifty vision with the good stuff. This is the best of it. A *Crimeline* special.

I shake my head and he laughs. You're one fucked-up kid, he says, although he's only a year older than me.

I take *Songthrush* alongside the *Susan Marie* which is tied up at the pier. The skipper gives me a basket of prawns. He helps me run the water and diesel hoses across his deck. He asks me if I'm making a trip and I tell him I'm thinking of dropping down west for a couple of days. It's summer so work is slack. We talk about his icebox which is giving trouble and I tell him it's the electrics and he should think about a rewind or a new coil. It's not my line of work. Maybe the end of the season, he says. It's always the same with the trawlers. Everything is the end of the season. They can't afford to miss a fine day until the whole thing burns out and then they miss weeks. I fill the tanks and a water-breaker and a twenty-five-litre diesel can. He tells me I should only show the prawns the boiling water. Two minutes at the most, he says. Any more and you'll make shit of them.

The *Susan Marie* is a trim ship. She rises and falls on the swell like a big-chested mother breathing steady. She's new-painted every year, a bright yellow hull with the name in red, but her compressor is shit. It doesn't bother him too much because it's inshore work. He doesn't need refrigeration. With quotas going the way they are, he says, he'll probably sell the boat in the near future.

The harbourmaster shouts and waves a letter out the office window. It's for me, I say, something about my daughter probably. I gave the office as the forwarding address.

You severed all ties, the skipper says, with the land.

Except for my daughter.

The skipper of the *Susan Marie* says nothing but I see by his face that he's sorry for my trouble. He has four kids, one doing deck officer in college. Sometimes I try to think of a future for Kaylie but it's all tangled up with Jazz and too complicated. I think I first of all need to know what she thinks about it herself, which I can't do while she's in care. Or maybe we just missed our chance. The letter is from social welfare. They want to do a welfare assessment pursuant to the Child Care Act 1991. It's a long time ago, I think. Max was already dying though we never knew in 1991. I didn't know there was any kind of an Act about to happen. I didn't know they were saving themselves up to make trouble for me at a later time. If I did I might have paid more attention.

Practising Funny Faces

I'm thinking of the pilotage in the entrance to the Trieux river. The tide makes at four knots, spring tides. I remember the lights are Moguedhier lateral starboard beacon tower, La Croix lighthouse, Vincre lateral port beacon, and Custom House Island, and after that you're in buoyage. I remember the skipper taking a short cut up the Moisie but the water was shallow. I remember the Pendrix beacon sticking up like a finger with the wooded shore behind. Places I can remember like pictures and places I can hardly see, like home.

I notice that the dashboard clock is becoming too faded to read. It's still morning anyway. Earlier I was wondering what we would be doing now if Jazz was alive. Probably I'd be down the yard; she might come down and bring sandwiches. Or, since it's summer and things are slack, we might go to the beach. I could see her walking Kaylie when she was maybe four, the water swirling white around their feet and then pulling back and they were up to their ankles in soft wet polished sand. I shift in the seat and try to get comfortable. I'm waiting three hours. People are giving me funny looks. There's a little girl pushing a toy pram up and down. She has two dolls in it, one about the right size for a baby, and one Barbie. What is this grown woman in her designer tracksuit doing in the same pram as a giant baby? The little girl doesn't care. She has no sense of proportion.

Then I see the door open and the mother comes out. I can see into the house as far as the kitchen. There's light coming through the back window and shining on something steel. Maybe a kettle. She puts shopping bags into the back seat of the car. She goes inside. She comes out with the father. He starts looking the tyres over. They're maybe low in thread or off balance or out of alignment. They talk for a while. They go back inside. The mother comes out again holding Kaylie's hand. She sits Kaylie in the back seat with the shopping bags. The father comes out again and leans against the door with his arms folded. Then he looks at one of the tyres again. They shake their heads. He goes back inside. The mother starts the car. I start the van. The mother reverses out the drive onto the road.

I follow her a car or two back.

She stops off at a dry cleaner's and leaves some stuff in from one of the bags. She talks to someone she meets coming out of the shop. She waves to a priest carrying a shopping bag on the pedestrian crossing. Then she goes to Tesco's. She parks near the carwash and turns around to Kaylie and talks for a bit. The mother gets out and takes the car keys with her. She takes shopping bags out of the boot. Ten paces away she turns around and presses the button on the key. The hazard lights flash once. The car beeps. She goes into Tesco's.

Over by the door the trolleys gleam like dwarf cages. She takes a small one – not much to buy today. She stops for a few seconds to talk to a man in a wheelchair selling scratch cards. She buys one. She's maybe thinking she'll give it to Kaylie to scratch when she gets back. I believe in this woman. I see she's a good person but she has my daughter and that's not right. People with the best intentions fuck up. Even Jazz wanted a big wedding. She went to see her brother. And I could have killed him but I didn't and everything else followed after. The doors slide back and take the woman in and close after her. The man in the wheelchair puts his earphones back. He has a Walkman on his lap.

I walk up to her car. I look in the back window and I see my daughter colouring in some fairy tale, maybe Little Red Riding Hood, only she's colouring the girl with a blue crayon. Her hood or coat is blue. Her hands are blue. She didn't start on her face yet but I notice that she's keeping exactly inside the lines, no mistakes, even though it's all the same colour. There's no wolf but there's trees in the background and maybe a house. I tap on the window but she doesn't react. Maybe she's still not hearing too good. I tap louder. She looks up. I'm filling the side window. I spread my arms out so I'm touching the windscreen too. I make a funny face against the glass and laugh out loud.

I point to the door and make opening signs. She thinks about it for a bit while I think about the queue in Tesco's, then she reaches in between the seats and presses the button with the red light and the locks clunk. I open the door and I squat down so I'm on her level.

Hi, love.

Hi, Dad.

What're you colouring?

She looks at the book like she only now realises what she's doing. She shrugs.

Want to go down the boatyard? I say.

She nods her head. All her movements are very small but definite.

Pete was asking for you.

She smiles. She likes Pete.

The guy who power-hoses the cars is watching me and the power-hose is spraying a rainbow over a silver Merc. He has that suspicious look. Earlier he had his back turned, now turning around he sees a man take a child out of a car. What could be wrong with that? But he's not sure. I put Kaylie into the van and I strap her in. As I drive away, I see that he's taking a mobile out of his pocket. He has maybe just got a text or maybe he's calling my number in. A woman comes out of the automatic door to Tesco's but she goes in a different direction. I pull out into the traffic and turn towards the sea.

In the Shrink-wrap

I said to Kaylie that we were changing our names to escape detection. I said it was all a big fairy story like in her colouring book. I would get her a new colouring book bigger than the old one and lots of crayons. She never said anything. She didn't look like she was listening but I didn't care. I talked my head off. It was the first time I was happy since Jazz passed away. Her new name was going to be Grace and mine would be Dan. I said I was giving Pete a present of the van and I was going to take her on a voyage of discovery in our new boat.

I drove into the yard and handed the van over to Pete. He was sitting there waiting for me in his best clothes. I told him I'd call him on the mobile when I got down west. Just to let him know how things were going, but if he didn't hear from me not to worry because we would be lying low.

He said: Hiya, Kaylie, and punched her lightly on the shoulder. She smiled at him and he got down on his knees and hugged her. I gave him the keys and told him that the shades would find it. I mentioned that the tie-rods were fucked and he'd want to get them replaced; she couldn't be tracked and she was burning tyres. I signed a note dated for a week before to say that the car changed hands. I gave him the reg. book. I said any tools I left in the back, they were his. I already took everything I needed out to *Songthrush*. He got in and started her up and then rolled down the window. He said: Good luck, man, and stay loose.

Bye bye, Kaylie baby, he said. Mind your daddy.

When he was gone we walked down to the slip and I helped her into the punt. It was only then I noticed that the harbour was blind with sea fog. I couldn't see the pier from where I was standing. As I rowed out I felt its wet cold closing in around. After fifty yards I couldn't see the slip. Now I was watching out for moorings. I passed a little motor boat that I recognised. I passed a yellow visitor's buoy. I passed a yacht. I heard an engine and stopped where I was. The engine went by quietly, somebody careful feeling his way in on a sounder or a GPS. Or maybe feeling his way out – in fog, directions don't make sense. I noticed that the tide was setting me down. The next boat I saw was a hundred yards further than I should be. I started to row hard. For every stroke that I moved forward, I felt the drag pulling me back a part of the boat's length. There was a crazy spring-tide tearing out. Bits of rubbish passed me, headed for eternity, another mooring, half drowned, pulled down by long sheets of rubbery weed, a plastic two-litre milk bottle tied to a rope, a dribble of baby barnacles around the lower edge. I saw a shape on my left that might be the pier. I could hear the rumble of a big compressor. Voices. The ice plant or a deep-sea trawler. Kaylie stared at me with eyes that might be infected by the sea fog, cold and uncertain and maybe unforgiving. For the first time I wondered if I was making a mistake. I wondered if I had the courage to take her back to the foster-parents. If maybe the system had something going for it and people like me shouldn't be in charge of children.

The pier was gone again and the compressor noise seemed to be coming from the fog itself. The space of water I could see was smaller than before. I saw a little Shetland motor boat with a crashed-out heron looking like someone took away something he badly needed to feel well.

I caught onto a mooring to try to get my bearings. I shipped the oars and twisted the pick-up line around the seat to take the pressure off. We're a bit lost, I said. I'm fairly sure the boat is around here somewhere. The trouble is I don't remember that Shetland.

I listened for a while. I could hear the tide running out against something. After a few minutes I heard the church bells ringing twelve. A car horn. I thought about Neilus Carey's prayers and what his god thought about a father and daughter hanging onto a mooring buoy in a bad fog and whether he might be calculating something that involved a trawler or a motor boat with the driver looking the other way. And whether a half-cracked scrap dealer had any influence.

In the end I pulled to my left, for want of a better idea, and we found *Songthrush* and climbed aboard.

I showed Kaylie around. Seeing it with her eyes it looked a bit rough. I noticed the damp feel to the upholstery, which anyway was worn through in places, a kind of wet-dog smell, the way salt on the timbers looked moist, that the place was small and old and not very girlie at all. So to make things better I showed her the picture in the pilot book of the place we were going. Daddy has a promise of a start there, I said. From the man who runs the harbour. He did him a favour before. That she'd be learning how to speak French. I told her I'd have to be Daddy and Mammy to her now. We would be getting new identities. When she would be Grace and I'd be Dan we'd be new people with a new future and maybe a new past that we could work out on the way over. She could be a princess and I'd be a prince and we'd be in disguise because someone was after stealing our country from under our noses. I didn't feel like a prince at that moment. I felt I was maybe making a big mistake. I left the pilot book open on the table in front of her. There was sun on the white houses of Lézardrieux and Pendrix. The water had bright coins on it. Down to the water's edge on one side came a forest that might hide the big bad wolf, and a crazy lighthouse marked the end. The tide goes so far out it looks like it won't make it back, I tell her. People fish for shrimp with big nets. The shrimp start out grey but they turn pink when they're cooked.

She stared at the new world. I think it didn't look like the promised land, from her point of view. It didn't look like any kind of future I could invent.

I put her lifejacket on. I poured her a mug of Fanta and put some biscuits on the table.

Then I went on deck and started the engine. The noise came back to me from every direction. I turned the steaming lights on. I heard the exhaust spitting and the glug-glug of water lifting in the impeller and spinning through the peculiar channels of the heat exchanger and back out again. I dropped the mooring and nudged her straight ahead. The bow swung lazily round in the current and fell away towards open water. I counted the moorings off until I cleared the last one. I had the following tide on the rudder and when it wasn't there any more I headed south-east. The boat started to feel the swell and I felt something loosening in my chest. I went over the lights again: Moguedhier lateral starboard beacon tower, La Croix lighthouse, Vincre lateral port beacon, and Custom House Island. Chances are, with my luck, I'd make my entrance in the dark. I remember Pierce saying to me once that the way up is the same as the way down.

I called Pete up and told him we were away and everything was mint. He was excited and I could hear the engine of the van running a bit fast in a low gear. I just passed a cop-car, he said. I was doing sixty-five in a forty zone. You might've just got penalty points. Sorry about that.

I told him the van was his now. They were his points. I told him to take care and stay off the mushies. He laughed.

Then I dropped the mobile over the side. I was almost out of credit anyway.

As we went out the fog moved in behind us, making a killing on what we lost. Everything was becoming; nothing was solid, nothing was definite. Water became air in the sun and air became water. Even the high houses saw nothing today, and it looked like someone ran an eraser round the shore. I kept my eyes on the compass and tried not to think about what I couldn't see. I was hoping any trawler that was moving had its radar on.

Kaylie came on deck and looked around her. She moved like some kind of flat insect in her lifejacket, a ladybird with her red middle maybe. She gave me a sad worried smile. She didn't ask where we were, or where everything else was. She sat down beside me and looked over the side at the sea.

I didn't know what to do next, now that my plan came together. It was like someone broke a window to gain access and then found himself barefoot among the pieces.

It was too dangerous to move.

But I thought about things that happened and things that were said and I remembered that whatever we're made of, there's enough of it. Stuff is taken away but more comes just when it looks like there's not enough.

I fell asleep at the tiller sometime long after midnight, and my head filled with dreams. So many dreams. Dreams of dying – the best I've had. Dreams of things I dreamed when I was out of my skull, birds and hospitals and cats and places I slept and burdens I carried. Dreams of Jazz. And I dreamed, among other things, that I was inside a car. My breath stank, my lips were cracked, and someone, maybe Kaylie, was banging on the window very slowly, probably because she was tired of waiting up for me to come home. I woke in the morning cold, maybe five o'clock. The sun was just up behind a thin cloud and the light made everything look iron. The fog was gone, and the breeze that blew it away during the night, and the boom was swinging over and back, and each time it came to the end of the mainsheet it had this small hollow collision against nothing. I dropped the sail and wound up the genoa which anyway was hanging like an empty sack from the forestay. Maybe when the sun burned off the cloud everything would be different; I had seen these dead days that turned into something else.

Then I noticed that the sea was covered in what looked like bubble-paper. There must have been ten million jellyfish hanging out together. They trailed their thin hair and pulsed their flaps. There were big purple rings and small ones that looked like pale cunts, and bronze coins and blobs of frosted glass. One looked like a face with a rusty hole in it. I wanted to start the engine to make my getaway but I was afraid the jelly would get sucked into the water-intake. I heard you could kill an engine that way. I was paralysed. I hoped Kaylie was asleep.

There was something terrible about it but I couldn't say what. They must be eating something; easy enough for the guys on the edge, but in the middle it was hard times. They didn't look like they could just decide to go shopping somewhere else. If they had brains they were maybe thinking things out, deciding this is the way it is, they better get used to it, it's nothing special. They were maybe thinking there's an advantage in not having visibility, being in with the gang, staying in the same place. Maybe they didn't notice that the ocean was moving away, that the scenery was changing, that their mates were passing on. Or maybe they felt it and it made them afraid, those strings trailing in the dark, they must know something.

I looked all round and the shrink-wrap stretched away so far into invisibility. First I thought they were just floating there, gathering round the hull for their own special intentions, but after a while I noticed a kind of sly pattern, a direction that you couldn't put down to any one individual, but that the whole congregation under-stood. Almost a purpose. They were headed somewhere, wherever the lowest brands of life go, the assembly-point of see-through beings, ghosts and nobodies and glass animals, and, for the time being anyway, it looked like we were going to that refuge too.

Waiting for the Day

Don't panic, I said because I panicked myself. Don't look over the side. She was looking over the side at what was happening to the sea in the iron light. She didn't say anything. She had on a pale blue pyjamas I bought to keep her warm at night. The label said one hundred per cent polyester wash in the delicate cycle inside out. Then she said: The toilet is stuck. I heard her a few minutes before pumping the handle and I knew from the sound that the jellyfish were up the intake and nothing was flushing. Or possibly I never opened the seacock yet. I don't know why I was afraid. I'll get it going, I said. I was watching her very closely and it seemed to me she was from another world. She didn't belong to the light or the plastic sea, she was pale and half awake and broken down in some way that maybe a father couldn't under-stand. I couldn't take the chance. I stood up and looked around me and after a minute or so I saw the low grey shape of the Fisheries Board about a mile away, going home after a night's snooping for drift-netters or intru-ders in the box. I called them up on the VHF and they agreed to tow me out of the jellyfish. The guy on the radio repeated everything I said, and I could hear the others laughing in the background. So they towed me out and afterwards, when the wind got up southerly, it was as easy go home as not. In a couple of hours I could see people walking around the lighthouse looking up and taking souvenir snapshots. And I could see people sitting around on the beach waiting for the sun to get hot. I could see cars driving out of the houses up on the hill, people who had to work on Saturdays. Everything was that close. Kaylie, I said, we won't go to France after all.

For the second time since she saw me in the car she smiled. I realised there's things that can't be said. And that there's more than one version. There was my mother in the caravan looking down at the blobs of sudsy grease in the sink, saying: What am I going to do at all? I always thought there was no answer, like she wasn't talking to me.

I said: Kaylie, you know I'm just waiting for the day?
Me too, Dad, she said.

I said it didn't work this time but there'd be other times. I said she'd have to promise to be a good girl which I know she always was. It was just something stupid to say. Like saying goodnight. Everybody in the world says it but nobody can make it happen.

The Old Men Have Their Say

I never heard of a bank robbery where I felt sorry for the bank. That maybe means I have some issues, and tourists and religious people and insurance agents don't have the same issues. This occurred to me later when counsel for the state was asking me about how I saw the car stop outside our house, and how they went up and down trying to work out the navigation. He talked to me like he used to be my father, like I was the result of something good he had once. The judge looks like my grandfather but he doesn't have the certain hands of a stonemason. The thing was I felt like a piece of shit for a lot of reasons, but mostly because before this everybody I knew got amnesia or an alibi, I was the first person I ever heard of from The Lawn with a good memory. I was like a spaceman hoping whatever I was attached to was going to fall far enough to bring me back.

This is the day the old men have their say, it's their country. They look up at the stars and we're blocking the light, out in space with no connections. They like a clear sky.

Another reason was that earlier they introduced into evidence a postcard. It was the old aerial shot with harbour and trawlers and the streets of the town. The address on the card was 19a Devonshire Street Lower. It was all wrinkled up and smudged from being wet. He asked me, did I recognise the writing.

He asked me what was my relationship to the person who lived at this address and I said: Which one? and he said: The person named on the card, and I said: Which relationship?

It would be the state's case, he told us, that this card passed through the hands of the victim's brother, then incarcerated in Mountjoy, and thence to the accused, pointing at the kid in the dock, watching everything with his know-all dog's eyes, from whom it was recovered during a search under warrant. Evidence would be introduced to that effect. The way they see it this is a tragic mistake brought about by sisterly love. But I remembered Jazz telling me she was going to save me, and maybe she did save me from something. She thought maybe words could stop the world: Hope you're keeping well. We're doing fine here. The baby is great. Tell Pat we're asking for him. Or maybe it was the pictures of a happy place that were going to break his heart. Or maybe she wrote him letters so pure and fine they could not be found by forensics. She asked me to take care of Stacey. But Stacey was missing now. She might be in England. She wouldn't be giving any evidence about why she gave Pat The Baker an aerial view of where we were hiding out. These are the days of memory. I spent half my time trying to forget.

The head of the DNA unit divided the body fluids and found the minor element belonged to Jazz and the rest was the personal trademark of the accused. She called him by name. She called it the minor element.

The state pathologist counted the wounds and bruises. He knew the shape of every wound. Life went out like a tide but was measured in ounces. The weight of blood in the human body is measured to the last drop, the rate of flow is known. A simple calculation gives us ten-fifteen. The time that Kaylie woke. Ten-forty when the shades came to see what all the fuss was about. Ten-fifty-six the ambulance. Once upon a time Pete asked me, did I ever see a stone anchor? He had one in his workshop, a stone with a hole for a rope. The holding is not good, he said, but when you lose it it's not so bad. I said: If that's all you have it might as well be made of three-one-six stainless when it's gone. Jazz had wounds in her hands where she tried to meet the blade. Kaylie gave evidence from some-place else. She tried to look round the video link like she thought she should be able to see who was guilty in that future time behind the camera miles away. I hid my face in my hands. Pete died in his best clothes like he was going somewhere, but Jazz was wearing slippers with eyes and ears on them. She was making tea. What can be said about Jazz at ten-fifteen on a Friday night? She was watching something, putting the kettle on in one break, making tea in the next. She was sleepy and not inclined to talk. She had her mobile beside her. She liked her tea weak with a lot of milk. When she saw the Pajero she thought she was an owner at last, getting a mortgage and other debts, the first step in the property ladder not subject to gravity.

This is the Country

I forgot to say Pierce Heskin died and I was in his will. My house and all the fittings and fixtures, the outhouses and yard together with such machinery – something like that. About machinery, I got the mangel slicer and the tractor that dropped dead again sometime after Jazz and I left. It keeps me occupied. I fixed the windows and cleaned things up and made representations concerning my new status as a householder to the social services which they're considering things in a positive light. At least since they decided not to prosecute over the temporary abduction. Pierce knew what he was doing. I'm not giving up the sea, I told him one night. I went into every room. I was stoned. Come out, you fucking Proddy ghost, I said. You won't turn me into a fucking bogger. He never came out, but going down the stairs I heard maybe a ghost's snigger, a creaky sarcastic kind. Once you heard it you never forget after. There's nothing like it.

After I moved in I got a visit from the shades with a summons to appear as a witness. They were going to nail the guy that got Jazz, they told me. It was like some special gift to me. Like they went out of their way for my sake. They had a good look around. This was the first occasion when they mentioned witness protection. If we could nail Pat The Baker, they said. We can connect him to this.

I like the we.

We have the guy that held you down, one of them said, when our Pat broke your legs. He's in witness protection. We could sort you too.

A change of identity wouldn't do you a bit of harm.

Our Pat is massive. He's Mister Big, know what I mean?

He has Asperger's, I said. It's his secret weapon.

They looked at each other. Asperger's what? They're going to look into it. They're careful men, they want to cover every angle. Who is this Asperger and why wasn't he interviewed?

Now I'd say you haven't anything illegal on the premises? If we looked we wouldn't find anything? Am I right or am I wrong?

This is the country you're talking about, I said. Everyone is clean.

They got back in the car and one window rolled down. Who got the land?

He was looking out at Pierce Heskin's fields, thinking if I owned the land maybe I was something. The kind of citizen the law has in mind. Most cops are boggers, they have that bogger thing about property. I was thinking it was maybe time for mushrooms. I couldn't remember when Pierce said they started. The blackberries were still green, I think. Pierce's old hat was still hanging behind the door waiting for him to come back.

A cousin, I said. He's contesting the will.

Blood is thicker than water.

That's a brilliant idea, you should go into politics, I said.

He said, Fuck you, Billy boy.

I would like to thank Clive Challoner for the engines, Niall Carey for technical details, and Rattley, Ian, the two Johns and Keith, for two years of mint talk.